YESTERDAY'S *child*

SONIA
LEVITIN

YESTERDAY'S
child

SIMON & SCHUSTER
BOOKS FOR YOUNG READERS

Many thanks to the following people for their generosity and kindness
in helping me with the research for this novel:
Karen Gaiger of Toronto
Peggy Parrish, Attorney, Fredricksburg, Virginia
Joanne Rochlin, Psychologist, Los Angeles, California
Lonnie Sturtevant, Probation Officer, Spotsylvania, Virginia

SIMON & SCHUSTER BOOKS FOR YOUNG READERS
An imprint of Simon & Schuster Children's Publishing Division
1230 Avenue of the Americas, New York, New York 10020

Library of Congress Cataloging-in-Publication Data
Levitin, Sonia, 1934–
Yesterday's child / by Sonia Levitin.
p.   cm.
Summary: After her mother's sudden death, high school student Laura starts
hunting for information that had always been mysteriously vague,
and in her search she uncovers some terrible secrets.
ISBN 0-689-80810-0 (hardcover)
[1. Mothers and daughters—Fiction. 2. Murder—Fiction.
3. Friendship—Fiction. 4. High schools—Fiction. 5. Schools—Fiction.] I. Title.
PZ7.L58Yf   1997   [Fic]—dc20   96-31649

YESTERDAY'S *child*

chapter / 1

Kim and I were walking home from school, as usual. And, as usual, Spider Margolis and Andy Tatum came by and called out, "Hi, Gorgeous!"

They meant Kim. I glanced at Kim, saw how she flipped her hand through her glossy hair, the color of ginger. We used to give each other "makeovers," even though Kim never needed it.

Kim gave them a grin and called out, "You sure creamed those guys from Presidio—way to go!" Then she whispered to me, "Say something to Spider!"

I turned and said, "Hi, Spider. Hi, Andy," but my tone wasn't bright.

"Spider's had his eye on you for weeks," Kim whispered. "Don't you think he's cute?"

"He's okay," I said. Actually, I liked Spider. He's a great athlete, both basketball and baseball. A few times I'd run with him on the track. I'm just not the drooling, swooning type, falling in love all over the place.

Kim turned to me, and I saw the sorrow and worry in her

face. It was like seeing a reflection of myself; we are so close. She said, "I wonder—that is, Jordan and I want to know whether you're still coming on the trip. After what happened, I—we—think it would be good for you."

I sighed. "Thanks. But how come everyone suddenly knows what's good for me?" I hated the bitterness in my voice, but I was still raw.

"You have to get your money in by Friday," Kim said in a businesslike tone. "Otherwise you'll lose your reservation."

"I know."

"Hey, this is our big trip, remember?" Kim was being enthusiastic for my sake. "The nation's capital, excitement, romance. Oh, please, Laura," Kim urged. "We've always wanted to take a trip together. You'll have fun, I promise. All these great guys are going. Marlene and Cissy and all those kids. There's even a waiting list."

"I don't care about those people," I said listlessly. "Do you?"

"You're my best friend," Kim said. "You know that. I'm trying to make it sound good to you. Laura, you can't just sit home."

"Why not?"

"Because it won't be any fun without you!"

"You'll have Jordan."

Kim made a face, then grinned. "It's not the same. Jordan doesn't do the same things you do."

"I should hope not," I said, starting to smile.

"Now, that's better," Kim said happily. "Will you go? Please-o!" The "please-o!" thing was a joke of ours from when we were in grammar school, that imploring, wide-eyed, goofy look.

I laughed. "I'll think about it. I have to talk it over with Father. I'm not sure what his plans are."

"Oh, he won't mind," Kim said quickly. "He's always so busy. We'll share a room, of course. We can go to the mall this weekend and buy stuff for the trip. I'll let you borrow my new angora sweater. Want to?"

"Sure. You can wear my new turtleneck."

We were pretending that things were the same as before, that we could talk and laugh half the night, gossiping, making elaborate plans for the future.

My smile faded. "Things are different now," I said.

Kim's eyes looked moist. "I know," she whispered, and put her arm around my shoulder.

We stood at the corner for a minute longer, then we separated with a wave and a perfunctory, "Call me later, okay?" as we'd done for the past six years, walking together from the school bus stop.

Kim lives about half a mile from me, at the bottom of the hill, while my house is up a winding road covered with brush and trees. I could see our front window gleaming in the afternoon sun as I approached, and Mrs. Sheffield standing there.

When I went in, Mrs. Sheffield was pretending to dust the living room, but I know she had been watching for me from the window. When she saw me, Mrs. Sheffield turned away, adjusting the pins in her gray hair. Briskly she untied her "cleaning apron" and smoothed down her dress—one of half a dozen she always wore, flowered, without any waistline.

"I'm glad you're home," she said with a smile. "I'll bet you'd like a snack. Did you have lunch?"

"I had a Power Bar," I said. "One hundred and fifty calories of pure protein. I'm fine."

Mrs. Sheffield only smiled. She never fussed at me about

eating, never criticized. My mother used to harangue me constantly about food.

"Skinny as a stick," she used to snort, helping herself to another piece of date nut bread, which she baked herself, adding extra walnuts.

"Well, young girls do burn off a lot of energy," Mrs. Sheffield would say, keeping the peace.

We went out into the kitchen and sat down at the round cherry wood table I'd helped select just last year when my mother decided to redecorate. Now that Mom was gone, everything fell into a different perspective. Would she have bought new furniture if she'd known she was going to die a year later?

Mrs. Sheffield had fixed some Jell-O with bits of fruit inside, topped with a dab of Kool Whip, and I ate it gratefully, for it was sweet and soothing. Mrs. Sheffield seemed to understand that I only wanted to eat boiled eggs and Jell-O; she didn't comment or judge, the way my mother always did with that awful guttural sound, part sigh and part groan.

That sound said more than words. It said, who can understand kids? They're like strangers on the planet—unpredictable little animals. I had always been a mystery to her and to Father. Somehow I knew, from the time I was very young, that they hadn't planned on having me, and further, hadn't the faintest idea of how to raise a child.

When I was small, sometimes Father would get down on the floor with me and start to paw at the carpet or make faint growling noises in his throat. It never amused me. Later they bought a stupid little counting game to play with me and pretended to be happily engrossed in it. But I saw through the charade, and they, too, realized it was useless. They didn't know how to play with a child. They told acquaintances "Laura's really so mature for her age. She never did act like a child. She prefers adult company and, really, she's quite content to play alone."

I told Mrs. Sheffield now, "Kim and Jordan still want me to go on the Washington, D.C. trip. I don't know," I said, testing the waters, "how it would look. I mean…" I let it drop, just as I let my spoon drop into the empty bowl.

"Now, nobody would think anything amiss, Laura," said Mrs. Sheffield. She always spoke that way, too, using outdated words, but coming from her they seemed exactly right. "Nobody with half a mind would think to criticize you for going with your class on a trip that's been planned for months."

"But what about Father?" I looked past Mrs. Sheffield to the wallpaper, little blue baskets filled with pink, blue, and yellow flowers.

Mrs. Sheffield's bosom rose as she inhaled deeply. Her soft skin suddenly crinkled into creases around her eyes, and I saw all the long years of work engraved on her face. "Well, your father has been talking about taking that Tokyo assignment after all. Of course, he has maintained from the start that he will stay here as long as you need him. But if you're thinking of going on that trip, he would be…well…"

Relieved, was the word Mrs. Sheffield didn't say. But it rang between us like a rip in the air.

I sat for a moment longer, then mumbled, "Excuse me," and fled to my room.

I sat down on the edge of my bed, and I allowed the thoughts to creep in around me. I probed at the memory, coaxed it out in every detail to let it be exposed fully, bringing its own special brand of pain. It's odd that pain can become so familiar, almost welcome, if it fills a void.

"Laura, you're wanted in the office."

"We'd like you to come home, dear. Don't mind about the rehearsal, just come along and your father will explain when you get here."

Of course, I'd thought that Father was going off somewhere halfway around the world on a consulting assignment, and that Mother had suddenly decided to go with him, that for some reason they had to leave immediately and wanted to say good-bye face to face. I was annoyed, I remember, at having to miss rehearsal. We were doing *Oklahoma!*, and I had a part in the chorus, a small part, but I loved it. I was thinking how inconsiderate it was of them to call me away like this, as if *my* life and *my* plans didn't matter at all.

I remember the front door was wide open. That was strange. Looking back, I see it all in slow motion, and I hear echoes of those words.

"Laura, I have to tell you something, and I'm going to need for you to be very brave."

"It wasn't anybody's fault."

"These things happen."

"Aneurysm."

Dr. Gunther, whom I've known forever, tried to explain it, as if understanding might make a difference. Words floated around me.

"Rupture. Artery wall. Fatal."

"Was it because she smoked?"

"It could have been a contributing factor, but…"

"Don't blame her, Laura."

"In a case like this, people always look for someone or something to blame. It's natural. But it's useless."

"Try to rest."

"Time will help. Time will heal."

Things happened as in a drama. Effects were created, somehow. A stage was set. People arrived. Heavy velvet curtains were parted to reveal a coffin, sleek and shiny as the body of a violin. The lid was raised. At this point in the memory I always became another Laura, and the story unfolded like a tragic fairy tale.

Laura thought of Snow White and the glass coffin, and the prince's reviving kiss.

Laura reached out. She laid her hand upon the pale, folded hands of the woman they said was Mother. But she looked so different. Her skin seemed stretched tight; the lip line was wrong. The flesh of her arm felt hard and unyielding, like the limb of a mannequin, and it was false in color.

Laura gagged.

People clustered around her; the smell of perfume and powder and detergents became suffocatingly strong.

"Call on us, Laura, for anything at all."

"We're there for you—you and your poor father."

Later I realized that about twenty kids from school were at the funeral. Father kept rubbing his eyes, saying, "Who are all these people?" Father had aged in the last few days. His hair seemed grayer, and he moved as if his spine were stiff.

"They're Laura's friends," Mrs. Sheffield told him. "From school."

"I didn't know..." Of course he didn't know them, because I hardly ever had anyone over at the house. My mother never seemed to like my friends. I was surprised that so many of them came.

Somehow I'd thought that after the funeral the pain would be over, things would be normal. But of course, it didn't happen that way. There was a gap, a hole in our house and in our lives.

Father and I didn't say anything, but I knew how aware he was of it, for the signs were everywhere—the empty chair, the silence at night when Mom used to watch "Inside Story," no smell of baked goods in the oven, the absence of cigarette smoke, of ashes spilled onto the table, of crossword puzzle books folded back, waiting for Mom to summon her considerable powers with words; no lights left on in all the rooms, no mail scattered on the hall table, no Beatles songs sounding from her room late at night. We were alone with the ghosts of these things, with our memories, and I with my guilt.

I came out of my room near dusk. My eyes felt swollen, although I had not cried.

"I'll make a salad," I told Mrs. Sheffield, by way of offering peace and normalcy. "I think I will go to Washington if it's really okay with Father."

"I think you should, dear. It will be a wonderful trip, and educational. You'll get your mind off your troubles."

"I wish I hadn't been so angry with her," I said. I chopped vigorously at the onions and herbs. "I didn't really forgive her, you know, for not wanting to chaperon."

"Then forgive yourself now, Laura," said Mrs. Sheffield. "Be more generous with yourself."

I had been furious, unable to express my anger. Because the truth was, I'd asked Mr. Langfeld to invite Mom not because I really wanted her along, but because I thought it was the right thing to do, for her sake. I thought she'd love the chance to get back to her old hometown in Virginia. I wanted to see her with friends for a change, enjoying herself. But she had thrown the gift back at me, with her usual scorn. "What? Who wants to see those old idiots? Not I, thank you very much. I have nothing in common with them, never did."

"You have nothing in common with anyone!" I had shouted.

Father intervened. "Go to your room, Laura. I won't have you upsetting your mother."

The two of them stood like soldiers, side by side against me. It was always that way. They were opposites, Father lean from running, with his gray hair, his loose cheeks and wide jaw. He was twenty years older than Mom. Mom was plump, with dark eyes and lovely skin, but her clothes were always ratty and uninteresting. It was obvious that she could be very attractive if she tried, and that she was much younger than Father. That was another thing I resented; nobody else's father was over sixty years old.

"What about upsetting me?" I had shouted. "Don't either of you ever think of me?" I felt a red-hot, explosive rage. It erased every other thought and feeling, a power that claimed me completely. I had felt such anger before, felt myself capable of anything, any violence, for in that moment I was blind.

"Go to your room."

I must not have moved, for in the next moment my father was there, grasping my arms, hard, shaking me. "Go to your room!" he yelled.

I went, still in the grip of that fury, and I turned on Pearl Jam, really loud, knowing how my mother hated it, wanting only to aggravate her. Not even the music could quiet my rage. The anger was like a terrible force, pounding inside me, needing to be set free.

That night, I remember, I dreamed of the sea, the pounding surf, Mother and I in a small boat, Mother rowing, and then the surf rose to a high, high tidal wave that swept over us both.

The next day I was still feeling upset from my anger and from the dream. On the way to school I told Kim everything, and we talked about how we were going to get away from our parents, away from stupid Mill Valley, away from everything that bothered us. "We'll go away to college, maybe to Los Angeles, UCLA. We won't stay in this town a minute longer than we have to. They think they can run our lives. They dominate us. It's unbelievable."

How we exaggerated! What was really unbelievable was that a few hours later, my mother was dead.

I finished the salad and took a shower, so that when Father came home I was neat and composed. I went to meet him at the door, the way Mother always used to do. He looked at me and smiled, a tired smile. I went to him and he held me, lightly, as if I were fragile.

"My brave girl," he said softly.

I told him about my decision to go on the class trip.

He nodded thoughtfully. "Well, that's fine, Laura. I think you should go. I'm doing that Tokyo assignment after all. We both need to get away from this house. When's your trip?"

"In four weeks. During spring vacation."

"Well, I'll be leaving in three weeks. Will that pose a problem for you? Will you and Mrs. Sheffield be able to manage?"

"Of course," I said. "We always do."

If he heard the reproach in my voice, Father gave no sign of it, but I felt rotten. I realized that I'd held out the impossible hope that Father and I might now spend some time together, find each other in a way that we never had before.

* * *

That night I had the dream again. Mother and I were in a boat, and she was rowing. Suddenly she dropped the oars and simply lay back, taking in the sun. Next, she was gone. Huge waves surged up around the boat, and as I turned, frantically rowing, I saw an enormous fish, its jaws opening to swallow me whole.

I woke up terrified. It didn't take a shrink to figure out the meaning of that dream. In the dark, alone, I let go and wept.

chapter / 2

After my mom died, I spent weekends at Kim's house, sleeping over on Friday and Saturday nights. We sat up talking until all hours, and Kim's parents never bothered us about going to sleep. When my mom was alive she was always on edge about my spending the night away from home. Still, she had to let me. I'd fuss and argue until she gave up.

"It's great that I can spend weekends here," I told Kim. "It's nice of your folks to let me."

"Oh, they love having you. Besides, it keeps me out of trouble."

"Ha! Remember all the trouble we used to get into?"

"Yeah." Kim grinned.

"The time we both came down with the measles?"

"And they wouldn't let us be sick together," Kim remembered, "until I refused to eat."

I laughed. "It was so much fun then, being sick together." Our mothers finally gave in, and I was moved over to Kim's house, because she had twin beds in her room. "All those paper dolls and coloring books and eating popcorn in bed."

"I don't think anyone ever enjoyed the measles like we did," Kim said, giggling. She picked up her large gray cat, Mongoose, and held him over her shoulder like a baby. I stroked the cat's soft head; he purred loudly.

"Remember when you saved him?" Kim asked.

"Sure. He knows it, too." Mongoose reached out with his paw, taking up a lock of my hair, making me laugh. I took Mongoose from Kim and held him close, his fur tickling my face.

"Maybe now," Kim said, "you can get a cat. Or a dog."

"Maybe." I sighed. "I read this booklet that the counselor gave me, about loss. It said that when someone you love dies, you feel guilty because, in a way, you're also relieved."

Kim nodded, looking deep into my eyes. "I can imagine. Like, you could have a pet now, but that doesn't mean you wanted your mother to die."

I said softly, "I know it sounds crazy, but sometimes I feel as if I killed her. I keep thinking, if I'd been better to her, if we'd been closer..."

"Laura, you know that's ridiculous. You just told me yourself that when someone you love dies, it makes you feel guilty. Everyone has things they regret."

"Yes," I sighed. "Unfinished business."

Kim turned on our favorite Madonna CD, "Bedtime Stories." It was beautiful, so soft and dreamy. My mother, of course, hated Madonna. "That tramp!" she'd say. She also hated Alanis, said it sounded like alley cats. Kim and I lay back on the bed, singing, then we played Pearl Jam and started jumping around like we used to do when we were kids, laughing and dancing. It was a way of escaping everything, our folks, boring school, boring Mill Valley with all the boring people we had known nearly all our lives. We were ready to break out and escape.

Kim kept talking about our trip to Washington, D.C. She was so excited. I was ambivalent. I still didn't feel quite right about going so soon after my mom's death, but Kim and Jordan were planning out each day, what we'd see, how we'd ride the Metro, hang out at the White House, meet important people. I guess, as the time grew closer, I was excited, not so much at the idea of seeing the sights, but at the thought of being free, out of this rut, away from memories.

At home, it was impossible to escape memories. While Mrs. Sheffield was around, it wasn't so bad. But at night, when she went home to her studio apartment, and if Father was out at some meeting, I'd be alone with the silence. The silence was deep and so heavy that it seemed hard to walk from room to room. Other times, small noises overwhelmed me: the rumbling starts and stops of the refrigerator, heat pumping through the vents, light buzzing through the fluorescent bulbs in the kitchen.

One night in March, when the wind made the windows creak and foghorns were bellowing out from the bay, I couldn't bear the loneliness anymore.

I went to stand at my mother's bedroom door. It was closed. In the past five weeks I had not opened it, and neither had Father. They had slept apart in adjoining rooms.

"Your father snores," Mother had told me long ago by way of explanation. I had assumed something different—that they really preferred not to be together.

I opened the door and was met by a rush of fragrances—traces of the Red Door perfume she always wore, the rose bubble bath that was part of her morning ritual, the bonsai plant on her bureau, the smell of the new powder blue carpet, and the jasmine blooming just outside her window.

"I've had the gardener plant a half a dozen jasmine," I remembered Father telling her so long ago. "Your namesake."
"Why, thank you, Ivan," Mother said, smiling at him.

I realized, suddenly, that they had been happy together, not like Kim's parents, laughing and joking. But in their way, my parents were well matched. Now that I thought of it, I never heard them fighting. They could sit in silence for hours, Father reading, Mother working on her crossword puzzles or doing some embroidery. I used to think it was unbelievably dull. Now, I knew that their togetherness had built a cocoon around me. I had felt safe.

I turned on the bedside lamp and laid down on my mother's bed. It was cold from disuse, and the room felt clammy. But soon, with all the lights on, it warmed up, and I sank back onto the pillows, feeling the softness around me.

Now that she was gone, I realized I had memorized every gesture of my mother's, the way she turned her lips when making a comment, one eyebrow lifted. I remembered how she would bend to take a tray of cookies or a pan of bread from the hot oven, eyes crinkled against the heat, assessing her creation with a softening of her lips—perfect. Her baked goods were always perfect, popping straight out of the pan without ever a burnt or crumbling residue. She was skilled, too, at fixing things—broken jewelry, mechanical pencils, can openers, even clocks. I remembered the fragrance of her clothes, the soft fullness of her upper arms and cheeks when I happened to brush up against her.

I lay on Mother's bed with my eyes closed, whispering her name, not the name I called her, but her given name. "Jasmine. Jasmine. Mother. Can you hear me?"

Maybe there are ways for the dead to break through, I thought. Maybe she can give me a sign.

The telephone rang. Startled, I leapt to my feet and picked it up, my tone frantic. "Hello!"

"Laura, what's wrong?" It was Kim.

"Nothing. I was just—sort of—dozing."

"Listen, Spider's going to call you. He asked Jordan for your phone number."

"Ryan," I said. "I hate the name Spider. His real name is Ryan. Why would he call me?" I asked Kim.

"Because he *likes* you, that's why."

"Oh. He hardly knows me."

"He knows you from running. He thinks you've got terrific legs and a great sense of humor. He thought you were fabulous in last year's *Lil Abner*."

Suspicious, I said, "Hey, did Jordan put him up to this? Just to be nice to me?"

"Honestly, Laura, I give up!" Kim said.

"What does Ryan want?" I asked.

"Why don't you get off the phone and find out when he calls?"

"Okay. I'm off. Thanks."

I hung up and sat down on the edge of Mom's bed, thinking about Ryan. Plenty of girls are in love with Spider Margolis, but they're like Marlene Madison and Cissy Cane, always falling in love, swooning and screaming. I've never been that emotional about boys—not in real life, that is. Only in fantasies.

Now in my line of vision was my mother's bureau with all her things. The realization struck: she wasn't coming back, not ever. Beside the bureau was a stand for her CDs and a player. She had every Beatles record ever made.

I stepped over to the upholstered bench where Mother so often sat brushing her hair, squinting at herself in the mirror, as if to refine the lines on her forehead and around her mouth. I picked up her hairbrush, tried it on my own hair, then opened the lipstick and pressed it to my lips. They said my mother was in the kitchen when it happened, standing at the counter filling the kettle with water. Her head struck the countertop and…that was it.

I sat down on the bench and stared at her things—beaded necklaces in a round glass box, an earring tree, cosmetics; a collection of small animals—a silver hippo, a glass mouse, a spotted ceramic cat, a large bird, and two dogs. It was odd for her to have such a collection, for my mother was afraid of animals, especially dogs.

Glancing up, I beheld my own image in the mirror, and I was startled, expecting, somehow, to see her instead.

In a way, I thought, I *was* seeing her. My eyes, like hers, are very dark brown. We have the same shape face, rather long, a dimpled chin, and my hair waves like my mother's, curling away from my face at the top. Only my hair is still blond, while hers had turned dark long ago.

Tentatively I opened the side drawer to look at my mother's things. Her underwear, in various pastel shades, was neatly folded. I opened the next drawer down. Panty hose and socks. The bottom drawer held several artificial flowers, some scarves, and a box that might once have contained stationery or sachet.

I had never seen this box before.

Was it right to do this? I asked myself, and then I shrugged. Dead people don't need privacy.

I took the box over to the bed, lifted the lid, then dumped everything out. There was a printed wedding announcement on a card. "Miss Jasmine Rogers and Mr. Ivan Inman announce their marriage…"

No formal wedding, just a trip to the Justice of the Peace in Carmel, no parents to give her in marriage. I had always known that my grandparents died in a car crash many years before I was born. Mother never talked much about it. Father had told me, rather sternly, "This is painful for your mother. If you need to talk about it, come to me."

I poked through the things: There was a faded flower on a tattered silver ribbon, several cards of congratulations from people I didn't know, and a few photographs. There were some menus from restaurants in San Francisco and Chicago, a painted souvenir fan from Singapore, the card from a tailor in Hong Kong, and a silver link bracelet, badly tarnished, on which hung many little silver hearts. It was, obviously, the kind of thing a young girl would wear, delicate and old-fashioned. I slipped the bracelet into my pocket, wanting desperately to own it, realizing with a jolt that now any of these things could be mine.

I started to put all the contents back into the box, then saw at the very bottom of the pile a letter, and just underneath it an item torn from a news magazine. It was a small picture of several men and a woman, standing at a lectern, and beneath it the caption, with parts of the message torn away: "...conference on fostering the North American Free Trade Agreement, Jacob Meistrander appears to be the leading candidate to replace the present minister.... His wife, Megan, has long been prominent in charity circles..."

Who were these people? My heart raced as I picked up the envelope, addressed in my mother's handwriting and sealed, but lacking a stamp. I held it up, read the address:

Mrs. Jacob Meistrander
138 Ellis Park Rd.
Toronto, Ontario
Canada

No zip code and no stamp: I was mystified. My mother had never mentioned knowing anyone in Canada, nor, to my knowledge, had my parents traveled there. Why had she never mailed the letter?

Suddenly I knew. I tore open the envelope, and saw immediately that my intuition was absolutely right. Mother had written this letter the very day before she died, had no doubt intended to mail it, after going to the post office to buy stamps and look up the zip code. The date on the top of the letter was February 7. The very next day, February 8, at eleven in the morning, she died.

These words, I thought, were among her last communications. I had asked for a sign. Maybe this was it.

chapter / 3

As I read the letter, it was like hearing my mother's voice.

"Dear Megan,"

I leapt up at the sudden screech of the telephone. I grabbed the receiver, shouted into it, "Hello!"

"Hey! Are you all right?"

"Yes. Sure. Who is this?" Of course, I knew.

"Ryan Margolis. Spider. Jordan gave me your number. What's going on?"

"Nothing. Nothing." I glanced at the letter; all I wanted was to get back to it.

"Well, I wanted to ask you—you know the trip to D.C.?"

"Yes, yes." I put the letter face down on the bed.

"Well, Kim told me you're going. It sounds like a great trip. I wasn't sure I could save enough money for the trip, so I had to get on the waiting list. Mr. Langfeld told me today that Marguerite Kaufman canceled, so I can go."

"Good for you." I tried to summon some enthusiasm. "Great."

"So, Langfeld told me that you guys have already had lots

of meetings, and he gave out maps and stuff. So I thought, maybe I could borrow yours. Have copies made, you know."

"Sure," I said. "I'll bring them to school tomorrow." All the while I thought, Why me? He could get this stuff from Kim or from Jordan. Maybe it was true that he liked me. "We could go to the Kopy Kat after school," Ryan suggested. "Have copies made. Go for pie at *Mama's*. How about it?"

"Yes." He's asking you for a date, a real date, a voice told me, that other "Laura" who watches and narrates. "That would be great."

"Cool!" Ryan enthused. "So I'll meet you out in front of the arches after school. Okay?"

"Sure. I'll bring the maps and instructions." I was certain that Mr. Langfeld had plenty of duplicates. I smiled to myself. He likes me!

"Well, 'bye," Ryan said.

"So long. Thanks." I bit my lip. What was I thanking him for? Why could I never think of anything clever to say? I started to dial Kim's number. We would go over every word of the conversation, and Kim would find all sorts of signs and innuendoes to get excited about.

But the letter lay there, like a presence. I picked it up and began again:

Dear Megan,

 I'm sure you'll be surprised to hear from me, just as I was surprised to find this clipping with your photograph. Imagine, you the wife of a government minister! This was always your desire, something very distinguished, almost royal. I offer you my congratulations. Really, I am happy for you.

 I am married and have a daughter. She is really a

*lovely girl, in high school now. Ironically, she is headed
for a school trip near our old hometown and even
invited me to go along. She thought I'd want to visit with
our old high school friends in Birch Bend. Twenty-five
years! It launched me into that sweet never-never land
of fantasy—what if Megan and I were to meet again?
Only in our dreams. I'm sure you have them, too.*

*Well, luv, not much more to say, though a lifetime
has passed. When all is said and done, there are only a
few things worth mentioning, a marriage, the birth of a
child, a career move (though I've never been able to
achieve such a thing), and, finally, forgiveness.*

Be happy.

Yours,

J.

I read the letter once again, then held the paper to my
cheek. Everything in it was so like Mother—the very signature, merely, "J.," the dreamy quality to it, the odd flow of
thoughts, and that word, "forgiveness." What did Mom mean
by "forgiveness"? Maybe she and Megan had had a fight long
ago. Or maybe it was just my mother's way of using words.
She used to savor words, like a poet.

I sat holding the letter against my chest, then read again
the words that clung to my heart. "I have a daughter...really
a lovely girl..."

Within the small pile of mementos, I now noticed two
small photographs, and I picked them up and studied them
for a long time. On the backs, my mother had written,
"Megan and me."

I had never seen a photograph of my mother as a young
girl. In fact, we seldom took pictures in our family. These girls

were about thirteen or fourteen, and I knew immediately that my mother was the taller of the two, her light, streaked hair pulled back and up into a ponytail, her eyes wide and expressive. She was wearing jeans and a long shirt and sneakers. Megan was dressed in shorts and a T-shirt, and her short, curly hair was tied back with a ribbon. They stood on the lawn in front of a house, laughing at the photographer. Both were pretty, each in a different way. My mother looked older and more sophisticated. Megan looked elfin, with bright eyes and an impish smile.

In the second photo, the girls sat on a low cinder-block wall with their arms around each other's waists. Their faces were turned toward each other, their smiles intimate and sweet. Someone might simply have snapped them unaware as they sat there on the wall, with a huge magnolia tree in the background.

I gazed at the pictures, unwilling to put them away. They provided a more tangible remembrance of my mother than any of her other things. I wished I had known her when she was fourteen. We would have been friends, like Kim and I, laughing and telling secrets.

I picked up the telephone and called Kim. She answered softly. Her parents were probably sleeping.

"Kim," I said, "I know it's late, but I've got to talk to you."

"Did Spider call?" Kim asked, breathless.

"Yes, and we've got a date for tomorrow. He's coming on the trip." My voice trembled, and I know Kim thought it was because of Ryan's call.

"Isn't it fabulous? He and Jordan will room together—isn't this awesome?"

"Kim," I said, my voice low, "I found some things of my mother's, a picture from a magazine. It's a friend of my mother's, married to a very important person in Canada, and there's a letter Mom wrote the very day before she died. I want to read it to you."

"Well—sure. Was it…"

"Listen." I read the letter very slowly, savoring each word. When I came to the part about "a lovely daughter," my throat tightened and I had to wait for a moment, then I whispered, "Oh, Kim, I've felt so terrible, thinking she was mad at me because of that scene about the trip. But she wrote to her friend and said I was a lovely girl. She loved me. She must have."

"Of course she did, Laura. You know she did."

"I'm going to write to this woman, Megan, in Canada. I should at least send Mother's letter to her. It was her last act, sort of. You know?"

"Sure. I think you should. Will you tell her your mom died?"

"Of course. I have to. She'd want to know, wouldn't she? And, Kim, I found something else. There were these photographs, old pictures, of my mother and her friend, sitting on this wall. They look so cute! On the back it says 'Megan and me.'"

Kim said, "It sounds as if they never saw each other after they grew up."

"Maybe they lost track of each other."

"They must have traveled in two different worlds," Kim said dramatically. "Your mom must have been surprised to see that picture in a magazine. Why wouldn't she have told you about it?"

"I don't know."

"Where would she have gotten the address?"

"Well, if her husband's in the government," I said, "it would be pretty easy to find."

Kim and I started imagining Megan, getting carried away, as usual.

Kim proposed, "Your mother and this woman, Megan, might have been best friends. She'll be so happy to hear from you! She'll probably want to take you under her wing."

"She can tell me things about my mother, when she was young. Maybe she has more photographs that she'll give me."

"Sounds like she's really famous. Maybe her husband is even going to run for president."

"Canada doesn't have a president," I said. "It's a prime minister."

Kim yawned and said, "Well, I'm really bushed. See you tomorrow. It's late. Let's go to sleep."

But I wasn't tired. In fact, I felt revitalized. I sat down at my mom's dressing table, and, using a piece of her lavender stationery, I wrote:

> *Dear Megan Meistrander:*
>
> *I am writing you this letter because, among my mother's things, I found this note to you and decided to send it along. I'm sorry to tell you the sad news that my mother died on February 8 of this year. It was a shock to all of us, a sudden heart failure.*

I glanced again at the photographs, then I added,

> *Please write to me. I would love to correspond with you. I will be leaving for Washington D.C. on a class trip in twelve days, and hope to receive your reply before then. I would really love to know more about my mother when she was young. Now that she is gone, it seems very important.*
>
> *Sincerely,*
> *Laura Inman*

After I wrote the letter I looked through my mother's collection of Beatles CDs and found the one with her favorite song, "Let It Be." I knew all the words, for she used to play it often at night. Now I put it on and sat back on her bed to listen, pretending that she was here beside me, listening, too.

> "When I find myself in times of trouble
> Mother Mary comes to me
> Speaking words of wisdom, let it be....
>
> And when the broken-hearted people
> Living in the world agree,
> There will be an answer, let it be."

The song was part of me; the words sang through my doubts, like prophecies. *There will be an answer, let it be.* I mailed the letter the next day and started searching through the mail for a reply. A week later I found my letter back in our mailbox, with the words, RETURN TO SENDER. NOT AT THIS ADDRESS. I was stunned.

I called Kim and we mulled this over for half an hour, with no solution.

My mother would never have made such a mistake. She was too precise. How had she gotten that address? Suddenly I knew. I raced into my father's study, turned on his computer and, in a matter of minutes, found myself cruising the Web.

MEISTRANDER, JACOB. It was so easy! I felt flushed with success, then instantly frustrated when only his address at the ministry appeared.

My heart thumping, I typed in MEISTRANDER, MEGAN. Up popped a title, "Director, Girls' Volunteer League of Ontario," and the Ellis Park Road address.

Now I was mystified. I had the right address. Why had my letter been returned?

I called Kim again. "Maybe Megan was on vacation," Kim suggested. "Maybe it was a post office foul-up." Maybe, maybe...

I was terribly disappointed, then disappointment gave way to determination. "I'm going to Birch Bend," I told Kim. "Maybe I won't find out anything about Megan Meistrander. But at least I can see the town where my mother was born, maybe even find the house she lived in. I want to go, Kim. I have to."

"But how can you? Isn't that in Virginia? Don't you remember the rules we signed? Nobody can leave the area, except on a group tour."

"Don't read me the rules," I snapped. "I'm not expecting you to come with me. But one thing's for sure, I'm not going to miss this chance to find out."

"To find out what?" Kim sounded almost frightened by my intensity.

"Everything," I said, composing myself. "I want to find out what she did, what she was like." Softly I added, "Then maybe I'll know who I am."

And then, I said inwardly, maybe I'll be able to let her go.

chapter /4

I was going to ask my father about Megan Meistrander, but it didn't work out. I'd put it off, knowing how annoyed my father always got when it came to questions about the past. "That's water over the dam," he'd say gruffly. "Why dredge it up again? Haven't you anything better to think about?"

Before he left, I did ask him about the silver bracelet with the little hearts. We were standing in the hallway. He was giving me last-minute instructions, along with a credit card and a kiss on the forehead. "You can reach me by telephone or fax anytime. Here are the numbers. And if you need anything on your trip, here is the American Express card. I've had your signature approved."

"Thanks, Father." Few girls I knew were so lucky, but Father knew I wouldn't take advantage of his trust.

"Buy yourself a nice souvenir," he said.

"Speaking of souvenirs," I said, and I reached into the pocket of my jeans for the silver bracelet I'd kept there since that night, "I found this bracelet in Mother's room. May I keep it?"

He looked alarmed. "What were you doing in your mother's room?" Father's face was drawn, almost gray. "What were you looking for?" His voice rose. "Don't you have anything else to do?"

"I'm sorry!" I cried. "I just wanted to—I miss her!"

He relented, his eyes looking very pained as he gazed at me and murmured, "Of course you do. Of course. It's just—you really must not spend so much time alone, Laura. It isn't good for you. You ought to go out more, with friends."

"I'm going to Washington, D.C.," I reminded him.

He looked relieved, but still his voice quavered. "We must think about having her things cleared out. After we both return from our trips. Until then…" He stopped and glanced down at the bracelet in my hand. "Of course you can have it," he said.

I took the bracelet to the Tick Tock Clock and Jewelry Shop in the village to have it cleaned. My mom had worked at the shop part-time, responding to old Harley Brimstone's plea that she help him out during the Christmas rush. After that she stayed on, and she seemed to enjoy having a job, though it certainly was no challenge for her. "Don't the clocks drive you crazy?" I asked her more than once.

"No, they don't bother me," she said. "I rather like the clocks. Each face is a little different, like people. Imagine, if they could talk! Would they chime out warnings?"

It was so like my mother to say something like that, but of course, then, I only shrugged it off. Now I recalled everything. I had wondered why my mother didn't have a real career, like most other moms I knew. Once, at the dinner table, I asked outright. "Why didn't you ever go to law school, Mom? You're so interested in those things—or teaching, like Kim's mother."

She had laughed at me, patting her hair, looking coy. "Now, Laura, what's the matter? Don't you want me at home with you?"

My father answered irritably, "Your mother doesn't have to work. Fortunately, I can provide for the family. Besides, I want her to be free to travel with me."

But I'd felt that the truth lay somewhere else. My mother seemed too nervous to hold down a regular job, with those spells of melancholy, and her dependence on Mrs. Sheffield.

While Harley was working on the bracelet, Kim and I went to The Depot Cafe for a soda and raisin muffins. We sat outside at one of the little round metal tables, watching the dogs that always romped in the square. "We'll have a great time in Washington," Kim said. "My mom said she went on a school trip in high school and it was one of her most precious memories."

"Good," I said grimly, "I need a precious memory." Then, we both burst out laughing. "Let's go look at some books," I said when we had settled down, and Kim agreed.

Part of The Depot is a bookstore, and we browsed for a while. I picked up a guidebook to Nepal. It looked so exotic and wonderful. Maybe Father and I…would we ever be close enough to want to travel together? I pushed the thought aside, making myself focus on the present.

Kim poked me and whispered under her breath, "Don't look now, but there're Darryl Lapkin and his pal Nate Ginnes. They're pretending they don't see us."

"Then let's pretend we don't see them," I whispered.

"They're looking at you." Kim started to giggle.

"Let's go," I said, putting back the book and turning to leave. Behind me I heard Nate Ginnes's rumbling voice.

"Hey, Inman—steal any scenes lately?" He laughed.

I swept past them, saw Darryl's thin, pale face and that look of loathing in his eyes. I went out to the square, trembling.

"Don't let them get to you," Kim advised.

"I won't," I said, though it wasn't true. Whenever I saw Darryl Lapkin I thought I'd die of embarrassment, remembering that awful play, *Moria McQueen*, the awful scene with Darryl.

I shrugged now and told Kim, "Let's go get the bracelet. I'm sure it's ready."

When Harley laid the bracelet out on a small maroon velvet pad, Kim and I were surprised at its loveliness. Now we could see the alternating inscriptions on each of the eight hearts: four said FRIENDS, and four said FOREVER, so that encircling my wrist were the words, four times repeated, FRIENDS FOREVER.

"That's so beautiful," Kim sighed.

"I'll never take it off," I said rashly. We pondered where my mother had gotten it. "Maybe it's from a lover," Kim said. "Or a best friend. Maybe they promised never to part."

The more we talked about my mother, the more my mother's image changed in our minds, until it seemed she was a saint. I forgot all about my anger and those sessions when Kim and I used to complain so bitterly about our mothers.

I also became obsessed with the idea of finding Megan Meistrander; through her I could bring my mother close.

"I'm going to phone Megan Meistrander," I told Kim resolutely. "It would be so great to talk to a friend of my mom's, a close friend."

"Let's go and call," Kim said. "Right now."

We rushed home and went into the den. I called information, asked for Toronto, gave Megan's name. "With a name like Meistrander," I whispered to Kim, "this should be easy."

But the operator said, "There is no listing under that name."

"Did you try Jacob? And Megan?" I persisted.

"There is no listing for that surname at all, ma'am."

"But—he's in the government," I argued. "Wouldn't he need a phone? Wouldn't he want people to be able to call?"

"I'm sorry," the operator repeated. "I have no listing for that name."

Disgusted, I banged down the receiver.

"Many prominent people have unlisted telephones," said Kim, having overheard. "Maybe there have been death threats against him," Kim said. "You never know."

"Will you stop!" I snapped irritably. "This is just a game to you, isn't it?" I cried out.

At the sight of Kim's pale, stricken face, I was overcome with guilt. "I'm sorry," I whispered. "I'm just..."

"You're one of the bravest people I know," Kim said stoutly, and I thought how forgiving she was, and I wondered why I couldn't be more like her.

My father had left for Tokyo. Mrs. Sheffield was asleep in the downstairs bedroom. It was late. I made my way along the hall and stood at the door to my mother's room, shivering with anticipation. I was drawn to this room as to a forbidden garden.

I had developed a little ritual. Now I sat down at her dressing table, brushed my hair with her silver-backed hairbrush, lightly applied the coral lipstick to my lips, then looked up, squinting at my reflection. Sometimes it almost seemed that my mother's shadowy image was reflected behind me. I'd sit there and try to feel her presence, think her thoughts, and sometimes words came to me. "Laura, will you run to the cupboard and get me a fresh towel?"

She was always changing her towels, her bed linen, her underclothes. It was more than a matter of cleanliness; I thought it was compulsive, and I had told her so.

"We all have our compulsions, dear. Don't you know, nobody's perfect? Except for my Laura."

I never knew whether she was being sarcastic or serious. Strange, disconnected bits of past conversations, ordinary and inconsequential, seemed captured in the air, returning now like whispers. "You're not afraid, are you?" How often she asked me that, when it came to staying home alone or meeting a large dog on the street or doing an errand in the dark. "You're not afraid, are you?"

"No, of course not," I'd say, laughing. "Are you?"

She never answered, except to murmur, "My brave girl."

I had prolonged my search through Mother's things to make it last. I had already gone over the closet, examining each dress, blouse, skirt, and jacket. Sometimes I wrapped myself in her clothes, to capture their smell. I had checked out all the dresser drawers but two, the small drawer on the left-hand side, and the cupboard beneath it, where my mother kept her purses. The little dresser drawer slid open easily. Inside it was a leather billfold, containing my mother's passport and some foreign currency. I opened the passport, looked at the photograph, saw her startled eyes and puffy cheeks. It was a terrible picture of her. Also in the drawer were a few old keys and hair ornaments, just junk, but then I saw another leather case. I held it for a moment, then reached inside and drew out four letters, all in my father's handwriting.

The first was tattered and yellowed. I skimmed the contents, then read again,

*"I have never met a girl quite like you. Your intensity
makes everyone else seem bland. The moment I saw
you, I knew I wanted to meet you…"*

The next letter was dated several weeks later.

*"I keep remembering our time together, repeating
every delicious moment in my mind. How the day flew!
I must be psychic or very wise indeed to have found
you—who else would quote Shakespeare with me, line
by line, or bend down to read Latin inscriptions on the
sides of a building? You are a treasure. No wonder I
have been alone so long—where were you?"*

The next was several months later.

*"Darling, I feel secure in the knowledge that we can
tell each other anything and everything, without fear or
shame. We need to learn to forget the past. The only
relevant thing is now, and our love. We are one. How
can anything about you ever repel me? Never use that
word again, my sweet."*

I was astounded. I had never imagined my father capable
of such sentiments.

I read the last letter, this one the most passionate, and my
cheeks burned as I imagined the two of them so long ago,
young and in love.

*"My adorable one! I can't bear the thought of
another week without you. Why do you torment me? I
have called your apartment a hundred times. Where are
you? Why don't you answer? Are you afraid of my
question?*

"Marry me. Marry me! It will be like beginning life

on a new planet. Nobody will intrude, ever. Let me love
you. Marry me! I'll go anywhere in the world that you
want to go."

I slipped the letters back into the leather case. It was only then that I saw the address: 29 Fulsome Road, London. The postmark was Dallas, Texas. How had they met, and where? Why had they settled in California, especially in this tiny town?

I knew my mother was born in Birch Bend, Virginia. But she'd never told me she had lived in London. I felt betrayed.

We left on a late afternoon flight, so that we'd arrive in D.C. at around midnight, too pooped, as Mr. Langfeld said, to do much damage the first night out. He was like that, always joking, saying how maybe D.C. wasn't ready for us yet, charging in there from old Mill Valley, California, set in the heart of the wild, wild West.

That always brought a laugh, because Mill Valley has to be one of the safest, quietest places in the world. Still, my mom always acted as if I was going out into a war zone. She seemed full of fears, now that I looked back. When we talked about this trip to Washington, I saw the sharp line between her brows deepen, and she gave my father a helpless, appealing look, but Father had murmured, "It will be all right, Jasmine. Really." What clinched it was that they met Mr. Langfeld and his wife, and they were about my father's age, "steady and experienced," as my father proclaimed.

Our third chaperon was Roz Zacharias, who works in the school office. All the boys are mad about her—she's barely thirty, I guess, with beautiful green eyes, dark complexion, and thick black hair, and she's always laughing and kidding around. We all call her Roz; she told us to.

I thought I'd known everyone who was going on the trip, but there'd obviously been some last-minute changes, because there was Darryl Lapkin, looking pale and nervous, as usual, but without his friend Nate.

"Some people canceled, others took their places," Mr. Langfeld explained, getting everyone acquainted. "It's open seating on this flight," he said. "You guys are free to choose your partners."

Out of the corner of my eye I saw Darryl retreating. Kim and I had planned to sit together but Jordan grabbed Kim, and as we entered the plane, the two of them sat down just behind the bulkhead. Ryan pulled me into the seat behind them, and across the aisle sat Roz with Darryl at the window seat beside her, looking away into the darkness. I was annoyed. Those guys were acting as if they owned us.

"What's with you and Darryl?" Spider whispered.

"Nothing," I said. "We were in a play together in ninth grade. I played the villain."

"Oh. He got a little carried away, is that it?"

"Not exactly," I said, and to change the subject I asked him, "Are there any blankets? It's cold in here."

Spider reached up and got a blanket for me from the over-head rack.

Our "date" had been fun, especially the looks I had gotten from kids hanging around at the village, seeing me with their hero, Spider Margolis. I guess I had been flattered that he'd kept wanting to put his arm around me, but I hadn't wanted him to get the wrong idea. I mean, I like Spider, but he's a lit-tle too physical. Now we talked. Spider started telling jokes, making me laugh. I wanted to keep it that way, just friendly and fun.

They brought us dinner, then showed a movie, but the

sound track was so bad we could hardly hear. I put away my earphones and settled down to sleep. I had closed my eyes and pulled the blanket over my shoulders and across my chest, and I was dozing contentedly, when I felt Spider's hand on my hair, then quickly it moved down, his fingers working overtime.

I sat upright. "Quit it!" I said sharply.

"What?" He smiled innocently.

"You know. Stop it."

"Sorry." He withdrew, pouting.

"Now I know why they call you Spider," I muttered.

Beside me, Roz started from her seat, frowning. She leaned toward us and pointed at Ryan. "Enough of that," she said sternly. "Why don't you go and sit with Jordan." She tapped Kim on the shoulder. "Time for a change," she said.

"What's all that about?" Kim whispered when we were sitting together.

"Oh, Ryan and his restless hands," I said. "Who does he think he is?"

Kim made a face. "They're all alike. It's a disease."

"Yeah. Called hormones." We giggled softly, our heads close together. After a while everything got quiet. The droning of the engines was soothing; I must have fallen asleep, for I was suddenly startled by a scream. I bolted forward, my hands tingling, head throbbing. Something seemed to weigh me down. I realized I was still on the airplane, and now I felt Kim's hand on my shoulder, shaking me. "Laura! Laura, are you okay?"

In the next moment Roz was out of her seat, squatting beside me. "Just a nightmare, Laura," she soothed. "Come on. Walk a bit. We'll get you a drink of water."

I was sweating from the terror of my dream. It began on a

vast plain, where I stood alone with only the howling wind and the waving grass. Voices gathered around me, saying isolated words, "My brave Laura. Aren't you afraid?"

Suddenly the prairie became an ocean, and I crouched in a very small boat with the swells all around me, the dark water rising higher and higher, and in its midst was the huge black fish, its mouth gaping wide. The small boat suddenly caught fire. I had to decide. Leap into the ocean? Or remain in the boat and be consumed?

"Want to talk about it?" Roz asked, as we stood by the door of the plane. She handed me a plastic cup of water.

"It's this same dream." I shuddered. "Only this time my mother wasn't in it." Now I understood the full impact of the dream; even there, my mother was gone.

"What do you think it means?" she asked.

"I don't know." I tried to smile. "You're the shrink." We all knew Roz was getting her master's degree in psychology.

"The dream belongs to the dreamer," Roz said gently. "It's for you to decipher."

"I never dreamed about fire before," I said. "But I suppose it's about fear."

"Everyone has fears," Roz said. "Like me." She smiled. "I was scared to come on this trip."

"Why? Fear of flying?"

"No. Fear of teenagers. Half a dozen people warned me against it. But—I've never been to Washington, D.C., and I really wanted to go on this trip. Besides, I happen to like you guys."

I didn't answer, for I suddenly felt nauseous, like when I was little and traveling in a car. It was a familiar feeling, a complete sense of doom settling over me. I wanted to hide, to burrow in my bed under the covers. Here, in the plane, there was no place to run. I drank all the water, trying to hold myself together. Then shakily I made my way back up the aisle and settled down beside Kim. She looked tense and worried.

"I'm sorry," I said. "I guess I'm lousy company. You'll be sorry you made me come on this trip."

"How can you say that?" Kim exclaimed. "You just had a bad dream. Listen, everyone thinks you're just terrific. I mean, you never complain or feel sorry for yourself. And it's awful to lose your mother the way you did."

I felt bathed in Kim's concern, warmer, better. "I want to show you something," I whispered, and I reached into my backpack and drew out my mother's leather case with the letters inside. "I found these letters before we left. I've been wanting to share them with you. Love letters," I said. "Want to hear?"

Kim's voice was breathless. "Is it okay?"

"Sure," I said. "My mother's memories belong to me now." Together we read the letters, and somehow I felt as if I were the one who had received them.

Now softly I told Kim, "I hear her voice all the time. It's like," I groped for words, "like, I'm sort of living my mother's life. Do you think that's crazy?"

"No, no," Kim soothed, but she looked frightened, too, and I saw her glance around for Roz. "You're just still upset. Nobody can blame you. Look, when we get to D.C. you'll be so busy you'll forget all this. Just wait and see."

I nodded, wanting so desperately to believe her. As I lifted my arms to pull the blanket around my shoulders, I heard the tinkling of the little silver hearts that said FRIENDS FOREVER.

chapter / **5**

Before the trip, Mr. Langfeld had made us read about Washington, D.C. We studied maps and photographs and reviewed
the important events in American history. It all seemed very
distant, even hypocritical. I mean, we kept hearing about this
country being founded with opportunity for everyone, yet the
daily papers were full of stories of racial hatred and killings
and politicians arguing about affirmative action; nobody ever
talked about unity or democracy.

My mom had always hated politics. "Big government, big
rip-off," my mother used to say. I don't think she ever voted,
said it was a waste of time. "One politician is as corrupt as
another," she stated.

If I ever pressed her about it, she just got that wry look on
her face and said, "Well—look at the war in Vietnam. Look at
Watergate. It's not like it says in the books. But of course,"
she added quickly, "one has to follow the rules. Just don't get
yourself disillusioned."

The thing was, as soon as we set down in Washington
D.C., and I saw those broad boulevards and enormous buildings and monuments I felt swept away. An actual chill ran

along my spine. The majesty of it, the hugeness, and flags flying, all made me feel proud. I'm sure my mother would have laughed and called me a fool. Or might she, too, have been impressed? It was hard to accept the fact that we'd never go anyplace together again.

I thought of the Beatles songs she used to play, one of them in particular, "Piggies," and how she would scoff about the "piggies" in Sacramento or Washington. She seemed so certain about her views. Now I questioned everything.

Our first day we saw so much—the Washington Monument, the Lincoln Memorial, Jefferson Memorial, the Capitol building, and the Vietnam Memorial. We had studied about the war. But this was different, suddenly real. Each name engraved in granite represented a real person, now dead. And what was it all for?

Later, when we went to Arlington Cemetery, the thought washed over me again, and again at the Holocaust Museum, where pictures of innocent people, even little children, had been taken just before they were murdered. The most awful thing was seeing that pile of shoes, thousands of them, all sizes. To know they had been worn by people, the young along with the old, and then they were killed for no reason at all, except that someone didn't like them—it seemed incredible. The photographs held me stunned and aching. What are we? Humans? Or monsters? These thoughts ran through my mind and floated through my dreams at night.

I tried to talk to Kim about it, but she shrugged it aside. "I don't want to make myself miserable, Laura. It's in the past. We can't do anything about it now."

"Everybody can help it, everyone together," I insisted.

"Look, I'm going across the hall. Marlene wants to show me some postcards she got."

Just then Ryan stepped out into the hall. He looked tired,

like me. "Want to go jogging in the morning?" he asked.

"Sure. Maybe that will help."

"I know what you mean," he said.

"It's not quite like reading about it in a book," I said.

"It's pretty intense," he said. I felt glad that at least some-one seemed to understand and share my mood.

The next morning there was a thump at our door, just after dawn. There stood Ryan in his running clothes, ready to go.

"Be with you in a minute!" I grinned and met him out in the hall five minutes later, hair still tangled, dressed in my jogging shorts and shirt.

"It's so great to get out really early," Ryan said, as we jogged slowly toward the mall, warming up. I agreed. It was a runner's paradise, the long stretch of grass leading to the Washington Monument, the air cool and slightly damp, and pink cherry blossoms floating down upon us as we ran.

"On Saturday, do you want to go on that tour to George-town?" Ryan asked. We ran side by side, matching our stride.

"No. Kim and I—that is, we're going on our own trip."

"Just the two of you?"

"Yup."

"Can I come along?" Spider flashed me a grin.

"You don't even know where we're going."

"It doesn't matter."

I laughed. He was flirting and running, and so was I. I felt good. "We're going to sneak off and go to the place where my mom was born, a little town in Virginia."

"You have relatives there?"

"No. I just want to snoop around."

"I'm good at snooping," Ryan said. "Let me come, too, and Jordan. We'll have a great time."

"Well, if that's what you want." I smiled to myself, thinking it would be fun to have the guys along. Besides, Jordan was good at reading maps and getting around.

"Okay. But we've got to fake it with Langfeld. Sign out for some place in D.C."

"Count me in, then," Spider said cheerfully.

We ran silently for a time. Then he asked, "Have you ever been back before?"

"Back here to my mom's home? No," I said. "My grandparents died long ago. We have no family here. I was born in San Francisco. I've never even been outside of California until now. Have you always lived in Mill Valley?"

We ran several paces before Ryan replied. "I was born in Chicago. My mom and I moved when I was nine."

"What about your dad? Didn't he come with you?"

"No, he didn't."

"You like Mill Valley?"

"Who wouldn't?"

I laughed. "You're right. It's like a storybook. You know, sometimes when I'm walking in the hills, I almost think I'll see a little squirrel house cut into one of the huge oaks, complete with little cupboards and beds."

"What an imagination!" Ryan exclaimed happily. "I'll remember that. The squirrels drive us crazy, running along our roof. My mom can't stand it. But then, there's lots of things my mom can't stand, like music and videos. Sometimes I know she can't stand me."

I said nothing, just kept on running.

"I'm sorry," Ryan said. "Guess it bums you out to hear kids saying things like that."

"No," I told him. "My mother and I had our off days. Most days, in fact. It's not that we argued a whole lot. We just didn't see eye to eye on most things."

"Like—what things?" We had reached the monument.

Ryan turned, jogging back down the mall, and I turned with him.

"Like, she wanted me to be plump. I'm naturally skinny."

"Well, from running," Ryan said.

"She didn't like my friends."

"You have great friends!" Spider exclaimed, shaking out his hands. "Look at me, for instance!"

I smiled and wiped my face; it was layered with sweat, and my body was steaming, altogether a good, healthy feeling. "We'd had a fight right before she died," I said.

"That's rough," said Ryan.

"But it's okay. I'm working it out."

"That's good. Hey, look at that tent!" Ryan ran onto the lawn. "Looks like someone's giving something away."

We stopped and gathered leaflets and lapel buttons about saving the environment, then we jogged back to the hotel to join the others for breakfast in the lobby. I felt that everything, at last, was getting sorted out and my life was back on track.

By Saturday we had seen so much of art and history that we were getting punchy, and I was glad for the chance to do something different. Ryan and Jordan enjoyed the idea of taking off, away from the group.

Marlene Madison, Cissy Cane, and Diane Ferguson were going on the Georgetown tour. All morning they talked about hanging out at the university shops, having lunch there, checking out the cute college boys. Kim didn't say anything, but I knew she wanted to be with those kids.

"You don't have to come to Birch Bend," I finally told her. "I can go myself, or else just with Ryan."

"Don't be silly," she snapped. "I said I'd go."

"Well, I know you like being with all those—groupies."

She glared at me. "Are you saying I'm a groupie?"

"I mean, I know you like Marlene and Cissy."

"They're not my best friends," Kim said pointedly. "And I don't break my promises. We're going. Just make sure we don't get caught."

We had to sign out, as usual. We put down that we were going on the Potomac River cruise, then to spend some time at the Smithsonian Air and Space exhibit. It sounded perfectly reasonable, wanting to relax on the riverboat after running around all week.

As I signed the ledger, I felt a moment of guilt. We were on our honor here. But then, it didn't seem so terrible, just a little white lie.

Jordan, who loved reading maps, was our planner. "We'll catch a tour bus," he said. He knew exactly where the ticket office was, how much the ride would cost. "We'll get off at the main stop—it's on Cedar and Armory Street, then we'll get a town map at a gas station. Do you know where you want to go?" he asked me.

"I just want to look around," I said, "see the high school, maybe find..." My voice trailed off. I didn't know exactly what I was looking for; I just wanted to feel the atmosphere of Birch Bend, let it enfold me and somehow end my longing.

The ride to Virginia took an hour and a half. While we were in that bus, speeding along the highway, I felt great, so free and happy. As we neared the station, there were butterflies in my stomach. I felt like opening night at the theater, afraid I'd forget my lines. I asked myself what I was doing here—did I hope to find a ghost of my mother? Now the whole idea seemed a little ridiculous, but I scampered out of the bus, pretending a lightheartedness that I certainly didn't feel.

As we walked along the main street, looking into shop windows, I became calm, a regular tourist, making comparisons between this place and home. Houses were different here, sturdier against the winter climate, and older. Even the trees had a different stateliness about them.

We came to a park with a duck pond and a bandstand painted a brilliant white. We sat down on the grass, and my fingers plucked at the soft green blades, and I lay back and gazed at a very blue, cloudless sky. Rows of dogwood were in bloom, and clumps of pink azaleas. I realized how much flowers had always been part of my life; I've always known their names, thanks to my mother. I looked for night-blooming jasmine, but found none.

I talked and laughed along with the other kids, but inside, underneath it all, I was aware of only one thing: My mother had walked these very streets. She had lived in one of these houses, maybe sat in the park on a summer afternoon with some boy she loved. From behind every tree and shrub I seemed to see her shadow darting out, only to disappear in a moment.

"Let's go get something to eat," I said, and we went around the corner to a grocery store and bought ice-cream bars.

"Let's look for an arcade or a mall or something," Ryan said, obviously getting bored.

"Maybe we could go to a movie," said Jordan.

I ran a few steps ahead, following the sounds of some celebration—people laughing, kids shrieking, some on bikes, some eating hot dogs. "Hey, it's a picnic," I called. "Let's go see."

"So what?" grumbled Jordan.

"It's—high school alumni," I said, now seeing the large

signs that had been stuck into the ground on posts: BIRCH BEND HIGH SCHOOL REUNION.

The vast area of lawns, picnic tables and barbecue pits was divided into sections for each of five different classes, and I could see the progression of years in the faces of the graduates—twenty-five years, twenty, fifteen, and so on down. Adults talked, reclined, cooked their hamburgers and hot dogs, passed out beer and Cokes. Little kids ran around screaming, playing, having fun. Nearby there were swings and a little carousel and a tall slide. Mothers and fathers and children made a constant, cheerful din. Someone had brought a CD player, and from it came the loud, melancholy strains of an old Beatles tune, "Yesterday."

Kim came to stand beside me. "Is this the school your mom went to?" she asked.

I nodded. "Sure. It's the only high school in town."

"What was her class again?"

"It was 1974."

"That's the group over there!" Kim pointed.

The boys took off, interjecting themselves into a casual football game with a bunch of little kids. I saw Ryan grab a handful of potato chips from somebody's lunch. A woman laughed, pretending to slap his hand. Jordan started clowning around, leaping to catch the ball, faking passes.

"Hormones," Kim and I said at the same time, and we started to giggle. We stopped at the same moment, sharing a thought without words, then stammering, "Isn't it weird?"

"This reunion..."

"Just when you were looking for..."

"I guess it was meant to be."

We watched the festivities for a moment, then I took a deep breath and said, "Let's go talk to them."

A group of ten or twelve people sat at a large redwood table, drinking beer and eating buffalo wings and chips. You could tell by their attitude, casual and teasing, that they'd all known each other for years. Every once in a while they glanced over to the baseball diamond, where a spirited game was going on, and they'd yell, "Way to go, yeah!" or they'd groan loudly over a strike.

Kim and I approached slowly. Nobody seemed to notice us. "Excuse me," I said. "I—my name's Laura Inman. My mother went to Birch Bend High. I think she was in this class."

A woman with bleached, frizzy hair leaned toward me, smiling in the mechanical way that is meant for little children. "What was her name, dear?"

"Jasmine. Jasmine Rogers."

The woman glanced at her companions, turned to me and said, "There's nobody by that name in our class. It must be one of the other classes."

"No," I said. "I don't think so."

One of the men yelled over to the next group. "Hey, you guys have a gal called Jasmine in your graduating class?" He raised his bottle of beer, as if in a salute.

"Naw," came the call back from several men. "Jasmine? We had a Rose. No Jasmine." Laughter billowed out from one group to the other. I stood there feeling awkward, and Kim clutched my hand for a moment, feeling it too.

A man came over from the baseball diamond, wiping his face with a bandanna. He wasn't tall, but his broad shoulders and muscular arms suggested that he must have been the class football idol.

"Hey, Monte—have a beer," the others greeted him. "Did we win?"

"We always win," said Monte. His blue eyes glistened, and

he smiled, emphasizing his wide mouth and prominent jaw. He must have been very handsome once, I thought. Now, I saw a coldness in his eyes as he nodded toward me. "Hi," he said. "Who are you? Somebody's kid?"

I told him our names. "We're from California, here on a school trip."

"To Birch Bend?" Everyone laughed; I felt like the straight man in a comedy routine.

"Our class came to Washington, D.C. We're just…"

"Slumming," said one of the women. She was perspiring, fanning herself with a paper.

"How'd you find this reunion?" asked the man called Monte, squinting against the sun.

"We just happened…" Kim began.

"It was a coincidence," I said.

His mouth tightened. Then he gave a grin. "There are no coincidences, haven't you heard?"

He was playing to the others, the women, who laughed and starting joking with him—yes, he was definitely the class king.

"Her mom's name was Jasmine Rogers," said one of the men. "We told her, there's nobody by that name in our class."

"This is a small town, honey. Everybody knows everybody."

"Probably got the wrong class."

"Or the wrong school."

"Or the wrong *town*, for God's sake—maybe she means Birch *Grove*. That's fifty miles east of here."

My heart began to pound, and I felt almost ill, embarrassed, the object of their jokes. "This is the right town," I said firmly. "It's the right school. I don't know why you are all…"

From the baseball field now another man appeared, heavy

set, his face red from exertion. His hair, the color of corn silk, clung to his face in damp wisps. He stopped and faced me, staring, mouth open, hand raised as if he knew me and was about to speak.

But one of the women called loudly, "Hey, Lester, sit down here, you old fool, you look ready to croak." She was a redhead wearing a bright red print shirt. "Have something to drink. You don't want to get dehydrated."

"Wouldn't hurt him to get dehydrated," someone laughed. "Lester could sure stand to lose a few pounds."

The man lurched down onto the bench. He cast another glance at me. Then he shook his head and called out, "I'm gettin' too old for these damn games. Next reunion, let's go to the races instead."

Everyone laughed. I felt like an intruder, but something kept me here, the feeling that I knew these people.

A tall, slim woman got up, opened a Coke, turned to me and said, "If your mom went to Birch Bend High, why didn't she come herself? Why'd she send you?"

From the CD player came one of Barbra Streisand's yearning tunes, "The Way We Were." One of the women sang along softly.

The football idol tipped back his head, swallowing beer. His throat pulsed. He sat forward, put the bottle down with a bang. "Listen, we don't know your mom. Get lost."

A blond woman frowned, touched his shoulder. "Take it easy, Monte. The kids made a mistake, is all."

"Well, why didn't her mom come herself? Angie's got the right question. Why?"

I faced him, feeling furious, almost shaking. "My mother is dead," I said. "That's why she didn't come. And she didn't send me. I told you. We happened to be walking here, and we thought—we thought people would be friendly."

The blond woman frowned. "I was class secretary," she said. "I knew everyone. There just wasn't any person like your ma. We're real sorry, hon. This must be real hard on you."

But the redhead scowled. "I don't even believe that about her mother. It's downright rude to bust in on people like this and spoil their party. I guess this is the way they allow kids to behave in California. Here in Virginia we don't let kids run wild. You go on home." She waved her hands to shoo us away. "Go on!"

I looked at Kim. She was pale, her eyes wide. Something in me rebelled, and I shouted out, "My mother *was* in the class of 1974! Why don't you remember her? Why won't you tell me?"

I was trembling now—hateful, stupid idiots—no wonder my mother didn't want to come and see them! My mother had told me they were nasty people—why didn't I believe her? Why did I have to go making a fool of myself?

I grabbed Kim's arm. "Come on," I said. "They're liars!" I rasped.

"Laura!" Kim's face was red. "Get a hold of yourself. Let's find the boys."

I shrugged her aside and ran toward the other group, and I called out, "Did you know Jasmine Rogers? Was she in your class?"

"No, no. We never heard of her."

"It could have been another class—seventy-six, maybe, or seventy-five," I said desperately.

"No way. This is a small school—we all knew each other. There was nobody by that name."

Someone muttered, "What's wrong with that girl? Think she's on something?"

I felt as if I were in a nightmare—worse, because this was real.

"Let's get out of here," I told Kim. She was biting her lip, totally embarrassed.

We looked all over, finally found the boys at the swings, goofing off, twisting the chains, spinning around.

"Come on, Jordan, Spider," Kim called. "We're leaving."

"Aw, Ma, do we have to go?" Ryan called in baby talk, and Jordan took up the plea, lisping, "No, no, Mommy, me don't wanna go yet—please!"

"Let's go," I said gruffly, turning away. "We don't need them."

"Come on, Laura," said Kim. "Lighten up."

"Don't tell me what to do!" I glared at her.

Spider came running. "Hey! Wait up. What happened? Did you find friends?"

"We found idiots," I said hotly.

"They said they didn't know her mom," Kim explained.

"So, what's the big deal?" Jordan said. "Why are you so upset?"

"Because they were downright nasty. And they lied!"

"Why would they lie?" Spider asked. "What could be their reason?"

"I don't know," I replied, furious. "But I'm going to find out."

"Come on, Laura," said Ryan. "Mellow out. It isn't worth it."

"Shut up, Spider," I cried. "How would you know?"

"I'm just trying to…"

"Just try leaving me alone!"

"Laura, he didn't mean…" Kim gave Ryan a helpless look.

I knew I had spoiled everything for the others, but I didn't even care. How could they say my mother had never gone to

Birch Bend High? It was as if they'd said she hadn't lived. I knew I'd have to get to the bottom of this, or I'd never have any peace. Then and there I decided to return to Birch Bend alone, to investigate.

chapter 6

"I don't think you should go alone," said Kim. It was early Monday morning. We sat on our beds eating the sweet rolls we had brought up from the breakfast bar. Here they called them "snails."

"Why not?" I said. "I can find my way. I'll take the same bus we took the other day. If I have a problem, I can go to an ATM. I've got a credit card."

"They were pretty weird at the picnic," Kim said. "I want to go with you."

I laughed. "You think they're on the lookout for us? I can just see it—a posse hunting for teenage party crashers. Look, you and Jordan have been talking about that FBI tour all week."

"I don't care about the tour." Kim tossed her hair over her shoulder. "Jordan's the one, and Spider. Guys enjoy that sort of stuff. I just want to be with you." She picked up her backpack. "Let's go."

The bus ride was like old times for Kim and me. We made up stories about people we saw, waved to kids standing in the road, talked about the boys and laughed a lot. When we got to Birch Bend I felt as if I already knew the town. Directions to the high school were simple, and once again I had the feeling of déjà vu, seeing the town through the eyes of my mother, years ago. A monologue hummed inside me: *"This is where she walked. This is the school she went to every day. Maybe that drugstore is where she shopped for makeup. Maybe they would still know her there."*

The high school building was solid and imposing, with a broad lawn and spreading maple trees, wide windows, orderly and silent, for it was still spring vacation.

We found the administration office at the front of the main building. Inside were the usual long counters, rows of chairs, and a secretary working on some files, simultaneously tending the telephones and replacing files in the cabinet. I motioned Kim to follow me, feeling secretive and excited.

In the hallways, two men were polishing the floor with a large buffing machine. Over the hum I asked, "Where's the library, please?"

The man jerked his chin backward over his shoulder, and Kim and I turned up another hallway and found ourselves in front of double doors marked LIBRARY.

One door was partly open, and we entered. Stacks of books stood on the counter and on trolleys, waiting to be shelved. A young girl, obviously hired as a temporary aide, stood in front of a trolley, sorting books, and in the back a librarian was bringing out reference volumes for a woman who sat at a table, writing notes.

"Where are the old yearbooks?" I asked the girl. She was dressed in jeans, and her hair was done in one long braid, hanging down her back.

"From this school?" she asked.

"Yes."

"How come you want them?" She seemed reluctant.

"I'm doing an article," I said "about sports at Birch Bend High. You know, comparing the old teams with the present. It's for a journalism assignment."

The girl pointed to a shelf far in the back. "They're all arranged according to year. You have to put them back yourself, though. We don't have time."

"Sure," I said. "We will."

Kim and I hurried to the back shelf. Kim whispered, "Why did you say that about writing an article?"

I shook my head. "I don't know. They were acting so strange at that picnic. My mother always said that the people in this town were snobs. If they thought we were outsiders, they might not want to help us."

"You're brilliant," Kim said.

"I hope the yearbooks go back far enough," I said. I pulled the step stool over to the shelves, climbed up, and scanned the topmost shelf. There it was, bound like all the other year-books in blue leather, with the lettering in gold, 1974.

Kim and I sat down at the table nearest the wall, where the shadows from the trees outside made patterns on the table and on our clothes. We were protected here from any prying eyes, and I felt the excitement of going on this quest. I opened the book, overwhelmed by the smell of glossy paper and print and the thought of finding my mother here.

Kim moved close, looking over my shoulder. "Look at those cute guys!" Kim whispered. "Look at their hair! Lots of them have ponytails."

I nodded. "Look at the girls. Those awful skirts."

We went through the book, page by page, gazing at the photographs of the graduates.

"There's something eerie about this," Kim whispered.

I nodded. "They seem so—real, all these kids. Don't you wonder what happened to them all?"

"We met some of them. We wouldn't even know which ones, they've changed so."

I stared at the photo of a very pretty, serious-looking girl. She gazed back at me almost as if she might speak, to clarify or apologize for being forever young, stuck in the past.

Slowly I turned the pages, savoring the impending moment of sudden discovery. We searched for the name Megan, and for Jasmine Rogers. There was only one Megan, an Asian girl. We found no picture of Jasmine Rogers at all.

I bit my lip, trying to piece this together—how could my mom be missing? Was she absent on the day they took the pictures? No—that was too simple. Besides, why wouldn't her classmates have remembered her? I was mystified and tense, then I remembered the expression of that towheaded man, Lester, who looked as if he knew me, as if he wanted to speak. Something strange was going on here.

Kim pushed back her hair, impatient and annoyed. "Well, maybe those guys were right, and your mom did go to school in a different town."

"No! She's got to be here." My voice rose, and the librarian came over.

"Something I can help you with, girls?" she asked. Her hair was a tangle of blond and silver-gray shoots standing up all around her head, and she wore a bright green knit dress.

"I was looking—through the yearbooks—for an article," I said, breathing heavily. "That is, also, my mother went to this school." What use was the pretense? My mother's picture was not here. It was as if she'd been obliterated from the earth.

"Her mother died," Kim explained in a low, tragic voice,

with an expression to match. She was overacting dreadfully. "We wanted to see, to sort of touch base with the past. We're sure her mom went to Birch Bend High. But why wouldn't her picture be in the yearbook?"

The librarian frowned and scooped up the yearbook in the deft way that librarians do. "Is it possible that her mother's family moved before graduation? Her picture might be in another volume." She scrambled up the step stool, pulled down several more volumes and laid them on the table. "Maybe she's in a group picture," the librarian suggested.

I flipped some pages. "I suppose it's possible."

"You girls look through these," the woman said, and she rustled away.

I picked up the book labeled 1972, quickly scanning the pages. The center of the volume was devoted to snapshots set into a collage, casual photographs of people at various activities. At the top of each photograph was a small number.

I looked at all of them briefly, then stopped. I glanced at Kim, thinking inexplicably, *I could just walk away now,* as if some foreknowledge warned me that this was the moment of turning. But I must have gasped aloud, for Kim rushed over and asked, "Did you find something? Do you see her?"

I pointed. It was a small photograph of two girls sitting on a low cinder-block wall, with a large magnolia tree in the background, a copy of the photograph I had found among my mother's things.

"That's it," I whispered. "It's my mother and her friend."

"What are those numbers on the photographs?" Kim asked.

"Maybe it's a code. Like footnotes." I turned to the back of the book. I was right. Each photograph had been numbered, and the names of the people were listed on this back page. I ran my finger down the column to number 22, which matched the number on the photograph. I saw the two names, "Megan Wynant and Jenny Rouseau."

I felt something spinning away from me, as if the floor had tilted. My mouth opened, but I did not speak.

"Jenny Rouseau?" Kim said. "Your mother's name was…"

"The same initials," I whispered. "J. R. Of course, it's her."

"What does it mean?" Kim asked, her voice high and anxious. "Why did she use a different name? Her name was Jasmine. When did she change it? Why?"

"Stop asking questions!" I said angrily. My own mother had lied to me about such a basic thing as her name. How could I answer Kim?

I clutched the book tightly to my chest, as if it were alive and could respond.

"Let's look through it again," Kim said. "Maybe there's a clue." I glanced up sharply at that word, *clue*. To Kim, this was a game, an exciting pastime. For me, it was everything.

Wordless I nodded, and carefully now we went page by page, scanning every face, every row of names. "She didn't graduate with her class," I said. "That's obvious. No graduation picture."

"They might have moved, like the librarian said." Kim frowned at me. "When did your grandparents die?"

"I'm not sure, exactly," I said. "Are you thinking…?"

"Maybe after they died your mom quit school. Maybe she never graduated. Maybe she went to work to support herself."

"It's possible," I said slowly. "But then, my mother was so smart. You said so yourself."

Kim tossed her hair over her shoulder. "Some people are self-educated, you know."

Suddenly I hated Kim's smugness. She and her mother were pals, her parents were normal, good-natured people, inviting her friends to the house all the time. How could Kim possibly understand my longing? I felt reckless and restless, wanting to run away to some far place, and for an instant I had the vision of picking up a chair and smashing it through the large library window.

I shuddered.

"Come on," Kim said. "This is getting us nowhere."

"Wait." I looked once again at the open yearbook, turning pages, and then Kim and I saw it simultaneously, and we both gasped.

"There's her name again," Kim said.

"She was in drama club," I said.

"Like us," Kim said.

"Did you girls find what you were looking for?" The librarian suddenly appeared and looked down at the open book.

"Her mother's name wasn't Jasmine Rogers," Kim said. "It was Jenny Rouseau."

All the muscles in the librarian's face seemed to contract. Her cheeks drew inward, her eyes became slits. "Well, I didn't know her," she said, her tone suddenly brittle. "But at least you found what you were looking for. You'll have to leave now. We're closing the library. It's—vacation time, you know."

She picked up the yearbooks, hurried up the step stool, and slipped the books firmly back into place. Then she moved behind us, her arms outspread as if to push us along. The girl with the long braid stared at us.

Outside, I looked at my wristwatch. "It's only eleven in the morning," I said. "That girl looked like she had plenty of work to last all day."

"You think they're not really closing the library?" Kim asked.

"I think that woman wanted to get us out of there," I said grimly.

"Why would she?"

"I don't know. Something's wrong."

Walking back to the bus stop, Kim and I went over the possibilities. Questions compounded, answers slipped away, elusive as little fishes. Why had my mother changed her name? Why had she never bothered to tell me that she was in drama, too? It would have made a bond between us, wouldn't it?

I recalled the time I was rehearsing for a scene from *The Taming of the Shrew.* My mother had stood at the doorway of my room, watching me as I spoke my lines in front of the mirror. Suddenly she came bursting in, her features contorted, her hair standing out wildly as she raked her fingers through it, calling, "No! No, Laura! That's not how it goes. You must put yourself in Kate's place, feel her anger, her disappointment, her pain and fear. Poor Kate! God, what a terrible thing, never to be married, especially in those days, when a woman's worth was measured mainly by her husband. Think! Put yourself into it—her father finds a husband for her sister, but not for her. Think of the anger, the shame, the outrage. 'What? You will not suffer me?'"

My mother shouted out the lines, her voice dripping with sarcasm, her eyes dark with emotion. "'Nay, now I see. She is your treasure, she must have a husband; I must dance barefoot on her wedding day and for your love to her lead apes in hell. Talk not to me: I will go sit and weep till I can find occasion of revenge.'"

I remember how I watched her and listened, fascinated, but she gave me no time to inquire or to applaud; my parents were going out that night. For me, she had become Kate in those moments. Now I understood: She had obviously played the part before.

I told Kim about it. We began to dream of my mother in the theater, a famous actress.

"Maybe she was on the stage in London," Kim said. "You told me she lived in London."

I nodded, imagining people tossing flowers up onto the stage, my mother bending and smiling to receive them.

Kim, suddenly excited, burst out, "Maybe your mother was a great star, and something tragic happened."

I nodded and took up the tale. "A scandal or something. Of course, it would have involved a rival. Or a man. So she left the theater…"

"Withdrew from society," Kim added, "moved to a small town. Mill Valley."

I shook my head. "This is silly. If my mother had been a star, surely I'd know it. Somebody would have recognized her."

"Maybe she'd put on a lot of weight," Kim argued. "Maybe she lost her looks."

"Stop it!" I shot back.

"I didn't mean it like that," Kim hastily said. "I'm sorry. Really. Look, there's lots of reasons why people change their names."

"What reasons?"

"She probably didn't like her name. Or maybe, maybe," Kim pulled the tip of her hair into her mouth, nibbling it nervously. "I don't know," she said with a sigh.

We had made our way to the bus, and now we entered and sat in the very back. We rode without speaking for a long time, while I tried to piece things together, picking through all the pictures in my mind.

"You know, Kim," I finally said, "my mother had a very unhappy childhood."

"Did she?"

"Well, her parents were killed when she was only in her teens. I've told you that. Why didn't I think of it? It explains everything. She obviously had to leave the town. Sure! That's why she went to London, to live with some relative there. Maybe an aunt or a real close friend of her parents'. While she was there, she changed her name to the aunt's name."

"That sounds logical," said Kim. "It would make things easier if they all had the same name. People wouldn't be asking questions all the time. Maybe the woman actually adopted your mom."

Suddenly it all fit, and I told it as if it were a long known certainty. "Look, probably this woman, Mrs. Rogers, really loved my mom and wanted her to share her name, to have her be like her own daughter. So my mother took her name. It was the least she could do, to show her appreciation."

"Then how come your mother never talked about this Mrs. Rogers?" Kim asked, her eyes narrowed now as she chewed at the ends of her hair.

"Maybe they had a fight. The relationship turned sour. That could happen, you know. My mother was very independent. Maybe this Mrs. Rogers was getting too domineering..."

"And after your mom met your dad, maybe the woman didn't approve of them going together. After all, your dad was so much older."

I took up the story, like forging links in a chain. "So my mom left London, angry because Mrs. Rogers didn't approve of the man she loved. Maybe it was easier to keep the name Rogers than to change again. Anyhow, what would have been the point?" My words came faster, and excitement burned in me as I connected one thought with the next. "She was changing her name again anyhow, getting married..."

"Then why didn't she tell you that her real name, her birth name, was Rouseau?"

Kim's words were like a dark shade, suddenly slamming down over the bright window.

"I don't know," I said. "I don't have to know everything!" I cried, feeling it all slipping away. "Maybe it's all so very simple. Maybe she just decided to change her name because it might change her luck. Maybe she just wanted to be a different person, a new person. Can't you understand that feeling?" I insisted. "I certainly can!"

"Okay, okay," Kim tried to soothe me. But it had been ruined, like a party that is ruined by rain. I felt chilled. Cold. Maybe I had a fever.

I wanted to crawl into my bed and stay there and not have to think about anything but sleep.

I did go to bed, shivering; I slept as if I'd been drugged. In the dream I was Kate from the play, dressed in a full-skirted frock with a deep-cut neckline, shouting the lines, "I must dance barefoot on her wedding day." I woke with sweat on my face and a sense of emptiness.

The others had whispered that they were going out to dinner and a lecture—did I want to come? I had pulled the covers over my head and willed myself to sink deep into sleep.

Now I was alone again, and all the unanswered questions came pushing toward me, like dark shapes that would never be vanquished.

My mother had allowed her life to be wrapped in secrets. Why? She had held herself apart from everyone, even me. She had lied, if not by words, then by omission. Why?

My mind began to race as I laid my plans. Next time I was going alone to Birch Bend. Next time I would find some answers.

chapter / 7

The next morning our entire group was booked for the White House tour. It was the highlight of our trip, seeing the White House, then having lunch with our congressman in the congressional dining room.

After waiting in line for over two hours, we went in, awed by the tall columns and gleaming hallways. The first thing I saw was a portrait of Jacqueline Kennedy Onassis. Kim, pressed close beside me in the crowd, whispered, "Isn't she beautiful?"

The sign "In Memoriam," brought a lump to my throat, as I recalled my mother telling me, "She was a perfect First Lady. No matter what happened to Jacqueline Kennedy, she rose to the occasion and kept her dignity."

Mother had admired Jacqueline Kennedy, and now both of them were dead. But Jackie Kennedy would be remembered forever.

I stared at the portrait, wishing my mother and I could have stood here together. I realized then, it wasn't the things we did together that I missed, but the things we had failed to do.

I glanced at Kim. She'd called her mother from the room last night. They had talked for nearly an hour. Afterward I tried to call my father in Tokyo, but I couldn't reach his hotel. I thought of phoning Mrs. Sheffield, but it was too late. I felt disappointed, but then Kim and I lay in bed talking, until we started giggling, just like old times.

Now we moved along with the stream of tourists, taking in all the glitter and beauty of the rooms and hallways, the elegant carpets, the huge vases of flowers, the chandeliers. We saw the beautiful Blue Room, the Red Room, the large reception hall, the grand dining hall.

We had lunch with our congressman, but the tables were crowded and Kim and I sat at the far end from our host. Jordan was in his element, sitting beside Roz and Mr. Langfeld, hanging on every word the congressman said. Roz's cheeks were flushed; the congressman kept looking at her, asking her opinion. Kim and I, at some distance, speculated and giggled—was he married? Was he hitting on her?

After lunch everyone split up, some to go shopping, others to go to the various museums. Kim and Jordan walked away holding hands. Jordan had been jealous and upset about Kim going off with me the day before.

"He doesn't own me," Kim had exclaimed angrily. "I wish he'd just get lost."

"Don't be mad," I defended Jordan. "He wants to spend some time with you. Why don't you guys do something together today after the tour?"

Kim had eyed me dubiously. "What about you?"

"I'll go back to the hotel and try to reach my dad. Maybe I'll get lucky this time. I want to tell him about the trip and everything."

"Will you tell him what you found out about your mom?"

I stared at her. "No. Maybe. I don't know."

"Well, I guess I'll see you later," Kim said. "We can all have dinner together and maybe go to the show."

"Great, great," I said with false enthusiasm. Now, I wanted only one thing, and that was to get back to Birch Bend.

So I slipped away and went to the bus depot, secure now about where I was going. Birch Bend was becoming familiar; I'd find the main library, do some basic research.

While I waited for the bus I bought a magazine, then a Coke, and I daydreamed about the wildness in me, that streak of independent yearning that I'd never shared with anybody, not even Kim. I thought of running away, changing my name, my life. It was what my mother had done. Maybe that was why I, too, felt that urgent desire to be somewhere else in somebody else's skin.

When I was nine, I had actually run away one day, though nobody ever knew it. We were living in San Francisco. My mom had gone to bed with a headache. I slipped out the back door, with four dollars in my pocket, and caught the California Street bus all the way to the park. I remember that excited feeling, the freedom to do exactly as I pleased. I walked around for about an hour, went up to the tea garden and ordered cookies and sat there alone, smiling to myself. But my smile ached after a while. I wanted someone to smile back at me. I wanted to be spoken to. Everything was empty and too gigantic. What had seemed like freedom now felt like abandonment.

How had my mother done it? Why? Jenny Rouseau, Jenny Rouseau, the name sang through my mind. Why did you give up your name, Jenny? Was it just that Jasmine was more glamorous? Is it all that simple? But why didn't you ever tell me? And why didn't you ever go back to Birch Bend?

The memories were simply too painful, Laura.

It was as if her voice had said the words. I looked up, and there beside me stood Ryan Spider Margolis. I gasped in surprise. "What are you doing here?"

"Glad to see me?"

"Hmm—I don't know," I said candidly. Since that afternoon at the picnic, I hadn't spent any time with Ryan, irritated at his silly behavior, disappointed by his lack of understanding.

"I'm sorry I was so—goofy," he finally said, looking downcast. "At that picnic, you know. We were just fooling around, and you..." He sighed. "It was serious for you."

I nodded. "It's okay, Ryan. I guess I was a little bit uptight."

"Like a spring."

We both laughed.

"Yeah. How did you know where I was?" I asked, glancing around. "I thought I covered my tracks pretty well."

He grinned shyly. "I guess I sort of followed you. Are you mad at me?"

I shook my head.

"Are you going back to Birch Bend?"

"Yes. Did Kim tell you what we discovered about my mother yesterday?"

"Sort of." He still seemed uncomfortable and kept looking over his shoulder. "Hey, that's our bus. Let's get on."

I smiled in spite of myself as Spider grabbed my hand and together we boarded the bus.

We sat down near the back, and for a while we rode without speaking. It would be fun if this were an ordinary date, I thought, if I didn't have this mysterious agenda. "Look," I said, "I understand perfectly if you're tired of all this—this chasing around looking for..." I took a deep breath and let out the word, "ghosts."

"Everybody has some ghosts," Ryan said lightly. "I came of my own free will, remember? You don't have to apologize."

I felt Ryan's warmth beside me, along my leg, my whole side, from hip to shoulder. I wanted to look at him, but was somehow afraid. I didn't want to like him. My life was complicated enough.

Suddenly I felt his hand covering mine, tentatively at first, as if he were afraid I might push him away. Gradually we both relaxed. Our fingers entwined. I said, "We found my mom's picture in one of the yearbooks, but under a different name. It was a name I never knew. And I can't explain it, not really."

"Kim told me you had a theory about your mother living with someone, using their name."

"Yes."

"I have another theory."

"Really? What is it?"

Spider took his hand from mine and rubbed the top of his head, so that his hair stood up, sort of spikey. "Maybe," he said, "your mother was married before. To a man named Rogers. Maybe it was an awful marriage, and they got divorced."

My heart thudded in my chest at the obvious conclusion: Maybe my mother even had another child before me. Maybe, somewhere, I had a half sister or brother.

"Look, Ryan," I said heavily, "it doesn't help to speculate. If my mother had been married before, she'd have told me." But the lie caught in my throat, and I think Ryan knew it.

"I wish you wouldn't call me Ryan," he said, and I glanced at him and saw that his face was flushed, his look very serious. "That's my dad's name. I'll be thinking you're talking to *him*."

"You like being called Spider?" I asked, incredulous. "I thought it was a nickname people gave you because of..."

"Actually, I thought of it myself."

"How come? When?"

"I was just a little kid. Nine years old. I'd started running and the little girl who lived next door came out laughing one day, yelling, 'Spider legs! Spider legs!'" He smiled almost self-consciously. "I was tall for my age, even then."

I nodded. "I've always been tall, too."

"Didn't anybody ever call you Spider?" he teased. "It's a compliment. Spiders are fast, independent, elusive, mysterious."

"Okay," I said, laughing. "I'll call you Spider. Just don't you call me anything but Laura."

"How about 'Gorgeous'?"

I didn't know what to say. Spider took my hand again, making his fingers dance along my wrist. The bus sped along. I was not eager for time to pass; this was one of those good times. I didn't want to rush away.

After a while I told Spider my plan. "I know my mother lived in Birch Bend. I thought if I could find the house where my mom lived, I could learn something more."

"The house might not be standing anymore," Spider said.

"But it might. Maybe there are still neighbors who knew her as a child."

"Could be," Spider said dubiously. Then he turned away and looked out the window.

"You think I should leave this alone, don't you," I said.

"Yes, I do. Poking around in the past usually causes trouble and grief."

"You sound like my father," I scoffed.

"I've had experience," Spider said soberly.

"What do you mean?"

"Nothing. It's—nothing."

He looked troubled, but he would say no more, and I didn't want to pry. The bus turned down the main street, headed for the depot.

"How would you go about finding the address?" I asked. "I thought I'd look for some old phone books at the library."

"I'm not sure," said Spider. "Phone company might be better. Or maybe the county clerk's office. I think they keep records of deeds and stuff."

"How come you're so smart?" I teased him.

He flexed his muscles, grinning. "It's from running. Sends blood to the brain."

The man at the bus depot directed us to the library. I believe he recognized me from previous times; he winked and called me "sister."

The library was three blocks from the high school, a sprawling, modern building. Inside there was a long counter with three computers waiting to provide information, and a librarian seated nearby, smiling as we entered, obviously pleased to go into action. The place was nearly empty.

"Excuse me," I said.

The librarian smiled brightly.

"I'm looking for old telephone books."

"How old?" She leaned toward me expectantly.

"Twenty-five years or so."

"Oh." The librarian looked sorrowful. "I'm afraid we don't go back that far."

I turned to Spider. Smugly he mouthed the words, "phone company."

I asked the librarian. "Would they have old books at the telephone company office?"

"Oh, no," she said. "They're at the historical society. That's where we send them after five years. Where we used to send them, that is. Now we put everything on microfiche."

I asked, "Can you give me the address of the historical society?"

"Certainly." She whipped out a small pad of paper and wrote down the address, tore it off, and handed it to me. "It's only five blocks from here, on Madison Street. A small brick building. You can't miss it."

"Would it be open now?"

The librarian checked the clock on the far wall. "Oh, yes. Every afternoon from two to five. Joeldeen Cunningham is the person you want to see. Tell her Ida May, from the library, sent you. Tell her not to forget the barbecue at my brother-in-law's place next Sunday." She laughed, a reedy sound, and self-satisfied.

The historical society building was an old two-story brick house with small windows and black shutters that shone with new, fresh paint. From a distance I saw the small, gracefully lettered sign hanging from a rusted chain: BIRCH BEND HISTORICAL SOCIETY, and in small script, "Open Two to Five Each Afternoon."

Spider and I went up the stone steps, deeply worn in the middle. "This place must be five hundred years old," I said.

"Maybe three hundred," he corrected me. "Country hasn't been here that long."

"Sorry. Didn't know you're a historian, too."

The narrow glass door was framed in black, hung from the inside with a faded flowered curtain. Things rustled as we entered, and a smell of oldness wafted out, paper and carpet dust, cloth and mold. But inside the narrow hall, everything sparkled as if it had just been polished; the glass lamps, the wall mirrors, and the bright cloth that covered a small antique table set with bric-a-brac.

A woman came toward us, rolling from side to side, and I saw that her feet were clad in flat leather slippers, pink, to match her polyester suit. Her face was whiter than was natural, her lipstick a bright rust color. She wore a necklace of large fake pearls and earrings to match, and her manner spoke of years ago, of loneliness, of gladness for visitors at last.

She smiled, showing uneven, darkish teeth. "Come in! Come in! Make yourselves at home. Don't mind the floor, it does slant a bit. People think it's their eyes!" She laughed happily.

I said, "Ida May from the library sent us. She asked us to remind you about the barbecue on Sunday."

This brought another bright laugh. "Oh, my. Oh, my."

"We came to see the old telephone books," Spider said. "From twenty-five years ago."

"Well, they're all in the back room. There's a bench if you want to take them out. This house is one of the oldest in town, you know, built by Filbert Cuttleson back in 1682.

Go on back! Help yourselves!" she sang out. "Call if you need anything!"

We went through the narrow hall, passing tiny rooms, each decorated with worn antique furniture, threadbare carpets and pillows, and tiny tables and chairs.

"Were people smaller three hundred years ago, do you think?" I asked Spider.

"Looks like it," he said, edging his way through the tight quarters out to the back porch. A large iron washtub was braced against the wall, and improvised floor-to-ceiling cupboards were painted a dull pea green. We opened several, all filled with file boxes, neatly labeled, until we came to a stack of telephone books packed in plastic wrappers.

"Here they are." Spider pulled them down. Dust accompanied them, spreading in puffs around us. "Whew! I'm..." He sneezed. "...allergic to dust."

"Here, let me." I undid the plastic cases and scanned the dates, going through seven packages before I found a telephone book for the late sixties. "This is it."

Spider opened the book, bending over it, his lanky body nearly touching the walls of the small room. "Rouseau. Rouseau. How do you spell that? One *s* or two?"

"One."

"Here it is. South Tyrol Street. Number 1421."

I held back, afraid to look, afraid everything might vanish, and I'd be left empty, as before. Softly I asked, "Is there only one Rouseau?"

Spider peered at the book again. He turned to face me. "Only one. Mr. and Mrs. George Rouseau."

"That's them. I know my mother's father's name was George. My grandmother's name was Jeanette. I always thought they sounded like a musical comedy team." I was nearly in tears trying to imagine them, imagining that I had grandparents like anyone else.

Spider closed the book and turned to me. "Now what?"

"We go there. Unless you don't want to. I could go alone."

"No way."

"Did you find what you needed?" The woman in pink polyester stood in the doorway, smiling expectantly.

"Yes, thank you for helping us."

"That's what we're here for," said the woman cheerfully.

We followed her through the narrow hall to the front foyer. "It's a beautiful old house," I said, smiling back at the woman as we left.

She settled back to watch us, and I could see that she was

lonely. She reminded me in a way of Mrs. Sheffield. I realized I hadn't even phoned Mrs. Sheffield once since I'd left home, and I resolved to phone her tonight.

It never happened.

chapter / 8

We stopped at a gas station for a cold drink and a street map. Tyrol Street was about two miles from the historical society building, due east.

As we walked, the neighborhood showed subtle changes. Houses were no longer attached, in rows, but stood separate, with lawns around them, and trees. It reminded me of Mill Valley, but an older version, more settled.

We came, at last, to the corner of Maple and Tyrol streets, and I stood there for a long moment, as if this were a tunnel to another time dimension, and I was just about to enter.

Spider took my hand. "You're cold," he said.

"Scared," I admitted.

"Of what?"

"Of being disappointed, I guess."

"We could go back."

"No way."

I was grateful that Spider didn't ask me what I was looking for or why I had come here: He seemed to know.

"How come you're so understanding?" I said.

"Am I?" He evaded me, but tightened his hold on my hand.

"Look." I pointed. "Fourteen-twenty-one. The house with the dark blue shutters."

Immediately I ached to run inside that house, to be in its rooms. I would stand and look from its windows, feel its walls sheltering me. Because it was my kind of house, pale gray wood with stone trim, a tidy front yard, a porch all around, with white posts and railings. Sheer curtains fluttered at the windows; I longed to look inside.

Carefully trimmed trees grew on either side of the porch. Several potted plants were filled with exuberant spring blossoms.

On the porch a hammock waited for someone to settle down and watch the slow-moving occasional traffic, or the orange cat sunning itself across the street.

I saw the mailman making his way on foot, hoisting his sack up higher on his back. Quickly I walked toward him, calming my features, trying to appear casual despite the urgent beating of my heart.

"Excuse me," I said. "Would you happen to know who lives in this house?"

"What house? What number?"

"Fourteen-twenty-one."

"Who wants to know?"

"I'm an old neighbor—my family used to live here. I just thought..."

"Oh, a nostalgia trip," he said, his face breaking up into deep smile lines. He was thin and nut-brown from his profession, and his hands were callused and nimble as he plucked out several letters. "Antonia Armenta," he said. "Used to be Mr. and Mrs. Only Mrs. is left now."

"Is she usually home?"

"You could ring the bell and see," he offered. "What have you got to lose?"

"Nothing. Thanks. We will."

We went up the walk, I ahead of Spider. I was glad he let me lead; this was my assignment, my own quest. I rang the bell, stared at the screen door. It sagged from too much slamming and pushing over the years. Maybe this was the very same screen door my mother had pushed against as a small child, learning to walk. "She's probably not home," Spider said, stepping up beside me. "Most people work during the day."

We were startled by a voice behind us. "I was out in the yard," said the woman. Her hair was dyed jet black, and she wore an orange and red flowered gardening smock, gardening gloves that were stained with mud spots, and she carried a trowel and a bucket. "Planting my dahlia and tuberous begonias. Think there's still time?"

I stared at her dumbly. "I think…" I said hesitantly, "dahlias go in right after the first frost. In California, sometimes we do them as early as March. Here, of course…" I let my voice trail away as the woman nodded vigorously.

"Do you use blood meal?"

"My mom does. Did. When we planted spring bulbs. Yes."

"Well, how rude of me." She pulled off her gardening glove and extended a slim, mottled hand. "I'm Antonia Armenta. And did you come along just to provide me with gardening assistance?" She smiled, showing perfect teeth, probably false, I thought.

"We're just visiting in the area," I said. "This is Spider Margolis. I'm Laura Inman. We're from California."

"Ah, Hollywood!" Mrs. Armenta exclaimed. "Do you see many stars there? A friend of mine went to Los Angeles and saw Sylvester Stallone having lunch. He was eating pasta. He had a bodyguard with him, my friend said. Have you ever seen Sylvester Stallone?"

"We're from northern California," Spider explained. "Laura's family used to live here," he added, obviously trying to get this conversation in gear.

"Here? On this street?"

"My mother lived in this house. Your house. Fourteen-twenty-one."

"Oh. *Oh*. Well, would you like to come in? Maybe you'd like a cold drink or a cup of tea. Do you drink tea?"

"Just water would be fine."

"Nonsense," said Mrs. Armenta as she led the way inside. "I have lemonade already made, shot with a little orange juice. I prefer it that way—always keep a pitcher of something cold. Unless it's winter, of course."

As she spoke Antonia Armenta led us through the hall, then the parlor, both filled with books and prints and needle-work. Tall stacks of books crowded the living room floor, covered the tables and chairs. Some were open, as if the reader had paused briefly and meant to return to the text.

Mrs. Armenta followed my glance and told us, with a wave of her hand, "My husband and I ran the used bookstore. Antonia's Antiquarian, we called it. I sold off most of them, but..." she turned to me with a smile, "I just couldn't let these go. My favorites. I love to read."

Mrs. Armenta led us into an old-fashioned kitchen, with see-through cabinets and shuttered windows. On the wide windowsill stood several decorative ceramic urns, variously glazed in blue, green, and tan. Two plants trailed down from hooks in the ceiling; it was a friendly, comfortable room.

"Lemonade?" Mrs. Armenta asked, taking a plastic container from the refrigerator.

"Yes. Thanks," said Spider, and I nodded.

We sat down, sipped our lemonade, and Mrs. Armenta looked at me quizzically. "Tell me about your mother," she said, with an intent gaze.

I was startled. "She's dead now," I said softly.

Mrs. Armenta nodded, as if she already knew, had seen it in my eyes. "I'm sorry," she said briskly. "Now, what is it you wanted to know about the house?"

"I'm not sure," I faltered. "I just wanted to see it, to hear about the people who lived in this neighborhood when she did."

"How long ago was that?"

"About twenty-five years, I guess."

The woman smiled. "I've only lived here eight years. Afraid I don't know much about the neighborhood. Except for rumor, you know. Here everything has a story. The high school administration office was once a one-room school-house. They say that President Jefferson's cousin went to school there." She smiled. "Who knows? The post office used to be a horse barn, and once a thief was hanged just outside it from that giant oak tree. Who knows if it's true? You probably noticed the house at the end of the street, the only one with a modern front. Kind of an eyesore, if you ask me. It certainly doesn't blend in with the others."

"Why's it so different?" Spider asked. I was grateful for his interest; I'd been thinking he must be bored to death.

"Well, there was a big fire, burned down that whole house. It was a real tragedy. Two people died in the fire. They had a child, too, but she was saved. Anyway, when they rebuilt the house, they made it all of glass and stone."

"When was the fire?" Spider asked.

"Long time ago. Maybe eighteen, twenty years ago. I'm not

sure, but it was long before my time. Funny, I came to retire here. The people we bought the house from went to retire someplace else. It's like musical chairs—or musical states," she said with a laugh, "people coming and going, making changes." She turned to me. "You still have friends and family here?"

"No. My grandparents died before I was born."

"Did they now, that's a shame. Were they local people? Born here?"

"I'm not sure. Their name was Rouseau."

"Not George Rouseau," said Mrs. Armenta, starting from her chair.

"Yes. Why do you...?"

Alarm and confusion showed in her eyes, as if she had been tricked and now feared we would hurt her.

"That's who we bought the house from!" the woman exclaimed. She got up, circled the table, all her movements flustered and tense. "Rouseau? Your grandparents?"

"How—how could you have—have bought the house from them? You bought it eight years ago, you said." Maybe she was senile, I thought, forgetful and confused. Everything seemed twisted and strange. I wanted to grasp her arms, shake the truth out of her, but I only stood there, staring.

"George and Jeanette Rouseau sold the house because they wanted to retire near the shore somewhere. They were moving away. But you told me they were dead. How could they be dead if they sold us the house? I mean, I met them. I saw them. George and Jeanette—could there be another couple by the same name?" Mrs. Armenta's eyes darted back and forth between Spider and me, as if to discover some hoax.

"I'm—I don't know what to say," I began. I felt suffocated. "I thought my grandparents had died years ago, when my mother was still in her teens. But now you say—they just left here eight years ago." I was filled with a rush of possibilities, an opening of new worlds, more than hope, more than happiness, I felt suddenly reborn. "Mrs. Armenta!" I summoned her by name, demanding the truth. "Are my grandparents still alive?"

Mrs. Armenta approached and faced me. Her face was creased and her voice wavered. "I can't say whether they are alive today. But I can tell you definitely they were alive eight years ago. Your grandmother, Jeanette, was one of the local artists. She made pottery."

Mrs. Armenta whirled around, pointing to the windowsill. "There! That's some of her work. I bought those ceramic pots at a sale from the local gift store just before your grandmother left. I believe they're signed on the bottom." She rushed to the windowsill, brought over one of the small pieces, turned it to reveal the signature scratched in white onto the underside: "J. Rouseau."

An odd feeling seized me, a weightless sensation, dizziness. This small ceramic urn that I held in my two hands was all I knew, all I had ever known of my grandmother. Her hands had worked this clay, had poured the glaze, had lifted the creation from the fire and scratched in her name. With the tip of my finger I traced the engraving, wishing for some knowledge to flow from the letters to me. When I spoke my voice was strange even to my own ears, very low, different. "Where did they say they were moving, Mrs. Armenta? Tell me. You have to tell me."

"My dear child!" she exclaimed. "I have no idea. Maybe I once knew." Mrs. Armenta's dark brows drew together, her forehead was creased, her lips taut. "I can't remember at all. I'm so sorry. I do have trouble remembering things ever since my husband…"

"Oh. Oh, God," I said softly. This house suddenly seemed too small, too close. I felt its heat overwhelming me, jarring my thoughts. How could I have come so close, only to lose them again? If I had grandparents, I thought, if I could see them and speak to them—a rush of loneliness engulfed me. My legs gave way. I found myself kneeling on the floor, hands flat in front of me, as if I had blacked out for a moment. The small urn lay on the floor beside me, miraculously intact.

"My dear, are you all right?" Mrs. Armenta asked anxiously.

"I'll be fine," I said, getting up. "Really."

Spider came to me. "We'd better go," he said. He led me to the door, his arm around my waist, holding me close. "We need to catch our bus back," he explained to Mrs. Armenta. "Thanks for the lemonade."

"Oh, you're very welcome."

Mrs. Armenta walked with us to the door. She said, "If I ever happen to hear from your grandparents, what shall I tell them?"

"Take my address," I said. Mrs. Armenta rushed inside for a pad of paper. I wrote down the number, and we said good-bye.

"Come back!" Mrs. Armenta called cheerfully.

"Thanks." I waved back at her. Spider and I continued up the street. I felt dazed. "I can't seem to think," I said.

"I know how that is," Spider said. "It's a shock to find out your grandparents might still be alive."

"To realize that my mother lied to me again. Lies!" I burst out. "Nothing but lies!"

"Maybe she lied because there were things she didn't want you to worry about."

"Like what?" I demanded.

"Like—maybe—I don't know." He shrugged, then stopped walking and turned to me, looking more serious than I'd ever seen him. "Listen, Laura," he said, "maybe you should leave this alone. Right now you're getting over—over your sadness. Things are just getting back to normal. I mean, you're on this trip and everything."

I wondered what he meant by "and everything." He reached out toward me; I stood there, perplexed. "What are you trying to tell me?"

He frowned and continued walking, slowly. "I—guess I sort of know how you feel," he said. "Remember you asked me why I took the name 'Spider'?"

I nodded and matched my steps to his and I listened intently, for his voice was very low, very serious.

"My folks split when I was only two," he said. "I couldn't remember my dad, but I had a sort of picture of him in my head. All the time, at night before I went to sleep, and whenever I went anyplace new or did anything fun, I'd think about my dad. Sometimes when the phone rang I'd run to answer it, imagining that it might be him."

"But he never called," I said.

"He never called," Ryan repeated. "The older I got, the more I thought about him. When I was in third grade, I guess I started acting up a lot. I mean, getting into fights, disrupting the class. My mom and the teacher decided I should go into therapy. The woman—this psychologist—did a whole lot of stuff with toys and pictures and puzzles. Finally she decided that I really had to see my dad, in the flesh, because I was getting too deep into this—this obsession."

Spider paused, and we stood there while he stared off into the distance, thrust his hands into his pockets, then said, "So Mom took me to see him. It was a far drive, about five hours.

All the way there I kept imagining what he'd be like. And when we got there—well, I won't go into the blow-by-blow account. The thing is, he was so different than I'd thought. He was—I guess he was sort of crude. Loud, you know? I mean, he talked loud, the kind of guy that goes around slapping people on the back all the time and telling lousy jokes. He needed a shave and a bath. You could tell. But that wasn't the worst of it. In the house was this woman. His new wife looked real young. And they had three little kids. The girl was hers from another marriage. But the two little boys were theirs. And when he came to the door, my dad had a boy in each arm. And they were hanging on to him, calling him Daddy, and they were…"

Spider broke off. He took a deep breath, then looked straight at me again. "They were his kids. They were his family. Not me. You want to know what he said to me? 'Ryan! My God—what a big kid. I wouldn't have recognized you on the street.' And that was just it. He wouldn't have recognized me, because he didn't really care. He had a whole new family, and I wasn't part of it."

I hesitated, then asked gently, "Had he known you were coming?"

"Oh, sure. My mom had called ahead."

"So that's when you started going by the name of 'Spider,'" I said. Spider gave me a quick, small smile.

I took his hand and we walked close together, and I felt his tension subsiding. I heard him give a sigh of relief. It made me feel good to know that in some way I'd helped him.

We walked along the street to the end. There was the house, the one Mrs. Armenta had said was an eyesore, all of stone, with a large glass front window rising to a peak. It was modern, utterly out of place, grotesque, in a way, the sort of house that simply didn't fit.

"Let's go," I said to Spider. But something made me turn back. A thought hugged the edge of my mind, an image of something I had seen before. Then I knew. Beyond the lawn was a low cinder-block wall. Behind the wall was a tree, a huge magnolia. The bark on the right side of the tree was blackened, scarred, where the tree had been singed by fire.

Now, as if I had been here long ago, watching, I could envision the two girls who sat on this low wall years ago, smiling at each other, imagining that they would be friends forever.

"It was Megan's house that burned down," I said, my voice trembling. "I'm sure of it."

As if my vision had opened, turning back the years, I could picture them, Megan and my mother, talking and laughing, carefree and happy. But that was before the fire, the fire that had killed Megan's parents and changed everything.

chapter / 9

When Spider and I got back to the hotel, it was about seven-thirty in the evening, already dark. We had stopped for a pizza on the way. I couldn't wait to tell Kim what had happened.

"Kim, oh, Kim!" I called out, racing into our room. "Wait until I tell you...Spider and I..."

"Oh, so you're back," she said, looking up from a pamphlet she was reading. Her eyes were smoldering. "Where were you?" she demanded. "Roz was up here questioning me."

"I went to Birch Bend," I said. "Kim, wait till you hear what we found out. My grandparents..."

"We?"

"Spider came with me. Listen, my grandparents..."

"You lied to me," Kim exclaimed. "You said you were coming back to the hotel. Instead, you went sneaking off with Spider. How do you think that makes me feel?"

"I didn't *lie*, exactly," I said, trying to soothe her. "Look, there are things I need to know, and it doesn't seem right to keep on involving you. That's why I decided to go alone."

"But you didn't go alone!" Her cheeks were flushed with anger. "You went with Spider!"

"I hadn't planned on going with Spider. He followed me. Kim, I was trying to be nice and considerate. You and Jordan wanted to go to the mint."

"That was Jordan's brilliant idea. All we did was stand in a stupid line for two hours. By the time we got in, they were ready to close the place. I hate standing in line! You were out having fun!"

"I was investigating," I exclaimed. "Kim, let me tell you…" but her face was still thunderous, and I tried to understand this sudden attack. "Is it because we had dinner without you guys? Look, we were starved and that pizza smelled so good. If you're hungry, I'll go out with you and…"

"No, it isn't dinner," she said in a mincing tone. "I can eat without you, you know."

"Then why are you so mad?"

Her voice sounded choked. "It's damned embarrassing when you and Spider go sneaking away. Everyone's talking."

"Well, why didn't you stop them? You know how I feel about Spider. He's a friend. That's all."

"I just don't like people looking at me like that."

"Like what?" I demanded.

"Like my best friend is a *slut*."

I wanted to slap her. Instead, I escaped into the bathroom, washed my hands and face, steaming inside. Don't overreact, I told myself, echoes of Father. If you're mad, wait, he always says. Usually I can't follow that advice, but this time I did.

When I went back into the bedroom Kim was standing in front of the mirror, her face and her body rigid. As I moved closer, she leaned toward the mirror, pretending to be totally engrossed in her reflection.

"What's wrong, Kim?" I said softly. I couldn't figure out why she was acting this way. I wanted to yell and shake her. But we've been friends for so long, through thick and thin, as they say. I touched her shoulder and said, "I just wanted to give you time alone with Jordan. He was already upset that we left him out yesterday. He wants to be with you."

She flinched, leapt back. "What makes you think I want time alone with Jordan? He's getting too possessive as it is."

"You're always saying how sweet he is. He's crazy about you, Kim."

"So what? Who cares?" Kim cried.

"I thought you cared about him. You've been going together for almost two years."

"Jordan's okay," she said, flipping her hair over her shoulder.

"But—I thought you—you were in love with Jordan."

"With Jordan? Are you kidding?" Her voice rose.

"Then why are you still going with him?" I asked, aghast.

"Why do I have to answer all these questions?" Kim exclaimed. "Get off my back, Laura!"

"So you're just using him," I accused.

"What a mean thing to say!"

"It's true."

"Jordan's not complaining!" she cried. "It's not your business anyway. It doesn't affect you. But when you go sneaking off with Spider it makes you look bad, and that reflects on me."

"Oh, poor Kimmy," I crooned, sarcastic in my anger. "Has to be friends with a big, bad tramp."

"Stop it."

"You're so hypocritical," I said.

"You're so manipulative. Always have to get your way. You insisted we all go on that wild-goose chase."

"See? That's exactly why I didn't want to take you along this time!" I cried.

"You're in trouble, you know," Kim said ominously. "Roz came up here looking for you. How do you think I felt when she questioned me? I didn't know what to say."

"Why didn't you just say I'd gone sightseeing?"

"I tried that. She wanted to know where. I don't like being put on the spot that way, Laura. I really hate it. Besides, I thought we were in this together. We started out together. Then you just dumped me."

I realized, then, how it looked to Kim, my going off without her. I realized, too, that she really needed me, maybe even more than I needed her. "I'm sorry," I said softly. "I hate it when we fight."

"Me too." She twisted a lock of hair around her finger.

"Don't you even want to know what happened to me today?"

"I do," she said. "Of course I do."

I took a deep breath, backed over to the bed, and sat down. Kim followed, watching me closely. Already, she was intrigued. That's how it's always been with us—we both loved a good story, an exciting drama.

"Well," I began, drawing it out, "Spider followed me to the bus station. So we took the bus to Birch Bend." I smiled. "We held hands. He's really sweet."

"So? What else?"

I lowered my voice. "We found out some really fantastic things. I saw the house where my mom lived. We went in it!" I recounted everything that Mrs. Armenta had told us. Then I continued. "My mother and Megan lived on the same block. Obviously, they were best friends. I'm sure it was Megan who gave my mom this bracelet."

I saw the gleam in Kim's eyes. She was captivated.

"Then Megan's house burned down. I know, because I saw the wall and the tree, the same ones that were in the photograph. It must have been the fire that separated them," I said. "Megan's parents were killed in that fire. Probably Megan was sent away to live with some relatives, and that must be why they never saw each other again."

I stopped to let Kim feel the impact of the tragedy. I bent toward her, conciliatory. "Look, I'm sorry I took off without you. But this is the most important day of my life. Mrs. Armenta bought that house from my grandparents only eight years ago. Don't you understand what this means? My grandparents might still be alive."

"Then why did your mother say they were dead?"

"I don't know! It's all too strange. I have to find some answers. And I need you to help me. I really need you."

"I don't want to go back there again, Laura," Kim said. "Roz is suspicious. We're going to get in trouble. My parents will just kill me."

"I'm not asking you to go anywhere with me," I said.

"I think you should leave this alone, Laura. Mellow out. We may never get here to Washington again."

"I may never again have the chance to find my grandparents!" I cried. "Don't you understand?"

I tried to fight back the sudden fury that came over me. After all the things I'd done for Kim, all the years of our friendship, now when I needed her she was backing off. The bracelet jingled as I shook my hand; FRIENDS FOREVER. I wanted to throw the bracelet at her, throw *something* at her. Kim went to the mirror and began brushing her hair in long, quick strokes. The movement infuriated me all the more. I started to speak, felt choked. Kim kept on brushing her hair, looking into the mirror at me. "Look, Laura," she said evenly, as if she'd rehearsed the words, "my parents spent a lot of money for me to go on this trip. I added some of my own savings."

"So what?" I glared at her through the mirror.

"We're going home on Saturday. Just four more days. We haven't even seen half of the Smithsonian. We missed the FBI tour. I wanted to see the African-American museum. I don't want to spend all my time chasing after people, figuring out what happened twenty-five years ago. What does it matter?"

"It matters to me!" I felt the heat of my anger. I stepped back, tried to breathe deeply.

"I mean, it's terrible that your mom died and everything, but I think we have to move on. I think we have to live in the present. You're taking this too far. It isn't even healthy."

I was trembling with rage. "Who said that?" I cried. "Your mother? Your precious mother, who never liked me, she's always criticizing—you said so yourself, you said you couldn't stand her!"

"Shut up, Laura!" Kim yelled back. "You're going off the deep end. Everybody says it's crazy, my dad and my mother, even Jordan and Cissy…"

"You told Cissy!" I screamed. "What did you tell her?" I grabbed Kim by the shoulders. "How dare you all talk about me behind my back? How dare you?"

"I didn't tell Cissy anything!" Kim cried, looking scared. "She just knows you left…"

"I needed you!" I pressed my fingers into her shoulders, wanted to shake her, wanted to push her, hard, against the wall. "I counted on you. Is this what you call being a friend?"

Kim twisted away, ran across the room. "What's the matter with you?" she cried. "Being friends doesn't mean I have to be your slave!" She stood silent for a moment, then went on, softer. "Look, Laura, take it easy. Don't waste this trip. Please. Be reasonable."

"How can you call this a waste?" I shouted. "This is *my* family, my life! I have to find Megan now. Maybe she knows where my grandparents are. They were all *neighbors*, Kim. They might have kept in touch. I have to talk to Megan. Why are you so stupid? Why can't you see that? *I have to see Megan!*"

"But she's in Toronto," Kim said.

"I'm going to Toronto," I said. I had not really decided until this moment.

"You can't," Kim said.

"Yes, I can. I have to."

"You can't!" she cried. "I'm not going to cover for you, Laura. What if something happened? It's too far, too much to ask."

"I'm going, with your help or without it," I said. "And I'm not going to to let you stand in my way."

"What are you going to do?" she demanded, breathing hard. "Strangle me?"

I drew back, feeling as if she had struck me.

"No." I sat down on the bed, felt the anger in me drain away as I remembered that awful scene from the play, *Moira McQueen*, Darryl's white face, his eyes filled with fear.

There was a pounding at our door. "Hey, Kim!" It was Marlene Madison in her high-pitched, "valley girl" voice. "What's going on in there? Sounds like World War Three." Someone else snickered.

"Nothing," I called back. "It's personal."

Kim pushed me aside and went to the door. Suddenly her whole demeanor changed, and she smiled sweetly at the three girls. "Oh, hi, guys. I'll meet you in the lobby in ten minutes, okay? I've just got to fix my hair."

"Sure, Kimmy," said Cissy. "But hurry. We don't want to miss the show."

Kim closed the door and faced me. "I—we're going to a show. It starts at eight-thirty. Want to come?"

"No, thanks. You go on with your friends."

"They're your friends, too!"

"No, they aren't."

I grabbed my jacket, my leather bag, and I pushed my way past Kim and into the hall. In a moment, Kim followed. "Laura! Come back here."

I didn't wait for the elevator, but rushed down the stairs, past the reception desk.

Roz was sitting at one of the small tables in the lounge, writing postcards and drinking tea from a flowered china cup. "Laura, wait a minute, please."

I kept my eyes downcast, but inside, I was cussing.

"I was looking for you this afternoon," Roz said. "You know the procedure, you're to be with at least one other person from the group, and you need to sign out. You are *not* free to take off with boys like that. The assumption was that you kids would go out in *groups*. Besides, we have to know where you are, in case of emergency. I thought that was clear."

"Yes, of course," I said. "I'm sorry. We were just sightseeing along the river. Then we stopped at a little cafe for pizza. I guess we lost track of time. I'm really sorry, Roz."

Roz bit her lip, looking stern. "Everyone has to follow the rules," she said. "Including you."

"I will," I said. "I'm really sorry. May I go now?"

"Where are you headed?"

"Just to the drugstore on the corner," I said meaningfully. "I

need some—um—supplies." At that moment I began to formulate my plan. I gave Roz a meaningful, woman-to-woman
look and put my hand to my abdomen. "Damn curse."

She smiled ruefully. "Other than that, are you enjoying the
trip?"

"Oh, yes. I can't wait to see Mt. Vernon." That was the
plan for tomorrow. The whole group was going on this all-day
bus tour. Only, I wasn't going to be there.

With a wave to Roz, I went out to the drugstore, snooped
around for a few minutes, bought some shampoo and a lipstick so that I'd come in carrying a paper bag, just in case Roz
was still sitting there. She was. I felt like a criminal, but also,
I felt great, like the world's greatest actress.

"You have to do this one little thing," I told Kim. "There's
nobody else I can depend on."

Kim pulled at her hair. "What if we get caught?"

"We won't if you play your part. Look, that's all you have
to do. Think of it as a bit of drama."

"Don't you think there's a difference," Kim said, "between
drama and real life?"

I stood staring at her. "I know the difference very well." My
voice was low, my heart beating so hard I felt shaken by it. "I
remember the time you were desperate, Kim. Remember the
night Mongoose disappeared?"

"I'm tired." She got in under her covers. "I want to go to
sleep."

"No." I followed her, sat down on her bed, bending close.

"Leave me alone!" Kim said.

"If it had been up to your parents," I said, "you never
would have found Mongoose. He'd have died, trapped in that
drainpipe, and you know it."

"That's your theory," Kim said, muffled.

"It's true. You weren't even going to go looking. Your parents said you had to stay in. Remember? They said the cat's old and probably went off someplace to die. That's exactly what your mom said, wasn't it?"

Kim sat upright, her eyes red. "Yes, damn you!" She looked about to cry.

"You called me on the phone," I whispered. "I waited until my folks were asleep. And I sneaked out. I did what you were scared to do, and it wasn't even my cat. I did it for you."

I'd been scared too, worried about what my parents would do if they caught me out at night like that. I was only eleven years old, always home by dark, never out alone.

"I came to your window," I said. "Do you remember?"

"Yes," Kim whispered, averting her eyes.

"And even then, you weren't going to come out with me. You were going to let me search alone. You weren't even willing to take the risk for your own cat, the one you said you loved so much."

"Stop it!" Kim clapped her hands over her ears.

"And when you finally came out with me, I had to lead you, all the way down to the beach. I knew she'd be there."

"How did you know?"

"Intuition. She used to play down there, looking for crabs. Don't you remember?"

"I hate that wind down there at night, Laura! And then we saw those guys—it's eerie out there in the dark. How come you weren't scared? Maybe I'm just a wimp."

"No, you're not. You just needed someone to help you. Like I need you now."

I re-created it now in every detail, reminded Kim how I'd crept down into the thick brush near the shore, where the

water drains out from the hill, how I'd heard that cat cry ringing out so desperately. I knew Mongoose was caught in the
drainpipe. I pulled at the rusted grating, hard, until it gave
way. The cat leapt out and clung to Kim's shoulder. "Remember how I cut my wrist? Remember all the blood?"

I had run back home in the dark, my wrist throbbing.
Home, I washed the cut and wrapped a napkin around it,
tight. In the morning I lied to my parents, told them I'd just
cut myself trying to fix some cantaloupe.

Now I turned my wrist and showed Kim the pale, raised
scar. "Look," I said.

"Don't, Laura," Kim whispered.

"It got infected," I said. "And I never told anyone. Your
folks still think that cat came home on his own."

"You were really great," Kim said. "And I owe you."

"Yes, you do."

"Okay. I'll do it."

"Okay. Now, go to sleep."

"What about you?"

"I've got some calls to make. Go to sleep, Kim. It's going to
be okay. Just do exactly what I tell you."

I made my calls, then set the clock for five A.M. The group
was leaving at six-thirty in the morning. By then, I'd be long
gone.

chapter / 10

The world is so enormous when you're out in it alone. It's totally different than when you have company, someone to cushion things. When you're alone, sounds seem magnified, everything glitters, and people hurry more.

I bought a scalding cup of coffee and a dry bran muffin, which I ate standing up at a counter alongside a dozen other people. Nobody spoke or looked at me. I thought about Kim and Jordan. Was she using him? Was I using her? In friendship, people do things for each other. In a relationship, how much is give and how much should one take?

I decided there weren't any pat answers, nor did I feel like worrying about it anymore. I dropped my scraps into a waste can and hurried along to my gate, passing a white-clad missionary holding a FEED THE HUNGRY basket. I dug into my purse, dropped in a handful of coins, feeling generous. Suddenly I loved this *largeness*, the wide stretch of time and space, all mine. I even loved that trickle of fear across my back, as a dozen "what ifs" went sliding through my mind: What if I get caught? What if we crash? What if I can't find

Megan's house? What if she's gone on vacation? What if I'm grounded in Toronto by a storm? All terrible. All delicious.

I sat at the boarding gate, holding my backpack and parka, watching the people. There were two nuns, their faces carefully cultivated and calm. You could tell who was the boss; the one who held the tickets, who decided where to sit, when to stop talking. An old married couple looked like mirror images of each other, wearing matching green nylon jackets and crepe sole shoes. A girl dressed in jeans and a loose pink sweatshirt clung to a tall blond boy with long hair. Every few minutes they dived into a kiss, emerging breathless and flushed.

There was a young mother with three little kids. Her toddler kept falling down and crying. An older girl chattered incessantly, while the four-year-old boy zoomed his toy airplane along the floor, nearly getting trampled in the process. The woman kept up a brave front, "There, there. Don't cry. Mandy, please stop talking. Douglas! Come sit down, honey."

Douglas paid his mom no attention whatsoever.

The poor woman looked worn out. She glanced at me. I gave her a smile. She smiled back, rolling her eyes and blowing out a long sigh. "Goin' home," she said.

I nodded. Was she asking or telling me?

I wished that I had a home in Toronto, a husband waiting, three little kids. My life would be full, then, without questions and gaps. I'd have a place in the world, people who needed me.

I felt overcome, suddenly, with a surge of grief. Nobody had ever really needed me. Maybe nobody ever would.

The agent's voice buzzed over the speaker, announcing our flight. I heard only the word "Toronto," and hurried to get on board. I was excited again, eager to be going.

I love flying, the take-off, the scene below, and then the

white mist of space. Maybe, I thought, I'd be a flight attendant. I watched the two attendants in their dark blue uniforms and white blouses, perfectly groomed, perfectly poised.

"What can I get you to drink?" the attendant asked me.

"Orange juice, please."

The woman smiled a lovely smile with white, even teeth. I noticed the color of her lipstick, bright plum. It almost matched my bulky chenille sweater. I smiled back at her, feeling good in my nice clothes, a long denim skirt and low cut boots. I had bought a pair of silver earrings at the mall, small silver leaves dangling down, glittering whenever I moved my head.

"Going home?" the woman beside me asked pleasantly.

"Visiting," I murmured, giving her a sideward glance.

She looked exotic and very professional, her sleek dark hair cut short, her bronze skin flawless. I wondered where she was from, but felt too shy to ask. She turned to her notebook, stuffed with memos and accounts.

I thought of Kim and the other kids on their way to Mt. Vernon. Kim and I had rehearsed the scene last night, over and over. I'm sure she played it superbly. Kim would rush out to the bus at the last possible moment, when the chaperons were already counting noses and everyone was impatient to leave. Kim would whisper to Mrs. Langfeld, "I'm so sorry to be late. But my roommate wasn't feeling well. She's got terrible cramps. She decided to stay at the hotel today."

The chaperon would frown and hesitate. "Oh? Maybe we ought to look in on her."

"No, no, she'll be fine." Kim would look embarrassed, explaining, "I ran out and got her some aspirin. She's sleeping now. She says that's the only thing that works for her when she feels like this."

Kim and I had gone over the whole story, word for word. I was sure nobody would think anything of it. And by the time they all returned from Mt. Vernon, I'd be back, too.

The stewardess brought around some dry-looking coffee cakes wrapped in waxed paper. I took one, wondering where I'd be eating my next meal.

Then it hit me. I had no plans. None. How was I going to get to Megan's house? And when I got there, what would I say?

Now the questions and problems rose up around me, like roadblocks. I turned to the woman beside me. "Actually, I'm just visiting my cousins," I said.

"Oh?" She smiled again and nodded. "It's nice to have relatives that one can visit. Mine are all in Manilla."

Ah. I felt rewarded, somehow.

"Have you been to Canada before?" I asked.

"Oh, yes. I come here on business twice a year."

"Then maybe you can tell me," I began, "if my cousins don't come for me, is there a bus I can take from the airport to Ellis Park Road?"

She paused, tapped her pencil against her lips. "Let's see— you'd take the Airport Express to Islington Station, then catch the subway to High Street."

"Where's that?"

"Near High Park," she said.

"I've never been there before," I admitted.

"Well, you'll like it. Beautiful park, enormous pond, nice trails for walking, but not at night," she said. "Don't go there alone at night."

"I won't," I said.

It occurred to me that I didn't have any Canadian money. Where could I get it? I'd have to find a bank. Maybe they'd give me a hard time. Why hadn't I thought this through?

Now the worries rattled through my mind like a train increasing in speed, repeating, repeating. What if Megan wasn't at that address? How could I have been so stupid to assume she'd be there? My letter had simply been returned. Maybe Megan had moved. Maybe she was dead! Why hadn't I thought this through?

Sweat broke out on my face and neck. That terrible sense of doom came over me. Fight it, I told myself, clinging to the words. No need to panic. Keep cool.

I forced my thoughts to the point; I had to find the answers to my questions. Where were my grandparents? Why had my mother told me they were dead? What happened in Birch Bend? Why wouldn't she ever go back? Why did she change her name to Jasmine? What was wrong with her name? What was wrong with *her*?

The plane took a sudden dip, hitting an air pocket at the very moment of insight. My mother *was* peculiar. I had always known it, never faced it before. Her strangeness was like a continual presence between us, holding us apart. I remembered her sudden melancholy moods, when she retreated to her bedroom, and I'd hear the throbbing Beatles songs: "Let it be…let it be." And my father always protected her, fielding questions and phone calls, saying, "Don't worry about that, Jasmine, I'll take care of it."

One moment she'd be fine, cracking walnuts, baking a cake. The next moment she'd go off to her room to lie down, sighing with fatigue. What triggered it? I never knew. Mood swings. I had read that description somewhere, in a magazine. It was a "Personal Quiz." *Do you suffer frequent mood swings?*

I felt the old dread descending upon me. I'd felt so great just a while ago, in the airport. Maybe whatever it was that pulled my mother down into depressions was a genetic defect, passed on to me. Maybe it would show under some kind of powerful microscope, a bent fiber, a weirdly twisted piece of DNA—I'd seen things like that in *Science World*.

The plane gave another lurch. The stewardess cautioned everyone to keep their seat belts fastened.

I checked my seat belt, pushed my seat back as far as I could, became aware of a scrambling in the aisle, roaring sounds. It was the little boy I'd seen in the lounge, pushing his toy plane along the aisle.

"Douglas! Douglas, get back here!" came the mother's fretful voice.

I lay back with my eyes closed.

The mother came rushing up, embarrassed, frantic. "Douglas! Douglas!"

I groaned. Give me a break. I opened my eyes, peered to the side. There was Douglas kneeling in the aisle, staring at me eye to eye.

"Hey!" the little boy said. "Hey!"

"Hi yourself," I said, smiling.

I could see gooey red traces inside his mouth and on his shirt front, from a sucker, probably. "You're all sticky," I said.

At that moment his mom caught his arm. "Douglas! I'm sorry," she murmured to everyone, distraught. She picked up the child. He seemed enormous in her arms. Poor woman, I thought, then, lucky woman to have that cute little boy. What was wrong with me? Why couldn't I decide even how I felt at this moment?

I wanted to cry.

Instead, I looked at the woman beside me. "Think it will be cold in Toronto?"

"Probably," she said. "Though the sun should come peeping

through by noontime." She reached into her bag and brought out a passport.

My stomach lurched. I asked, "Do you need a passport to go to Canada?"

"Well, certainly," the woman replied, giving me a strange look. "Canada is a foreign country, after all." My stomach felt queasy, my breath came in quick gasps. Passports. How could I be so stupid? I'd shown my driver's license for a photo I.D. when I checked in at the airport, for security reasons, they'd said. Nobody had told me anything about a passport. Why hadn't I thought of it? What would happen to me if I got caught without a passport?

I imagined being interrogated in some small room, a man in uniform calling the hotel in Washington, barking out, "We've got one of your students here, a runaway. What do you want us to do with her?"

I whispered to the woman beside me. "What if a person doesn't have a passport?"

"Oh, you can use a birth certificate for identification, too," she said with a smile.

Sure. I just happen to have my birth certificate on me.

I tried to look disinterested. "How about a driver's license?" I asked hopefully.

The woman laughed. "I don't think so. They want proof that you were born. A driver's license only shows that you can drive." She thought this was pretty hilarious. I felt dazed, sick.

I sat there, straining to make time stop so I could think. But from the window I saw the ramp being brought to the plane. The flight attendant pushed down the door handle. People began looking around for their belongings, buttoning up their jackets, for gusts of cold wind had entered the cabin.

Deep inside, I felt a twinge of silent laughter. This had to be a joke. Sometimes things are so terrible that they actually seem funny. I was afraid that I'd start to laugh any moment, collapsing, finally, into tears. Hysterical. I bit my lips together, trying to remain calm.

People started to pull their bags from the overhead racks, pushing and crowding into the aisle. I picked up my stuff and hurried out of the plane, following the signs, watching people rush to line up at the little booths underneath huge signs: *Visitors to Canada. Canadian Citizens.*

I stood for a moment, watching the procedure. People showed their passports, paused to answer a question or two while the official in uniform looked them over. My mind went blank.

Suddenly I heard shouts and commotion behind me. "Douglas! Douglas, honey, stay with Mommy!" I saw the young mother rifling through her huge bag, bringing out a fistful of documents, glancing around frantically, trying to keep her small brood together.

"Douglas! Hold Mandy's hand—where's the baby?"

I heard a smack, a scream. The toddler had fallen down again. The mom ran for the baby, scooped her up.

Without a further thought I dashed over and intercepted Douglas, grabbed his arm, hoisted him up onto my hip and started jogging alongside the mother. "I've got him," I panted.

"Oh, thank you—he's such a handful."

"It's okay," I gasped.

Douglas, meanwhile, started picking through my hair, as if he were looking for bugs. We shot into line, the mother carrying the screaming toddler, the older girl hanging on to the strap of her shoulder bag, weighting her over to one side.

"Coming home?" asked the official, eyeing the chaos.

"Yes. We've been to the States for a wedding—here's my

passport. Mandy! Let go, for God's sake!" A compact and lip-stick and several coins spilled out of the woman's purse.

I dived down and retrieved her things, handed them to her.

"Thanks, thanks," she said, utterly distracted, jiggling the baby, peering ahead into the crowd. "This your family?" the man asked me.

"Sister," I said quickly, reaching into my backpack for the small leather billfold I kept there, hoping somehow to bluff my way through. I wondered whether he could see the hot flush on my face, whether the lie was evident in my wavering voice.

The official held out his hand.

At my ear Douglas began to shriek, "Daddy! Daddy!"

The woman dashed forward. "Oh, there's my husband, thank God. Lucas! Lucas!"

I ran after her, Douglas clinging to my neck so tightly that I gagged. My side ached, but we were clear. I felt nested inside the eye of a small hurricane, as mother, father, and children launched into their reunion.

Gladly I set down the burden that was Douglas; his father scooped him up, giving me a grin. "Oh, thank you!" he said exuberantly, but the mother was already rattling on about their trip.

I went on, following the sign: Downtown Express. Some-one had figured out exactly what travelers need. Beside the express booth was a small cubicle that proclaimed Banque — Change. I took fifty dollars from my billfold and moments later received a handful of Canadian bills and some coins.

Trembling with relief and triumph at my narrow escape, I was ready to roll.

chapter / 11

I had never been alone in a foreign city, and the feeling it gave me was like being suddenly launched into a new life. It was as if all my senses were sharper now, taking in the sounds of the city, its traffic, and its bustle.

The trees were still bare, their limbs looking pale gray in the morning light. The sky was very blue, with traces of white clouds racing by. It was cold. I saw a few boys skateboarding, wearing caps and jackets. I pulled my parka closer around me, leaning into the window of the bus, feeling the vibration and gentle shimmying, and the strange sort of floating sensation that comes from being borne away without the slightest knowledge of what's coming next.

I gazed at all the buildings, office towers, large apartment houses, an occasional flower bed with slim fingers of green just breaking through, a few clusters of yellow daffodils bobbing in the breeze.

Strange, I wasn't worrying about the next step now, and I thought of the Beatles song my mother had loved, "Let It Be."

The bus rode past the waterfront with its docks and huge

canisters of cargo. At a distance I saw a high, spindle-shaped tower resting on a rounded base. On the top was some sort of lookout, probably a restaurant, I thought, and I wished I could go there. Maybe after talking to Megan I'd have time for sightseeing. My flight wasn't leaving until four in the afternoon.

I glanced at my watch. It was only eight-thirty in the morning, but I felt as if I'd been traveling all day. "Islington Station," called the driver. I got out and stood listening to the jangle of voices, the English a shade firmer, more literary sounding, I thought, and now and then I heard bits of French. I saw a taxi and decided to take it. I gave the address, which I had memorized: 138 Ellis Park Road. I asked, "Is it far?"

"About eight kilometers, Miss," said the driver, eyeing me closely. His eyes were red and watery, his lips dry.

"Very well," I said, feeling sophisticated and independent.

I got in.

"Mind if I smoke?" the driver asked.

"No," I said, though I did mind. He opened the window to let the smoke blow out. I settled back, but was astonished to find that in no time the ride was over.

"Here you are, Miss." The driver pointed to the house, set in the middle of the block alongside other similar structures, all two- or three-story brick. The houses were old and soot stained; their windows looked solid and heavy.

I paid the taxi driver and got out. The patch of grass around the porch was a strange muddy color, brown just turning green, and there was a muddy smell in the air, as if the ground had long been saturated and was just starting to settle.

A gust of wind pulled at me. I buttoned up my parka, checked the house number again, looked up at the dark windows, felt my heart thumping as if I'd been running. This was the moment; now, I felt unprepared. I went up the steps, stood on the porch, hesitating. Then I rang.

Cars streaked past. The wind rattled some stray newspaper pages along the gutter. I rang again and knocked, too, for good measure. The door swung open. It was a boy, about eighteen, I guessed, squinting in the morning glare.

"Uh—hello!" he stammered, surprised. "Why—I guess…" He faltered, stepped back. He was tall and solid looking, his angular face indicating surprise and a bursting energy, a sudden smile. "Have you come to see Father about a job?"

I shook my head, laughing a little, and he smiled back at me. I immediately noticed his eyes, gray-green and very bright, filled with life. He had straight dark hair, high cheekbones and a wide mouth. There was an energy about him that almost made me gasp, but I kept my cool while he appraised me with a quick, oblique glance.

"Come in, come in," he said, preceding me. He moved with the strength and sureness of an athlete, and I thought he was probably a runner.

"Father's gone to the office already," he said. "I'm Thomas Meistrander. And you would be…?"

Beyond him, I caught a flash of rich Oriental carpet, a thick, curved banister, gleaming crystal.

"I'm Laura Inman," I introduced myself. "Actually, I didn't come here to meet your father," I said. I met his gaze fully. "I've come to see your mother."

"But, you're an American!" he cried delightedly. "From where?"

"California."

"Oh, I've always wanted to travel," he said. "I'd love to go to California."

"I've been to Washington, D.C. on a class trip, and let me

tell you, that is really a fabulous place. Have you been there?"

He shook his head, smiling. "I'd like to go," he said, and I could see his frustration.

I went on eagerly. "I'd never traveled at all, until this trip. Now I've seen more monuments and museums in the past week than in my entire life, except for San Francisco, of course, which is pretty close to us." I stopped, realizing that I was rattling on as if I'd known Thomas Meistrander forever, and we were still only standing in the foyer.

Thomas seemed to realize it, too, and he laughed suddenly and led me into the parlor. "Have a seat. Let me take your jacket," he said. "Mum should be home any time now. She went over to check on some floral centerpieces for a luncheon she's organizing today. It's a big charity function." He nodded, indicating a chair.

I sat down on a stiff wing chair of cream-colored satin, which matched the large sofa. The room was filled with ornaments and heavy, overstuffed furniture upholstered in colors that stunned me—a blue and red print loveseat, a red ottoman edged with gold braid. On the walls hung glittering crystal sconces, and on the mantle stood an elaborate marble clock, also touched with gold.

I could see right away that these rooms were not right for Thomas, that he would much prefer a large leather sofa, a few comfortable chairs, and things that were easy and tasteful and low key. Everything here spoke of money and status and formality. To me, the first impression was somewhat suffocating. But then I looked at Thomas, and the air was fresh again, sweet, for he was smiling at me, watching me take it all in.

"Pretty elaborate, isn't it," he said without bitterness. "Mum loves to decorate. She never stops. Her friends like to use the house for teas and meetings. She always lets them."

"That's very nice of her," I said.

"She would strangle me now, for not having offered you something. How about a soda? Cup of tea? Coke? Please say you'll have something."

I smiled. "Sure. Anything."

"I'll be back in a moment."

I took this time to survey the many pictures that stood in ornate silver frames on a marble table. There were several portraits of a large, dignified man with a mustache, wearing a three-piece suit, looking very regal, somewhat stern. I could see that the brow and the straight hair were the same as Thomas's, and unaccountably I felt a jolt of familiarity that had no real basis. After all, I'd met Thomas less than ten minutes ago. There were photographs of Thomas wearing an athletic uniform, holding a hockey stick. He looked robust and happy. There were several pictures of Thomas with his parents. I peered at his mother Megan's face, trying to see in it the young girl from my mother's snapshot. The hair was fuller and lighter; obviously she had it streaked now. I gazed at the slanted brows that still gave her a pixie look, the pointed mouth, its expression almost sharp. Then I looked carefully at her eyes and saw in them none of the joy or warmth that shone from Thomas's, and in spite of myself, I shivered.

Surely a photograph doesn't reveal anything much, I told myself. Just then Thomas came in, carrying a lacquer tray set with sodas and a plate of tiny scones, along with a small tub of jelly and another of whipped butter.

"How beautiful!" I exclaimed. Never before had a boy served me food, and I'm sure none of the ones I knew would have done it so well and so readily.

"My mom trained me to serve her ladies," he said. "Of

course, we have a day maid that comes in. I wouldn't want you to think..."

"I think this looks delicious," I said, helping myself to one of the scones and a sip of soda.

"You came to see Mum?" Thomas prompted. He sat back watching me, half smiling.

"Yes."

"Well, she should be home any time now," he said.

I could tell he was curious about my visit, but too well mannered to ask me outright. I liked that.

Thomas popped three little scones into his mouth, one after the other. He ate heartily, then asked, "Where are you from in California? Near Hollywood?"

"No. It's a little town near San Francisco called Mill Valley. I'm sure you've never heard of it."

"Oh, but I have!" he exclaimed. "Years ago I heard this song on the radio. It was sung by a chorus of children. *Mill Valley.* It was sweet, made the place sound like a bit of heaven, you know, peaceful. I always wondered whether it was a real place."

"It's real, all right," I said. "And it is peaceful. The biggest event is our summer crafts fair. We're just a few minutes from Muir Beach, down over the hills, and a little farther up the coast is Stinson Beach. It's wonderful hiking. Do you like to hike?"

"I love to hike. More than anything."

I couldn't tell whether or not he was kidding.

"I love it there," I said, and was astonished to discover that this was true.

"Do you surf?" Thomas asked.

"No, you can't surf there. But the cliffs are beautiful and high and green. In the summer my friend and I like to go to Stinson and hang out all day."

"You have lots of friends," he said.

"No, not lots," I said. "My mother just died a couple of months ago," I found myself saying, "and about twenty kids from school came to the funeral."

"Was it an accident?" Thomas asked.

"That they came?"

"That she died."

"It was an aneurysm. A hemorrhage, I guess, of an artery. It was very—sudden."

"How horrible."

"I'm just sort of getting over it now. That's one reason I went on this trip, you see, to get away from..."

The front door opened and shut with a firm sound, and I rose to my feet, as did Thomas, while he called out, "Mum! Someone's here to see you, a girl."

There was an extended stillness, then she entered, with an unmistakable aura of command. Her wool suit, a deep purple color, satin blouse, and gold jewelry, all were elegant and perfect. Almost too perfect. In that first glance I saw her intellect, and something else, a deep secretiveness or suspiciousness, I could not tell which. I glanced from mother to son, saw how different they were; Thomas's expression was bright and welcoming—open. His mother's features were drawn, her eyes narrowed, then widened, like an owl.

I felt submerged, overwhelmed by those darting eyes and the intense energy that radiated from her. She breathed rapidly, watching me, as if I had come here to steal something away.

But Megan's voice belied her expression. She moved toward me, hands outstretched in a theatrical pose, exclaiming in a high, chirping voice, "Who have we here?" She smiled a pointed, pixie smile. "Have you come about the Girls' Volunteer League?"

"No—I'm from California," I said, meeting her eyes.

"California? Ah." It was a sigh, a strong exhalation. "What is it you want? How do you come to me?" Her tone was sharp.

"Mother," murmured Thomas.

Megan breathed deeply, pursed her lips and said, "Forgive me. I don't mean to be rude. It's just…" She turned to her son. "There have been incidents involving the minister. I don't like to burden you, but…one can't be too careful. I'm sorry, I didn't mean to sound inhospitable." Composed, she said, "What can I do for you, my dear?"

I drew the letter from my pocket, the one I had sent Megan, and which was returned to me. "You and my mother were friends once," I said, softly. "You grew up together in Birch Bend. Jasmine—that is, Jenny. Jenny Rouseau. She had changed her name, you know. She wrote you this letter just before she died."

Megan seemed to sway. For a moment I feared she might faint. "Died?" she whispered. "Jenny is dead? And you are her daughter?"

I saw, deep in her eyes, a look of terrible trouble and sorrow. She had suffered. I wanted, suddenly to touch her. This was as close as I would ever get to my own mother, her friend in the flesh, so different from my mother, muscular and tall and tense, but alive. Here and alive.

Megan reached out and took the letter. Her gaze froze upon me, as if she were searching my face for a different truth. "Jenny's daughter," she repeated.

"Why don't you open the letter, Mum?" said Thomas.

Megan shook her head and said in a husky tone, "Yes, of course."

I stood there while she read the contents of both letters, first mine, then my mother's. Thomas stood looking over her shoulder. I had memorized my mother's letter to Megan, and the words hummed in my mind as I waited… "I am married and have a daughter…a lovely girl…twenty-five years! What if Megan and I were to meet again? Only in our dreams… finally, forgiveness."

When they had finished they both turned to me. Megan's face had now changed utterly; she was pale, almost ghostly.

"Sit down," she said, leading me to the sofa. "Your mother is dead?"

"Yes. I'm sorry to be the one to tell you."

She shook her head, quite distracted. "I don't know— what to say, my dear." She sat down, facing me. "What a shock. What a dreadful shock. You must forgive me, I'm quite overwhelmed. Thomas, dear, run and bring me a sip of water or some tea. Yes, a cup of tea. I really must compose myself."

"Why didn't you accept my letter? Why was it returned to me?" I asked, feeling tears gathering in my chest and throat.

"Laura, you must understand," Megan said. "We get so much mail, you know, asking for donations and such. And, with my husband in politics, it's not wise. There have been letter bombs, threats…" She waved her hand vaguely. "I'm sure you understand."

I sighed, nodding. She sat back against the cushions, breathing deeply. Then she glanced at me and asked, "What had your mother told you about us?"

I was startled by the question, but quickly I answered, "Nothing at all. I never knew about you until after Mother died. Then I found this letter and your photograph. Mother never talked about the past. It was a—a thing with her."

"But were you close? The two of you?" Now Megan leaned toward me, her eyes searching mine.

"I—well…" I hesitated.

Thomas came in carrying a tea tray. We filled the awkward space with pouring tea into cups, stirring, sipping.

"Tell me about her," Megan murmured at last.

And I told her everything; the sudden death, father leaving for Tokyo, my trip to Washington D.C., and that awful picnic where nobody had the slightest knowledge of Jasmine Rogers.

"But, she had changed her name," I concluded. "I found out by looking in the school yearbook."

"Clever girl," murmured Megan. She looked beyond me, her mouth pursed in concentration. "Then what?"

"Not much else. I went to the house where Mother used to live and found out my grandparents might still be alive. They lived there up until eight years ago."

"Yes? What else did you discover?"

"Nothing. That's why I came here. I need some answers!" I said, bending toward her. "Why did my mother tell me my grandparents were dead? Can you tell me what happened to them? Are they still alive? Why did my mother change her name?"

I picked up my tea cup, set it down, rattling on the saucer. "There are so many things missing in my life! I want more than anything to fill in the gaps!" I burst out. "Mother died so suddenly, and my father won't..."

"He is in pain," said Megan. "He can't bear to talk about her."

"Yes." I ached with grief rekindled, felt Megan's hand on my arm, firm and warm.

"I understand, my dear," Megan said. "I'll tell you all I can."

chapter / 12

Megan settled herself against the cushions, gazing off into the distance. "Your mother and I hadn't seen each other for twenty-five years," she began. "We had a falling out."

I said, "I assumed that, because of her line, you know, about forgiveness."

"Of course, I forgave her long ago," Megan said with a sigh.

"Mother never holds a grudge," Thomas put in. He helped himself to another scone and several salted almonds.

"That's sweet, Thomas," Megan acknowledged with her pixie smile. "But Laura didn't come here to talk about me. She came to find her grandparents and to learn about her mother. I can understand that," she said, with emotion. "It's terrible to lose a parent, especially so unexpectedly. It's like—time has suddenly stopped, leaving you abandoned somewhere."

I bit my lips, holding back sounds. Megan had read the facts of my life, given words to my secret grief.

"I have to tell you right off," Megan said, "that I don't know the whereabouts of your grandparents."

I felt numb. I could barely speak, but I whispered, "Why did she tell me they were dead?"

Megan sighed. "Your mother hated her parents. Sad, but true. She told you they were dead because she never wanted you to see them."

I had heard of such things, children divorcing their parents, so to speak. "What did they do to her?" I whispered.

Megan lifted her hands helplessly. "Nothing. Who can explain such things as resentment and sheer hatred? It's beyond me."

I thought of the times I'd been angry at my mother, but I never hated her, never.

Megan waited for a moment, then went on. "As far as your mother and I—we were inseparable. When I wasn't at her house, she was at mine, sleeping, eating, doing our schoolwork. We had all the same hopes and dreams. We had such plans! We were going to go to boarding school and, after graduation, we wanted to go to Europe together, take a year of study abroad. It was quite the thing to do in those days."

"It still is," said Thomas with a laugh.

Megan turned to him with her little pointed smile. "My darling Thomas, I know you're angling to go study in the States." She turned to me. "He brings it up at every provocation. He can't wait to get away from his mum, can you, Thomas?"

I blushed, embarrassed for him. But Thomas only stared at me unabashed. I felt as if we were somehow joined in a conspiracy. I wanted to talk to him, to see his smile; then Megan's voice pulled me back.

"As for these mysterious circumstances, all that you've told me about our classmates' behavior at the reunion picnic, your mother's strange behavior, changing her name and all that, it's easily explained. I will tell you everything, my dear." Megan took my hand and held it in her own. Her hand was cold and strong. "You are very different from your mother, I can see that already," she said.

I felt warmed by Megan's voice, by her obvious approval of me. She lifted her tea cup to her lips, sipping the last of her tea. She closed her eyes briefly, then continued, speaking animatedly, her voice full of passion. "I'm not at all surprised at the way those people treated you at the reunion," Megan said. "Jenny and I could never stand those people. If it hadn't been for Jenny…" Megan pursed her lips, shook her head. "I had moved from Ohio. I don't know where your mother lived before, but she'd only been in Birch Bend for less than a year, and she already hated it. I was the new kid, and we were both disgusted and fed up with small-town stupidity. That's how your mother put it. She used to make up funny, silly names for people. Jenny had a great gift for mimicry. Ah, she was so very gifted, so very bright!"

Megan went on, speaking rapidly. I glanced at Thomas, saw that he, too, was totally absorbed. "We met one day at the drinking fountain at school, and we started talking, and before we knew it an hour had passed, and we missed our class and were both punished. They kept us after school for detention. We didn't care. We sat there writing notes to each other the whole hour, and loving it. The amazing thing was, we were absolutely on the same wavelength about everything. I was twelve, she was half a year older, but we were in the same class, because I'd skipped a grade in grammar school. From that very first day we became inseparable."

Megan glanced at her son. "You've got your hockey team and your summer buddies. It's different for girls. They get so very close, so bonded." Megan turned to me. "Do you understand?"

I nodded. "I have a friend like that. Her name is Kim."

"Of course you would," said Megan with a slight smile, then she continued, her hands pressed together almost as if in prayer. "Jenny and I did everything together. Jenny was a vast reader. By the time she was thirteen, I think she had read all of Shakespeare. She used to read me parts. In winter, we'd sit in front of the fire and she read to me, acting out scenes. God! She was exciting, and what an imagination! She'd picture the entire setting for me. I don't know where she got it from. God knows, her parents weren't nearly that literary—her mother made pottery and loved to garden. Her father was an accountant, a dear man, but intellectually he couldn't hold a candle to Jenny. Very few people could."

"You could," Thomas put in.

"I suppose so," Megan said. "But you mustn't think we were eggheads, only interested in books and drama. We went skating all winter long, and in the summer we found this very deep swimming hole with a small waterfall above, and we'd leap down into this hole—oh, I'm amazed to think of it. It was at least twenty-five feet from the cliff into the water, and freezing cold."

"I never knew you were such a daredevil, Mum!" said Thomas, much amused. He smiled at me. "It's a good thing you popped in," he said. "Now I'm learning all the family secrets."

"Hush now, Thomas!" she snapped. "Where was I?" Megan frowned, then continued. "The thing is, Jenny's parents were plain people, good people, but they were entirely unsuited to Jenny. Utterly incompatible. They constantly rubbed each other the wrong way. Jenny wanted freedom, total freedom. Of course, her parents had other ideas. Jenny always wanted to be an actress. She wanted to do Shakespeare in London. It was her dream."

I said softly, "Once she helped me, when I was doing a scene from *The Taming of the Shrew*. She was wonderful. But she never even told me she'd done acting. She didn't tell me anything!" I accused.

Megan nodded. "Dear Jenny, she *would* be so secretive. The things she loved most, Jenny kept to herself. She had this intensity, you see. That was why she and I were so close. We shared everything that we could not tell anyone else. We were like sisters—no, closer than sisters, like clones. We used to turn on the radio and dance, waving long scarves, pretending to be priestesses in the temple of Venus—you can't imagine all the things she brought to me, visions of the ancient world, and she was funny. So funny. Nobody could make me laugh the way Jenny did."

I couldn't help thinking how much Megan and my mother were like Kim and me.

"You loved her," Thomas suddenly said.

"Yes," Megan said. "I loved Jenny very much."

"What happened? How did you lose touch?" Thomas reached for another handful of salted almonds, and I smiled to myself at the difference between men and women. My stomach was knotted with anticipation and involvement in Megan's tale, while Thomas thought only of the bottom line, the ultimate outcome.

"Well, you know that my parents died when I was nearly fifteen." Megan turned to me. "A terrible accident."

"Don't," said Thomas. "Don't go into it, Mum. Please."

Megan took a deep breath, nodding. "I won't."

"Terrible migraines, she gets," Thomas said.

"Jenny and I had made plans to go away to school in the north," Megan said. "There's a wonderful girls' preparatory school in New Hampshire, called Quincy Academy. Jenny had learned about it and sent for the catalogues, and she had developed the whole idea. For over a year she begged and indoctrinated her parents, until they said she could go in her junior year. Of course, the plan was for us to go together."

"Ah, so you wanted to go off to school!" Thomas exclaimed, looking pleased with himself.

Megan waved him aside. "My parents weren't thrilled about the idea, but they finally relented. They made several conditions, however. I had to maintain excellent grades and to earn money during vacations, to help with the finances."

"She always got excellent grades," Thomas said. "Talk about Jenny being smart..."

"All right, son. I don't take credit for it—it's in the genes. My parents were both..."

"Brilliant," Thomas put in.

"Anyhow, my parents made these conditions. I think they wanted to see whether this was just another half-baked idea of ours, or whether I was willing to make some sacrifices for it. Of course, I was. Jenny and I talked of nothing else except going away to school, how wonderful that would be, the academic environment, the extracurricular activities—they had soccer and French and ballet and drama at that school. It sounded like paradise."

Megan sat back, breathing heavily. Then she said, "There was an accident. My parents were killed."

I thought of the fire, but said nothing. What could I say? I've always felt awkward in the face of tragedy.

"After that," Megan said very softly, "everything changed. Jenny's parents were wonderful to me. They took me in. They cared for me. I was half crazy with grief. You can imagine."

"Mum. Don't, please," said Thomas.

"I have to tell her, darling! Laura needs to know—she's entitled to know. Look," she said to me, "I think something happened in Jenny's mind. Guilt, maybe, because my parents had died and her parents were still alive, because I was destitute and she..."

"Wasn't there any insurance money?" Thomas asked.

"That was the awful thing, the unexplainable thing. There was nothing. My parents, brilliant as they were in academic matters, were utterly helpless when it came to managing money. It turned out they were deeply in debt. The house was double mortgaged. There was, in fact, no money at all for my keep."

"What did you do?" I gasped. "Where did you go?"

"Well, as I said, I stayed with Jenny and her parents for a time, about three months, all the while receiving these imploring letters from my Aunt Marcia who lived in Canada. She's dead, now, these many years. Thomas never even knew her. But she came down for the funeral and immediately took a liking to me and wanted me to come and live with her. She was unmarried and very lonely. What else could I do? Here was my only blood kin in the world, and she needed me and wanted me. And I couldn't impose on the Rouseaus' kindness forever, could I?"

"So you went to live with your aunt," I said. "And my mother..."

"Your mother simply could not understand that I would leave her. That was how she put it. 'You're leaving me! How can you leave me? You promised we'd be together. You promised we'd go to Quincy—how can you live with yourself, liar that you are!' She became..." Megan stared at me, hesitating, then doggedly she continued. "She became enraged, abusive, she even threatened...she threatened to kill herself if I left her."

"No!" I cried out. But I knew, deep down, that this was all true, for I knew my mother's strangeness, her moods, her anger.

"I'm sorry." Megan's lips were taut, her hands clenched. "I shouldn't have..."

"Yes, yes!" I cried. "I want to know. I need to know everything. Please tell me."

Megan poured herself another cup of tea, but let it sit while she continued. "One day your mother, Jenny, was simply gone. She left a note. It was simple, direct. 'Don't try to find me or to follow me. If you do, we will all regret it.'"

"Where did she go? Why?"

"She said she was going away to the stage, London, New York, Hollywood. She said she would change her name. There was nothing for her in Birch Bend."

"Nothing?" I echoed. "What about her parents?"

"That's what was so awful," Megan said. "Jenny had talked before about running away. It was sort of a continuing fantasy of hers. We used to talk about stowing away on a ship, hopping a train, or getting a ride with a trucker. For me, it was just a fantasy, an amusement. But Jenny used to get that look on her face..."

"I know the look," I whispered.

"Then I realized she really meant it," Megan said. "We argued about it many times. The thing was, she felt no—no ties at all to her parents. It was odd. As if she was—incapable of feeling—" Megan hesitated, whispered the word, "love."

Megan was frowning and biting her lip. "When Jenny left, it didn't surprise me. Her parents, of course, were devastated. We all thought she'd gone to California, you know, the mecca for aspiring starlets. Her parents sent out fliers, contacted the police, made calls to shelters. Her father even traveled to San Francisco and Los Angeles looking for her. There were so many runaways in those days! I suspect she got mixed up with a drug crowd. She'd been involved before."

"My mom was doing drugs?"

Megan looked down at her hands, then straight at me. "Laura, I'm not saying your mother was a criminal. She experimented. We both did. Smoked some marijuana. I drew the line when it came to LSD and stronger stuff, I mean, that scared me. But Jenny—Jenny was fearless. Don't judge her, Laura. I always thought she was a troubled soul. Too bright, too smart, too bold for this world. She was unique."

"I never really knew her," I said, and there was a terrible ache in my throat. "She didn't let me."

"I know, I know, dear," Megan said, reaching toward me, then placing her hand on my arm.

"Did she ever have any success on the stage?" I wondered aloud.

"I doubt it," said Megan. "I think we would have heard, even though she changed her name. We would have recognized her. You have to realize that thousands of young girls were stagestruck like Jenny. Very few realized their dream."

"She was in London for a while," I said. "That's where she met my father. I found some old letters."

"Oh? Interesting. Perhaps she did do some theater there. She never mentioned it?"

"No. Never." Again, I felt bereft.

Megan sighed. "I wish I could have spared you all this. Of course, I suppose Jenny's parents never really got over her disappearance. I felt so sorry for them. After I moved to Canada, I corresponded with them for a while. Then I went away to university, did some traveling, got married. You know how things go. We lost touch. And it really seemed better for me to get out of their lives. It would have been painful for them each time they heard my name. It would have made them think of Jenny, and their loss."

"How cruel of her!" I burst out. "How selfish!"

"Don't judge her," Megan said again. "You don't know— she was so very independent."

"Not lately," I said. "She depended on my father for everything. She rarely went anyplace. She hardly had any friends."

"So you see how differently you two turned out," Thomas said, and I was startled by his voice, for I had almost forgotten his presence. "Mum is the most sociable creature in the world. She has hundreds of friends, all these activities…"

"Good heavens!" Megan cried, glancing at her watch and leaping up. "I've almost forgotten myself completely. I'm due at the hotel before eleven. Laura, what shall we do with you? When is your flight back?" she asked.

"Four this afternoon."

"Well, I'll take you back to the bus station on my way to my engagement. You could walk in the park a bit, and there are shops on Bloor Street, boutiques and many little restaurants. Do you have money?"

"Yes, thank you. And thank you so much for seeing me. I probably shouldn't have come bursting in this way. You're so busy, and I…"

"It's quite all right, Laura," said Megan, walking beside me to the doorway. "I'm only sorry we won't be able to take you around. If I'd known ahead of time…"

"Oh, please," I said quickly, feeling flustered. "I didn't expect to be entertained. I just needed to see you."

"Of course. And Thomas has an exam at noon, don't you?"

"Yes. Geography," Thomas said with a groan. "Of course, I could make it up, say I was ill, or a long-lost relative popped in." He grinned at me engagingly. "Mum, I could use a day off."

"No!" exclaimed his mother with such force that I flinched. "No," she repeated. "You must discharge your responsibilities, Thomas, you know how your father feels about that. We were not especially pleased with last quarter's report."

"All right, Mum," Thomas said tensely.

But she persisted, hands braced, leaning toward her son angrily. "What if all the rest of us simply walked away from our responsibilities? What then? Your father is at the office by seven every morning. I don't understand that you have time to waste. A day off, indeed."

I felt hugely embarrassed—wouldn't she ever stop? Poor Thomas tensed visibly, his lips pale, his entire body looking as if he were warding off blows.

Megan's storm of words ended as suddenly as it had begun. I glanced at Thomas. He gave me a quick wink. How wonderful, I thought, that he could get over his mother's tirade so quickly.

Megan took a deep breath, then turned to me, smiling. She placed her hands on my shoulders. I thought for a moment that she would kiss me, but she only gave me that burning look and said stoutly, "Go on with your life, Laura. Don't look back anymore."

There was hardly time for Thomas and me to say goodbye. In a twinkling we were settled in Megan's Subaru. She drove fast, spinning in and out of lanes, honking, looking back over her shoulder and waving signals out the window.

"Let me off here," I said, seeing a large expanse of green. "This looks lovely. I might even run a bit."

"Very well." Megan stopped the car. I got out. I wanted to say something about seeing her again, something that might keep us connected.

But Megan sped off without another word, and I was left alone again, more desolate than ever. I was in no mood to run. I walked slowly toward a large pond, where ducks and geese and a few swans floated silently, their bright eyes fixed and staring. Willow branches hung like fine green lace over the water, and the ripples made delicate, whispering sounds.

I sat down on a bench. It was beautiful here, green and alive, but without anyone beside me, the beauty was oppressive. Several young mothers walked past, wheeling their babies in buggies. A couple strolled by, oblivious, obviously lovers.

I felt a terrible ache inside me and thought of the Beatles song, "All The Lonely People," the tune playing itself over and over in my mind.

"All the lonely people,
Where do they all come from?"

"Laura! Laura!"

Incredibly, everything changed, the sun flashed out over the pond. It was Thomas, running up to meet me.

chapter / **13**

Thomas came running toward me, grinning, and I'm sure my expression matched his. He looked so very pleased with himself!

"Hi! Hi!" he called out, arms waving. "I knew I'd find you here!"

"How did you know?" I was so happy to see him that I felt suddenly shy.

Thomas, too, stopped short and stood there looking at me. He was breathless from his run. Then he said, "I knew you'd be driving past the park, and that you'd see Grenadier Pond, and you'd want to walk about."

I loved the way he said "about." It sounded like "a boot."

"I knew you'd be attracted by the ducks and geese."

"Wrong," I exclaimed, triumphant. "It was the swans."

"I have plans to show you the sights," Thomas said. "If that's okay with you."

"What about your exam?"

"I called in sick," he said. "See what a terrible person I am! Playing hooky, disobeying my mother."

"Lying," I added to his list of infractions.

"No. Truth is, it did make me sick to think about letting this day go by without showing you the city. It's the least I can do," he added, "to improve U.S.-Canadian relations."

"I didn't know they needed improving," I bantered.

"Oh, they do," said Thomas, beaming.

We walked at the edge of the enormous pond, listening to the ripples in the water, the soft lapping at the edges. I felt the great serenity of being in the moment so completely that time didn't matter at all. For now, I was in an endless space, forever fresh and new and clear.

"Sorry my mother got so intense," Thomas suddenly said.

"No problem," I replied.

"She gets these moods. Sweet one minute, furious the next, then it's all sweetness again."

"My mother was like that," I admitted. I felt a momentary heaviness in my chest at remembering. "She'd go off into her room and listen endlessly to the Beatles. She'd get—depressed."

"I don't think Mum gets depressed. She just gets angry."

"It's the same thing."

He gave me a startled look. "How do you know?"

"I believe I read it somewhere. Depression is anger turned inward."

"Ah. Well, my mother never turns anything inward—no, it's all battered out at me and my pop. We don't care. Mum's not a bad sort. A little high strung." He grinned. "I guess Pop and I drive her crazy."

We saw a furious shaking of tree branches, then several squirrels leapt out, chattering and chasing across the dull grass. "Those squirrels," I exclaimed, "they're *black*."

"Why wouldn't they be?" Thomas said.

"At home the squirrels are gray."

"Strange." He made a face. "What color are the trees?"

"Lavender," I said, laughing. "And the sky is yellow."

"Sounds beautiful. Can't wait to go to California and see that sky. Say, do you like animals?"

"I adore animals."

"Then we'll stop by at the zoo. It's just a small zoo here in the park, with llamas and deer and some foxes, I think. Do you have a dog at home?"

"No," I said. "My mother was terrified of dogs."

Thomas stopped and turned to me. "Really? So's my mom. She'll go miles out of her way to avoid getting near a dog. I used to beg for one. It made her furious."

"Is she allergic?"

"No, I don't think so. She just tenses up."

We walked on for a time without speaking. Once or twice my shoulder brushed Thomas's arm. I liked being close to him; I liked it very much.

"Do you think they were alike because they were such good friends?" Thomas suddenly asked.

"Maybe they were good friends because they were alike," I countered. "Except, your mom is so fashionable, and mine didn't even like to dress up. Your mother obviously has hundreds of friends and activities. My mother was sort of—well, a recluse."

"Really?" He seemed fascinated.

"She didn't like joining groups. She hardly ever went out, except to go traveling with my father."

"Did she like decorating the house?"

"No, not much," I said, laughing. "Our place is pretty casual. But you'd like it, I think."

"I know I would."

We had come to the animal enclosures, where several small children were ringed around the petting zoo, squealing with delight at the goats and ducks and the miniature pig.

Thomas watched the little kids, smiling.

"Do you have a younger sister or brother?"

"No. I'm the only one. A surprise package." I was startled by my own words. What a thing to say to a virtual stranger! But somehow I felt an intimacy with Thomas, as if we had known each other long ago, perhaps even in another incarnation, although I'm not at all sure I believe in things like that. I asked him. "Do you believe in reincarnation?"

"Not actively," he said soberly. "But I'm willing to be open minded." He looked down at me, half smiling. "Do you think you're reincarnated?"

"No. It's just—a feeling that we know each other."

"Maybe that comes from the intimacy of our mothers," Thomas said.

"I suppose that could be. Just think, if they hadn't had that fight, we might have known each other since we were babies."

"I don't understand what the fight was about, exactly," Thomas said.

"My mother was mad because your mother was leaving to go to Canada. She was very possessive, always."

"Wouldn't let you go places? Didn't want you out of her sight?" Thomas's eyes flashed and he breathed heavily, flexing his hands, as if something were holding him down.

"Yes," I said. "She always made a fuss if I wanted to spend the night with a friend."

"You heard my mother getting all huffy about my wanting to go away to school, didn't you?"

"I guess a lot of parents are a little over-protective," I said.

"She wants to keep me tied to her apron strings," Thomas said, his tone sharp now and bitter. "I've got to start living my own life. My father says so, too. He says I can apply to schools away, maybe in Montreal. Maybe in the States. I'd love to go to Stanford University," he said longingly.

"That's less than an hour from Mill Valley," I said.

"Are you going there?"

I shrugged. "Haven't thought about it. I'm just a junior."

"I graduate this June."

"And you haven't applied for college yet?"

"It's been a war," Thomas said. "I've sent all sorts of applications, but there's a constant fight. She wants me to stay here. I don't know why."

"Because she loves you, needs you," I said with a smile.

"My mother doesn't need anybody," he said sharply.

"But it sounds like she's so involved with people…"

"She organizes things. She plans. That doesn't mean she really gets involved."

"What are you saying, Thomas?" The look on his face almost frightened me.

"I don't know. I've always felt that she keeps people—me included—at a distance. It's hard to explain."

"You don't have to," I said softly. "I know exactly what you mean. I went to Birch Bend," I said, "because I felt the same way. I didn't really know my mother at all. She built this wall around herself. Now that she's gone, how can I know her? How can I know myself? That's why I had to come to Toronto."

"I'm glad you came."

We walked on silently. Then Thomas said, "Maybe it's because they were so bright. Some people are just different, too complex, too unique to be understood really. It makes them difficult to live with. Pop says my mother's a genius."

"Mine was bright, too. Very. She could quote you things—Shakespeare, things about science. She was a whiz at cross-word puzzles. I always thought that if she'd just get out a little, make friends, things would change."

Now I told Thomas about how I'd wanted my mother to come on this trip as a chaperon, how she refused, scorning the people at Birch Bend. "So I decided to go there," I said. "It's really a lovely place. Sort of old-fashioned. Did your mom tell you much about it?"

"She never told me anything about it," Thomas said. "I never even knew the name of the place until today."

"You're kidding!"

"My mother never talked about her childhood. I guess it was because..."

We had come to the edge of the park, to an intersection of speeding traffic and blinking lights. "How about lunch? Are you starved?"

"I could eat," I said, realizing that I was very hungry.

"We'll walk along Bloor Village and you can pick what you like," Thomas said, leading me across the street to the boulevard with its small shops and countless tearooms and restaurants.

Couples were walking hand in hand, pausing to look at shop windows, sitting close together on a bench in a patch of sunshine. Now I felt that I was part of the entire picture, no longer an outcast or a misfit, alone in a society where everybody went in twos. Thomas and I stood together, our images reflected in a large plate glass window. My head reached just above his shoulder. He took my hand in his. We stood there, hands clasped. I felt warm, then cool, excited and happy.

"We look good together," Thomas suddenly said.

"Shall we eat here?" I suggested. From the window I saw a huge selection of cheeses, meats, sausages, all sorts of jams and breads. "I like the iron dog."

"Did you see the parrot?"

I smiled. Everything was so lovely, so charming.

"I have an idea," Thomas said. "We'll eat our way along Bloor street, a progressive lunch."

"How shall we start?"

"Some samples of cheese with crackers. Sparkling cider. Then we'll go to Fiasco's."

"What's that?"

"Italian. Do you like pizza?"

"One of my favorite foods in the world."

"They have one with pesto and goat cheese."

"Heaven!" I thought of the last pizza I'd eaten, with Spider. It seemed like a year ago. It was, in fact, only last night. I looked at Thomas, suddenly overwhelmed with all sorts of mixed feelings, and he must have seen something strange in my eyes, for suddenly he drew closer and asked me, "Are you going with anyone? Do you have a boyfriend back home?"

I shook my head. "No," I whispered. "How about you?"

He put his arm around my waist, drew me near. "I went with a girl about a year ago. Mum hated her. Anyhow, she was much too demanding. A Barbie doll."

"Oh, you've got those here, too?"

"Do we ever!" I felt his fingertips on the ends of my hair, barely touching, and I felt the bliss of being admired and wanted by someone so wonderful that I could hardly believe any of this was real.

We ate our way along Bloor Street, ending at a Ukrainian bakery where we sat at a small round table nibbling custard tarts topped with strawberries and whipped cream.

I sighed, shook my head. "I can't eat another bite."

"Want to walk some more?"

"Need to walk some more."

Outside, the sun through the new leaves was casting dappled shadows on the sidewalk. Everything seemed touched with deeper color than I had ever remembered. The bricks on the buildings were solid and deep rusty red; windows sparkled, with patches of blue sky reflected in them. A few daffodils just settling in for spring nodded and danced, moving their bright yellow heads in rhythm with the breeze. In the dull gray sidewalk I now saw tiny chips of mica, like miniature diamonds.

"I thought about what you said," Thomas told me, looking serious and still. "About depression. It never occurred to me before that Mum is depressed. Nobody would think it, because she's always rushing about, this luncheon, that tea for a fundraising, black-tie dinners—she's never still. But as long as she's rushing about, she's fine. When the phone isn't ringing, when nothing's going on, she gets upset. I suppose she simply can't stand to be alone. And you say your mother was never sociable. It makes them opposites, in a way, doesn't it?"

"So? I've heard that opposites attract," I said.

"Do you believe it?"

I smiled. "No. I like people who are like me."

"And what are you like?"

"Like you," I said boldly, and I felt the swift pressure of Thomas's hand around mine.

We walked and talked, sat in the faint sunshine, walked and talked again. I found myself telling Thomas about incidents and thoughts I'd never mentioned to anyone, not even Kim. I told Thomas about my nightmares, and he held my hand. I told him how afraid I was, sometimes, that the huge despondency that had claimed so much of my mother's life would overtake me, too, like a tidal wave, and Thomas understood.

"When I was little," he said, "I always thought it was my fault when Mum got upset. I'd be sitting there with her, and suddenly she would take offense to something, get very shrill and angry, and I never knew exactly what I'd said or done, only that I must have been very, very bad."

"How did you get over it?" I asked.

"I'm not sure I have. Oh, Pop and I put up a good front. We joke and try to shrug it off. But we can't, completely. Maybe if I got away," he said wistfully.

"Getting away helps," I said, "seeing new things, meeting new people."

I told Thomas about the strange things I had discovered since my mother's death. "It's as if she was always laying traps for me," I said, and I felt a flash of anger. "She lied to me all the time, and yet she insisted that I always tell her the truth! Now I find out she ran away from her parents, left them devastated. I never imagined my mother could do such a thing."

Thomas's gray-green eyes became hazy with emotion. "That's how it is," he murmured. "We expect our parents to be good—even perfect. And they are, after all, just *human*."

Suddenly it was three in the afternoon, and Thomas said with a shout, "Look at the time! I've got to get you to the airport!"

"Do you have a car?"

"Parked it at the entrance. I suppose we could run," he said, eyeing me dubiously.

I pulled off my parka, gathered it in my arms and took off.

Shouting and laughing, Thomas took off after me, and we

ran and ran along the pathways in the park, beside Grenadier Pond, all the way to the gate, where at last I stopped, exhausted and exhilarated both at once.

Thomas drove fast to the airport, swung the car into a parking stall and hurried around to open my door. Then he clasped my arm and we made our way into the terminal, up to the boarding area, and I saw that people were already starting to line up.

I turned to Thomas with a sinking inside me, a feeling of utter loss and confusion. I should say something polite, what a nice time I'd had, how glad I was to have met him.

"Thomas, I..." I began. And then his arms were around me, and his mouth was on mine, and all words and thoughts melted away. I moved close, closer. Everything else was blotted out, only Thomas's lips and his breath, his skin and the smell of him, the firmness of his arms, the warmth of his chest, the beating pulse at his throat—only this was real.

"Oh, Laura," he whispered, "don't leave."

"I have to!" I breathed. "I wish I could stay."

"Stay another hour," he begged. "There's another flight at five, another an hour later."

"They'll find out. I wasn't even supposed to be here. I tricked them."

"You mean you sneaked away? Didn't even get permission?" Thomas gave a laugh. "You are a bold one! When did you decide? Just spur of the moment?"

"I can be pretty impulsive," I said. Laughing, I told Thomas how I'd attached myself to that harried young mother to avoid the passport issue.

"You were lucky," Thomas said. "Minors traveling alone are supposed to have a letter from their parents. Of course, you look so innocent." He squeezed my hand.

We stepped apart, our hands still joined. "When I went to Birch Bend and learned about the fire that killed your grandparents, I realized I had to meet your mom. Somehow I had the strongest feeling that everything was connected to that fire."

"What are you saying?" Thomas interrupted. "What fire?"

"The fire that killed your grandparents," I repeated. "I didn't want to bring it up to your mother. It must still be so painful for her. But now, at least, I can put a few pieces together."

I stopped, seeing the expression on Thomas's face, stunned and disbelieving. "What's wrong?"

"You said there was a fire, that my grandparents died in a fire?"

"Yes! The woman I met told me. I saw the house, rebuilt—I'm sure our mothers were together the night it happened. Your mom said they were always sleeping at each other's houses. Can't you imagine how horrible..."

"But my grandparents didn't die in a fire," Thomas said. "My mother told me they were killed in a car crash."

"No!" I cried. "My grandparents died in a car crash. At least that's what my mother told me."

"Laura, this is preposterous. It all sounds so—so sinister. How can we find out the truth? Are you going back to Birch Bend?"

"I suppose I could," I said. "But why? What'll I look for?"

"I don't know, exactly," Thomas said. "There's something very strange. Somehow I feel that it's important. For us. Oh, Laura, maybe we..."

I never heard the rest of it, for the announcement came, "Now boarding flight 212 for Dulles Airport..."

"Wait!" Thomas put his hands on my shoulders. "Where can I reach you? This is too strange. We have to talk."

"I'm staying at the New Hampshire Hotel," I said. I reached into my bag, drew out a brochure I had brought along, in case of emergency, thinking of the irony of how my mother had always prepared me for emergencies. "The phone number is there on the back. And here's my phone number at home in Mill Valley, in case…"

"I'll call you later tonight," he said.

"Thomas…" I began. All possible words of farewell eluded me as I looked into his face, trying to memorize his features, the warmth in his eyes, the way he smiled.

"This isn't good-bye, you know," he said.

I looked into his eyes. "I know," I whispered. "Will you come to California?"

"Of course." Thomas moved with me into the line.

He put his arm around me. I felt his closeness. I almost couldn't bear it.

"Laura!" he said, his tone soft but so urgent that several people turned to stare.

"Yes?" I reached up and touched his cheek. It seemed the most intimate gesture imaginable.

"I'll call you," he said. "We need to talk." Thomas bent to kiss me once more, and then he let me go.

chapter / 14

"My grandparents didn't die in a fire…"

"Your mother ran away to be on the stage…she said she'd change her name…"

"Jenny hated her parents…"

"This isn't good-bye, you know."

"Will you come to California?"

"My grandparents didn't die in a fire."

On the plane back to Washington, D.C. I fell asleep, exhausted from all of it. Still the words kept revolving in my mind, and I relived every moment of the day: the fears, the revelations, the love.

Is it possible to fall in love all at once? Is there such a thing as love at first sight? I would never ask those questions again. I knew something now that I had not known even a few hours ago.

Now I began to wonder and to worry about Thomas, his past, his future. What did it mean, that his mother had lied to him, too? What could it mean, except that somehow our families were linked in lies.

I decided I had to go back to Birch Bend, though how I would accomplish this I could not imagine. I'd left the group three times already, twice to go to Birch Bend, and then all the way to Toronto. Someone would surely get suspicious. And what if I went back and found nothing more?

I had a sudden, exhilarating thought. Could Thomas possibly come to Washington? We'd go to Birch Bend together, maybe solve the mystery. Or he might have a talk with his mother, ask her about that car accident story. She'd be forced to reveal everything. Perhaps there was a very simple explanation, some reason things were hidden. There could have been a scandal. So what! We were all modern and savvy. Maybe there was a love affair, maybe even a pregnancy. Maybe Megan and my mom had made some sort of a pact.

Forgiveness… The word from my mother's letter haunted my thoughts. What was there to forgive? Who had been wronged? It was a man, I thought, with certainty. Both were in love with the same person. Something happened. A wrong was committed. For years, they never spoke, never wrote, until that final letter, my mother offering forgiveness. Or maybe it was the parents, some scandal with them—two sets of parents were involved here. Yes, surely it was a sexual thing, maybe between the *parents!* I was shocked for a moment. Maybe there was something going on—it became public knowledge. The girls, Megan and Jenny, were shamed; decided, after they grew up, to leave town and never return, shunning their parents forever. Maybe none of the parents had died, but all were still alive, being treated *as if they were dead.*

Now I began to wonder whether Mrs. Armenta really had her information straight. Maybe nobody was killed in a fire. She admitted she wasn't living in Birch Bend at the time. It was only a rumor. Of course, I'd seen the scarred tree, but that didn't prove much.

I felt flushed, burning with anxiety. I wanted to turn around and go straight back to Toronto to face Megan and demand to know the truth. The plane circled and circled. Outside the sky grew dark; the engines of the plane droned on and on. I felt imprisoned, locked into my endless, unresolved thoughts.

After what seemed a long time the flight attendant finally announced our arrival at Dulles Airport. Thankfully, I tightened my seat belt and gathered my things, ready for landing.

Thomas had said he'd phone me. When? Already, I was counting the minutes since we'd said good-bye. Maybe I'd phone him when I got back to the hotel. Then I realized with a sinking feeling that I didn't even have his phone number. Now I didn't care about anything except hearing his voice again.

Oh, God, I thought to myself, I've got it bad. I couldn't wait to tell Kim about Thomas.

I followed the other passengers off the plane, into the terminal, proceeding at a fast clip, thinking only of getting back to the hotel now without being caught.

"Just a moment, young lady." Someone grasped my arm.

I whirled around, startled. "Yes? What's wrong?"

"You walked right past the immigration checkpoint. Didn't you see the signs?"

"I—no. I guess not. I'm sorry."

A large man, dressed in a dark uniform and wearing a picture ID badge pinned to his shirt, stood directly in front of me, blocking my way. He examined my face, as if he were looking for signs of a crime. "May I see your passport, please?"

My heart began to pound. I glanced about, saw no help. "I

don't have a passport," I said. "I—I'm an American."

"Oh? How did you get into Canada?" His eyes were hard; I saw years of aggravation in them, years of hearing lame excuses, of dealing with liars.

I said, "I was with friends."

"I see. And what were you doing in Canada?"

"Visiting. My boyfriend."

"What's his name?" he shot back.

"Thomas Meistrander. He lives on Ellis Park Road in Toronto. You can call and ask!" I flung out defiantly.

"No need to get excited, young lady," the man said, his tone milder now. "All I need is some sort of identification. Do you have anything with a photo on it?"

"My driver's license."

"That's fine."

"Fine? Really?" I almost laughed with relief and surprise. How strange life is; awful things come down when you least expect them. Then, when you fear the worst, everything's suddenly cool.

"I need you to sign this form," the officer continued, "telling where you've been, the date—no big deal." He propped his clipboard on his knee, wrote something, then looked up at me. "Your folks know about this boyfriend?"

"Oh, sure."

He held the clipboard toward me, tapped the bottom of the form. "Just sign here."

I signed.

"Have a good evening," he said.

"Thanks! I will!"

Outside the terminal I saw that it had rained. The streets were slick and black, with headlights making fluid-looking tracks along the roadway. I shivered, hoping I wasn't late, hoping the group was still on the way back from Mt. Vernon.

I took the airport shuttle to the central district, hurried along the streets to the hotel, passing business people rushing home, vagrants huddled in doorways and squatting over vents. I felt competent now, a seasoned tourist; I knew how to get around. Things looked different all around me. The world was altered by what I had experienced today, mostly by meeting Thomas. How odd—yesterday I hadn't known he existed. Today he filled up my thoughts. I wondered whether he had already phoned, whether he'd left a message, wondered when I'd hear his voice again, thought to myself for the second time, oh, God, I've got it bad. No, not bad, it's good. Not just good—great!

I wanted to spin along the street. I felt like running. I'm a fool, I thought, a nut case. All I did was spend an afternoon with a boy. All we did was talk and kiss twice. All I did was fall in love. And he loves me, too. I know it!

It was like a small convocation in our room: the trio from across the hall—Marlene Madison, Diane Letton, and Cissy Cane—were gathered there with Kim, and I heard them talking as I came toward the door.

"Laura always was a little weird, you know? I mean, it's awful that her mom died and everything, but that doesn't mean she isn't weird." It was Diane's voice.

"Don't blame yourself, Kimmy. It's not your fault if Laura ran away. Even if she did something drastic. After all, just 'cause you're friends, doesn't mean she isn't her own person." I heard Marlene's, "valley girl" drawl and hated her.

"My mom has a friend whose daughter committed suicide." This contribution came from Cissy.

"Look, guys, I don't feel like talking about it," said Kim. I heard the quiver in her voice; I heard the anxiety and the dread. Still, I didn't go in, for I was curious and fascinated to hear more.

"We're only trying to help you, Kimmy," drawled Marlene. "You're not responsible for Laura. You're just too sweet and nice. I always did wonder why…"

Fiercely Cissy broke in. "I'll bet Mr. Langfeld is calling the cops. Oh, damn, they might want to question all of us. I hate cops. Why should we all be put on the spot like a bunch of criminals, just because Laura…"

"Shut up, Cissy!" Kim cried out. "I don't want to hear this!"

"If you know where she went," said Diane, taking up the call for action, "you ought to tell. Why should you take the heat? Why should you get involved?"

"Because Laura's my best friend in the world! I'd do anything for her!"

I pushed the door open. From the doorway I watched as the four of them turned to stare at me, as if I was a cadaver come back to life. Cissy looked stunned. Marlene got red-faced. Diane pointed and gasped, "You!"

But it was the look on Kim's face that told me what I wanted to know, and then her arms were around me, and we were hugging and crying, and the other girls grumbled and left.

"Oh, Laura, I was so worried!" Kim exclaimed. She pulled me over to the small sofa. "Tell me everything. What happened? Why are you so late? I tried to stall them—all day I kept looking at the clock, wondering where you were and what you were doing."

"The flight was delayed nearly an hour for landing. Too much air traffic or fog or something." I shrugged. "Kim, I have to tell you. I found out things about my mom. She ran away to go on the stage! It was almost like we said. And I met the greatest guy. Megan's son."

"Her son! What's he like? What's she like?"

"He's eighteen, a senior at this great prep school, and he's gorgeous and smart and athletic and wonderful and he's going to come to California to see me!"

"Laura! Laura, how great!" Kim's eyes glowed, and her breath came swiftly with excitement. "What's his name? When's he coming? Did he kiss you?"

"Yes." I felt myself blushing. "Yes, he did. And it was—oh, Kim."

The door burst open. "So there you are."

Roz stormed into the room. Her eyes were narrowed, her tone brittle with anger. "I want to talk to you, Laura."

Kim stood up. She glanced about uncertainly, her cheeks flushed. "Do you want me to leave?" she whispered.

"Yes," said Roz.

Kim went out, perhaps to the stares and questions of those stupid girls, I thought resentfully. They couldn't wait to see me get in trouble.

Roz faced me squarely, eyes blazing. "I want to know exactly where you were all day, with whom, and why you deliberately lied to everyone and disobeyed the rules. And I want you to know that unless you have some very good reasons for taking off like this, I intend to telephone your father and let him know we're putting you on the very next flight back to California!"

I stepped back, biting my lip, stalling for time. "Where is Mr. Langfeld? I want to talk to him."

"Forget it! He and Mrs. Langfeld had theater tickets for tonight. I'm handling this. They deserve a night off, after herding you kids around all week, and now—how do you think we felt when we came up here and saw this room empty? Have you any idea?" Roz was shaking with anger.

I sank down on the sofa, covering my face with my hands, and I thought of tragic things, of the double suicide of Romeo and Juliet, of love lost forever, of the passion of St. Bernadette, of my mother in her coffin, and I managed to work up a storm of tears.

I had needed to weep before, on stage. Begun with great concentration and effort, however, these tears took on a vitality of their own. The act became reality. Soon I was sobbing uncontrollably as the many dimensions of my sad life raced before my eyes—parents cool and distant, no extended family at all (and I wept for aunts, uncles, and grandparents I'd never known, never would know). I wept for all the many years of grief, trying to get close to Mom, and for that final door slamming in my face on the day she died. I wept for the hope I had harbored as I went to Toronto, and now at the realization that even if my grandparents were still alive, I'd never find them, and if I did, perhaps I would hate them as my mother had hated them. Lastly, I wept for the loss of Thomas, for that surge of love I'd felt earlier today, which was now forever gone.

I felt Roz's hand on my shoulder. I looked up and saw that her eyes were misty with tears. She drew up a chair and sat down opposite me.

"Laura, Laura," she said, "please, let's try to work this out. Let me help you. I'm not your enemy. I don't want to hurt you."

"You—it's not you," I gasped, wiping the tears from my face. "I'm just—I don't know what to do anymore. Everything is lost."

"No, no, that can't be," Roz soothed. Her brows drew

together, troubled, and she leaned toward me with great concern. "Tell me what happened today. You can't carry these burdens all alone, Laura. You don't have to."

I took a deep breath, reached for a tissue and composed myself. "I was at my mother's old home town," I said. "Birch Bend. It's over an hour away, in Virginia."

Roz hesitated before asking, "What were you doing there?"

Tears started again, unbidden, and I went on, brushing them away as I spoke. "I was looking up an old friend of my family. Her name is Antonia Armenta, and she lives in that town. She knew my grandparents. I thought she could tell me something about my past. My heritage. Being here in Washington, D.C., is so painful!"

Roz gazed at me intently and she murmured, "Why is that?"

"Because I also have a heritage, but I don't have anyone to tell me about it! My father… he's always gone. And now my mother… she never told me anything. But now I know that my grandparents might still be alive. Mrs. Armenta told me so. She was going to do some research for me. She said she'd try to make some contacts." I was amazed at how easily the lies came to me; they seemed ready and waiting in the wings.

"Wait a minute, Laura," Roz said. "If this was so important, why didn't you just tell us about it and get permission to go?"

I looked down at my hands, clenched in my lap. "I was afraid you wouldn't let me go that far. The rules said we had to stay in the city, unless we were all together on a tour bus. I knew you wouldn't take the whole class to Birch Bend! Neither would I want everyone along to see…" Again, the tears started.

"All right. All right. I can understand that this is a private matter, Laura, but you might have trusted me. You might have considered that I'd understand."

I held my breath, hung my head. "I'm sorry," I murmured. "I was scared. Once permission was denied, I'd have no chance at all. Don't you see?" I was appalled and amazed at how easily the fabrications rolled from my tongue. Genius! Liar! The two descriptions battled in my consciousness even as I went on.

"Mrs. Armenta invited me to come to her house again tomorrow. She said she'd look up some old photographs and try to get more information for me. Roz, I feel so empty! I have nothing left! Nothing!"

"Hush!" Roz commanded. She sat stiff and silent for a long moment, arms folded across her chest. Then she said, "Give me this woman's telephone number."

"I don't have it."

"But you must have called her before."

"It's in my little notebook. I left my little notebook there by mistake. But I can get it again from information."

Sternly she said, "Do so."

I hurried to the telephone, silently praying that Mrs. Armenta had a listed number, that she'd be home.

The scheme rushed so swiftly, so effortlessly into my head; I was amazed. It's a gift, I thought. I felt like a criminal—deliciously so, congratulating myself. It was all so easy!

From the operator I got the number, swiftly memorized it and dialed. Mrs. Armenta answered almost immediately, in the high, breathless tone of a person given to both fear and hope whenever the telephone rings.

"Mrs. Armenta," I said quickly, eagerly, "this is Laura, the Rouseaus' granddaughter. I'm here with my counselor. She asked me to call you. She wants to talk to you. I'm planning to come and see you tomorrow. Is that okay?"

Remembering Mrs. Armenta's sudden bouts of vagueness, I paused to let the significance of this statement sink in.

"Why—why—yes," she finally replied. "I suppose that would be just fine. You're coming over tomorrow, you say? What time?"

"I could be there in the morning at ten," I said, casting a glance at Roz, who was listening hard.

Roz reached out for the telephone. I handed her the receiver. "Mrs. Armenta, this is Roz Zacharias. I'm one of the chaperons for this trip, and it's our policy to check it out when our pupils leave the tour area. I'm sure you understand."

There was silence for a moment, then Roz said, "Laura tells me that you are an old friend of the family. Oh. Her grandparents? Yes, she mentioned that."

I waited, holding my breath, wondering what possible kind of luck could make Mrs. Armenta understand and sympathize with my predicament. I crossed my fingers behind my back, hoping that Mrs. Armenta might be just confused enough and perhaps lonely enough that she would focus only on the idea of having a visitor tomorrow. She might gloss over the fact that we hadn't made any plans to meet again.

I could tell, from Roz's murmurs, that Mrs. Armenta was explaining how she had bought the house from my grandparents, and I heard her say, "Such a nice young girl."

Then Roz said, "Well, since you are such an old friend of the family.... I know what a rough time Laura has had.... Sometimes we have to know when to make allowances."

Roz hung up the phone and turned to me. "You may go tomorrow, Laura, but these are the rules. You're to be back here at the hotel by four P.M., and no excuses whatsoever."

"Yes, ma'am."

"And you will under no circumstances go alone."

I did my best to look mollified and humble, while inside I was bursting with self-congratulation.

"Can Ryan Margolis come with me?" I asked, my eyes wide in innocence.

"No way," said Roz flatly. "You take Kim."

"Pride goeth before a fall." This was one of my mother's favorite sayings. She peppered me with it whenever things were going really well. If she'd been here now, it's what she would have said, because I was so proud of myself.

My fall came very soon, very hard.

chapter / 15

The first thing Kim and I did when we got to Birch Bend was to walk to Tyrol Street. I showed Kim the strangely miscast house, the burned tree and the cinder-block wall.

"This is definitely where the photograph was taken," Kim said. I had brought the snapshot with me, and we made the comparison. "This is where they were sitting," Kim said, and she sat down on the wall.

I went to sit beside her. On the bus on the way to Birch Bend I had told Kim everything that Megan told me, that my mother had hated her parents, how she had run away, changed her name, tried to lose herself. I told Kim about Thomas, and that last revelation that Megan had also lied to her son. "Something is very wrong here," I said now. "Two sets of parents wouldn't both have died in car crashes, unless they were all together."

"Maybe that's it," said Kim. "Maybe the four of them were going someplace, and both sets of parents were killed. That would be enough to make anyone crazy."

"Could be," I murmured. "But then, what about the fire?"

"Do we know for sure that there was a fire?" Kim asked.

"Well, Mrs. Armenta said so. Then, there's the burn on this tree." I nodded toward the magnolia.

"Well, maybe there was a fire," said Kim, "but Megan's parents weren't killed in it."

"It's possible," I agreed. "There might have been a fire first, then the car crash."

"Sometimes bad luck comes in threes," Kim said.

"If Megan lied about the way her parents died," I said, "maybe she also lied about my mother running away."

"Why would she lie?" Kim asked.

I sighed. "That's what I want to find out."

We sat for a few minutes on the wall, quietly pondering.

"How are we going to investigate?" Kim asked.

"We'll check old newspapers. We'll start with the fire. If there was a fire, it would be in the papers."

"Does anyone keep newspapers around for twenty-five years?" Kim wondered.

"We'll find out," I said. "But first, I want to talk to Mrs. Armenta, in case Roz calls her again later."

We walked the half block to the gray house with blue shutters. As we stood there I imagined it being twenty-five years earlier, and that Kim and I were really Megan and Jenny. It was a strange, eerie feeling.

Mrs. Armenta came to the door. She threw up her hands, smiling, then drew me inside. "Laura! My stars. I was so astonished by that telephone call—what happened? Where were you yesterday? My, my that counselor was upset. Did I help?"

I burst out laughing. "You mean…."

"I know a fib when I hear one," she said stoutly. "And I know when a young girl needs an alibi. I'll bet it had something to do with a boy. Am I right?"

"You're right," I said happily, and I introduced Kim. "Kim is my best friend," I said warmly.

Mrs. Armenta smiled broadly, looking deep into Kim's eyes. "My dear, I'm glad to meet you. Will you come in and have a soda? Or some lemonade?"

"We can't stay," I said quickly. "I just wanted to thank you for covering for me. Why did you do it?"

Mrs. Armenta smiled. "I remember what it's like to be in love, the little white lies you have to tell. By the way, I remembered something yesterday after you'd left."

Kim and I exchanged glances. "Yes?" My heart was beating powerfully. I felt like an explorer on the edge of discovery. Every nuance held a clue. "What did you remember?"

"Well, I told you that the folks who lived in that house had a daughter. After her folks died, the girl was shipped off to Canada. I thought maybe you could talk to her."

"But Laura already…"

I interrupted Kim. "That's good to know, Mrs. Armenta," I said. "It could be very helpful."

"I'm keeping your phone number right here in this little drawer," said Mrs. Armenta. She showed us a small, bright papier-mâché cabinet, the drawers filled with papers and cards. "If I remember anything else, I'll be sure to get in touch with you."

"Thank you so much," I said. We went to the door. "If anyone should call and ask about us…" I began.

Mrs. Armenta smiled, then put her finger to her lips in an exaggerated gesture of conspiracy. "I'll say you were with me all day."

I rushed over and gave her a hug. It surprised us both, I think, for Mrs. Armenta hugged me back, then smiled broadly and said, "Come back. Come back anytime and see me."

When we were out of earshot Kim asked, "Why didn't you tell her you'd already been to see Megan?"

"I don't know," I said.

"How does she know about Thomas?"

"She doesn't," I said. "She thinks I'm in love with Spider." I felt like a conspirator or a detective, keeping secrets. I recalled my mother's admonitions: never tell anybody everything. The less talk, the better. Yes, she had closed herself off. Was I doing the same thing? Would I, too, end up suspicious, without friends, my main companions being old songs? So many of Mother's attitudes had made their way into my actions. I wondered whether I would ever be free of them.

"Where to?" Kim asked.

"Library."

"Last time that librarian gave us a hard time," she said.

"We're going to the public library," I said. "It's over on State Street."

"You sound as if you've lived here."

"I almost feel that I have."

And in fact, the library was familiar from the other day, with Spider. The same woman sat there at the computer, waiting to be helpful. I walked up to her and said Kim and I were doing research on the town. Did they save old local newspapers? Oh, yes, she assured us. On microfiche.

She pointed to the room with the machines. Did we know how to use them?

"Sure," I said.

"Everything is arranged by date in those shelves," she called after us. "If you need help reaching anything, just ask."

Kim and I went to the microfiche room, with its many machines and shelves filled with cartridges, all neatly labeled.

"What years should we look at?" Kim asked. Then she

said, "If we get done early, let's go walk on Main Street. I saw some cute stores last time."

"Sure, sure," I said automatically. I scanned the shelves. "We don't know when the fire happened—if there was a fire. Mrs. Armenta said it was about twenty years ago, but she's pretty vague. We do know that my mother was probably in the class of 1974," I said. "Except that she didn't graduate with her class, so we know she'd left town by then."

"How old was your mom?" Kim asked.

"I'm not sure. She never said."

"Really?"

"She'd just tell me, kind of joking, you know, that a woman's age is her own business."

"If she was in the class of 1974, she'd have been eighteen that year," Kim reasoned.

"Sometimes people skip a grade or something," I pointed out. "She could have been younger."

"We should look from 1970, I guess," said Kim. "Let's get started." She reached up and took two cartridges labeled "1970" from a high shelf and carried them over to a machine.

I stood there, reluctant to begin. I suppose I was as reluctant to uncover the truth as I had been eager for it. Because once the truth is out, there is no more imagining or wishing. What did I imagine? What did I wish? I couldn't say. I only know that I hesitated, finally reaching up to take the cassettes for the years 1974, 1973, and 1972.

"Need help with that?" I turned and saw a heavyset man with a shock of light hair, the color of corn silk. It astonished me, for I recognized him from the picnic. He gave no sign of knowing us. Probably he had forgotten, I thought, and I was just as glad.

"We know how to use these," I said.

"Turn the machines off when you're done," he said. "And don't bother to reshelve the cartridges. The library staff likes to do it, instead of having things all messed up."

"Yes, sir."

The man gave me a swift glance, then moved out of the mircrofiche area to a row of computers at the other end of the long room.

I put in the first tape, wound the crank and sat back to ponder the past. At another machine a few feet away sat Kim, slowly turning pages, squinting closely at the old news.

"Hey, listen to this!" she called. "Here's an article about the Beatles. 'Paul McCartney announced he was leaving the Beatles, thereby disbanding the most successful pop music group in history. McCartney said the split was the result of "personal differences." '"

"Hmm," I murmured, scanning an article about a protest rally, during which some boys burned their draft cards, and someone set an American flag on fire.

"Listen to this!" Kim called out again. "Some American soldiers killed a whole bunch of Vietnamese people in this little village. They just shot them in cold blood. This is about the trial—five hundred and sixteen people, they killed. They called it a massacre. The My Lai Massacre. I never thought that our soliders would…"

"That's awful," I said. "It was a bad time for us."

"For us?" Kim chuckled. "We weren't even born."

"For our country. Our folks." I went over to Kim, glanced at her screen.

She said, "Look, there was this protest rally at Kent State University. The National Guard killed eight students—can you believe this?"

Incredible things were flashing before me, not stories, but

real events about real people. The present and the past seemed fused together. I remembered the Vietnam memorial we'd seen just the other day, all those names, each one representing a real person who was killed.

"Look for local news," I told Kim, as I went back to my machine. I felt very tired as I continued scanning the microfiche. We continued at our screens. Kim got up and brought back other cartridges. After a while she called out, "Hey! Come look at this!"

I rushed over to her station to see her beaming, pointing to the screen. "Look! It's an announcement of an art sale. 'Pottery by Jeanette Rouseau.' Wasn't that your grandma?"

"Yes!" I felt goose bumps, thrills I'd never imagined, just seeing her name in print. "What year is this?"

"Nineteen seventy-five. June." Kim read the words out loud. "Crofton's Gift Gallery: Summer Arts and Crafts Sale, Paintings by Don W. Jorrey, sculpture by Oliver Sorenson and Nancy Blake, pottery by local artist Jeanette Rouseau."

Local artist. The words sang to me. Artist. Grandma. She was clever, she was talented. I wished I could have seen her sitting at her potter's wheel, her hands slick with water and clay, her feet pumping the treadle. I pictured her, hair done up, a few strands escaping, her face dewy with perspiration as she concentrated on her craft.

"Anything else?" I asked.

"Nothing."

"Try going back a couple of years," I suggested. "I've finished seventy-three and -four. Maybe you want to check them. I might have missed something."

Kim laughed. "You never miss anything."

I finished my cartridge and put in the next, 1972, now going right for the local news. I scanned the articles, about the completion of a new library, the pride of the town, on State Street. Again I had that eerie feeling of being in two time frames at once. I read about weddings, promotions, a freak storm that knocked out the local power plant. All the events of the town, large and small, seemed collected here, transferred from this screen to me, as if I were to be the repository of the town's past—dog shows and Halloween parties, school open houses, political campaign speeches, the race for mayor, the accusations of a woman running for city council—the fire.

MIDNIGHT BLAZE CONSUMES HOME—TWO DEAD.

It was on the third page of the newspaper.

I felt as if I'd been knocked in the stomach. My eyes fastened on the headline. Under the headline was a row of smaller type: "Officials Investigate Cause of Fire."

The article continued: "Hugo and Eloise Wynant were apparently asleep in the upstairs bedroom when the fire broke out in their kitchen. Neighbors called the fire department, but the house was so completely engulfed in flames that the entire structure collapsed soon after firefighters arrived. They were able to enter the dwelling and extract the body of Hugo Wynant. His wife, however, had apparently remained upstairs, where she was trapped after the staircase gave way. Mrs. Wynant's remains were identified by dental records.

"Their daughter, fourteen-year-old Megan Wynant, was spending the night at the home of a friend and neighbor, Jennifer Rouseau. Miss Wynant, informed by police and fire officials of the tragedy, is said to have collapsed. She was the only child. The family dog, a mixed terrier called Sasha, apparently fled the house. Its severely charred remains were found in the front yard. Fire officials speculate that the dog's fur caught on fire, and that the flames flared up as the animal tried to escape from the house. 'The dog was a living torch,' said Sgt. Mercer.

"Several neighbors said it was the dog's cries that alerted them to the tragedy. Fire officials are investigating the cause of the blaze, speculating that a faulty kitchen appliance might have been responsible."

I don't know how long I sat there rereading the article, my heart pounding so violently that I thought I'd burst. No wonder, I thought dully, my chest aching, that neither my mother nor Megan could bear the sight of a dog. They must have loved that terrier, Sasha. To imagine her as a "living torch" would be so horrible that neither of them would ever want to expose themselves to such pain again.

I felt Kim beside me. I heard her heavy breathing, realized she was reading over my shoulder. "My God," she whispered.

"Horrible," I whispered back.

I turned the crank, flipping past several pages, searching for another article. There it was, this time on the second page.

INVESTIGATORS QUESTION DAUGHTER OF FIRE VICTIMS

I read on, mesmerized.

"Fire officials are questioning fourteen-year-old Megan Wynant in their investigation into the blaze that caused the death of her parents, Hugo and Eloise Wynant last Friday night. According to the girl, she knew nothing of the fire until police officers informed her at about one A.M.

"Investigators have discovered that gas was emitted from the kitchen stove. A burning candle nearby ignited the gas, causing the house to be swiftly enveloped in flames. 'This explains the explosive nature of the fire,' said Sgt. Mercer of the Birch Bend Fire Department. 'The whole house went up like a tinder box. We also found traces of gasoline, and we are questioning Miss Wynant as to whether her parents kept gasoline or other flammable substances on the premises.' Homeowners, said Mercer, are urged not to store flammable substances in and around their homes."

Kim spoke first. "Sounds like somebody left the gas stove on."

"And a candle."

"That's stupid!" Kim exclaimed. "Nobody would do such a thing."

"People make mistakes," I said.

Kim gave me a strange look. "A deadly mistake," she said.

I turned the crank again, straining to find some explanation to make it seem less terrible. If Megan's parents died in a fire, why did she tell Thomas it was a car crash? Why did she distort the truth? Did she lose her mind?

Anything was possible.

I turned the crank very slowly now, searching every page, every column. Then I saw it. This time the article was on page one, big news, heart-stopping news.

DAUGHTER ACCUSED IN FATAL FIRE

"Authorities now believe that the fire that killed Mr. and Mrs. Hugo Wynant was purposely set by their daughter Megan, 14, acting together with her friend, Jennifer Rouseau, age 15. The two girls…"

It echoed, like a stone tossed into a well. The two girls… two girls…two girls…

There was a roaring in my ears. Then I went numb. It was like being anesthetized, stunned, before the pain rushed upon me.

I couldn't speak or move. Only my eyes moved back to the

screen, to the words: "Acting together with her friend, Jennifer Rouseau..."

In a way, it was like coming to the end of a road. Those dreams of mine, being swallowed alive, capsizing in a boat on the vast, dark ocean—it had all been leading to this. This was the darkness I had dreaded. It had a name. Murder. My mother had committed the worst possible crime. Surely the taint of it was in me, too.

chapter / 16

I know that people react in various ways to shock. Some get hysterical. Some people scream and cry, some run away. Others get very quiet, almost coldly calculating, thinking about what to do next, how they can survive.

That's how I am. When they told me my mom had died, I went on remote control. My feelings were frozen, while my mind raced ahead with a thousand questions.

It was this way now. My hands and feet felt cold, icy cold, and my mind exploded with questions that I knew, no matter what, I must answer. Even if it took me forever, if it took everything I ever had or was, I'd find the answers.

Beside me, Kim stood motionless. Her face was frozen in an expression I had never seen before. Her hands were clasped together under her chin.

"Come on," I said. "We have to get busy." My voice sounded cold and distant.

"What are you talking about?" It was a whisper.

"We have to read. There's more. This was…" I held my breath, then released the word slowly, barely audibly. "Murder."

"No!" Kim cried.

"What else would you call it?" I flung back. "They killed Megan's parents, don't you understand? They set the fire. They did it on purpose."

"But maybe it was an accident!" Kim cried. "Maybe they were just doing it for insurance money, didn't know her parents would be in the house, and they never planned to kill them. Laura, how could you think…?"

"Look." I had found the next article, and I sat down now on the stool, outwardly calm, as if I were a stranger and uninvolved, while my heart still beat like a hammer, wildly, painfully in my chest. I spotted the isolated words, strung together now as I flipped the microfiche forward, saw that page after page was filled with what must have been the story of the decade: "MURDER…ACCOMPLICE…PLOTTED… CHILDREN…HATED…

"I'm staying here," I whispered fiercely, "until I've read every word."

Beside me Kim nodded silently. I glanced at her pale face, her stunned expression. As I moved my hand I heard and felt the bracelet with the little hearts, FRIENDS FOREVER.

Ah, well, I thought, at the edge of hysteria, of course they couldn't remain friends. After you've committed a murder together, how can you go on just fooling around, listening to music, playing games? No, once you've stepped over that line, into the big world, into the evil—no, you can never go back to being a child. Yesterday's child, I thought, suddenly overcome with grief, can't ever be a child again. And for a long moment I knew what it was like for my mother to have stepped across that chasm, one moment a simple, ordinary girl—*only fifteen years old!*—the next moment a killer.

All those thousands of questions leapt through my head at

once—how did they do it? What were the reasons? What did they tell themselves, how did they go from talk to action, from fantasy to *murder*? My head ached violently, my stomach too. I breathed in deeply, fighting nausea.

"You don't have to stay here with me, Kim," I said. "In fact, I'd rather you didn't. Why don't you go on back to Washington, to the hotel. Tell Roz—I don't care what you tell her. Tell her I ran away. Tell her…"

"I'm not leaving you, Laura," Kim said.

"Why would you stay?" Now I felt tears starting, and I swallowed them down. "Why would you want to? This is grotesque! You don't have to be involved. You can just go home. It's not your life."

"I'm not leaving you," she repeated. "Keep going. Let's get it all."

Once or twice, as we were reading, mesmerized, the librarian walked by, glanced at us and asked brightly, "Everything okay?"

"Yes, yes," we responded, giving her brittle little smiles. Then, like addicts, we turned back to the microfiche machine, pulled in by its eerie glow, its gentle hum, its terrifying, astounding revelations.

DAUGHTER CONFESSES TO MURDER PLOT

"Megan Wynant, the pretty, vivacious fourteen-year-old daughter of Hugo and Eloise Wynant, confessed yesterday that she had been discussing the murder of her parents 'for many weeks,' with her friend Jenny Rouseau. 'We talked about it. It was sort of a game, you know. My friend and I used to pretend we'd buy a gun and—do things. Of course, I don't really believe in guns. We made plans—stories, really, about committing crimes. It was just a game. I didn't know Jenny was so dead serious. She was the one who suggested the fire.'

"On the advice of counsel employed by her parents, fifteen-year-old Jennifer Rouseau refused to comment on her friend's allegations."

Kim would not look at me. I felt her presence, stony, quiet. I knew she was thinking about us, how the ideas for pranks and tricks had always been mine. The time we stayed out all night with the horses, each telling our parents that we'd be at the other's house—that was my idea. The night we rescued Mongoose, sneaking out again—my idea. The time we took my mother's cigarettes and smoked them all one Saturday morning on the mountain, until we threw up. I was the instigator, the bad seed. Like mother, like daughter.

My whole body was chilled now, my hands clammy as I wound the crank on to the next article. Now the newspaper was filled with the story, day after day, they explored this "heinous crime" from all angles, no considerations too personal or too devastating.

GIRLS KILL FOR REVENGE, FREEDOM

"...It was after her father whipped her with a belt for stealing $20 from his wallet, that Megan Wynant began to plot the murder of both parents. 'My mother just watched him beating me. She never said anything or tried to stop him.'

"The girl said that she and her friend, Jennifer Rouseau, had plans to go away to boarding school in New England. 'My parents were always threatening that they wouldn't let me go,' she said, 'even after they promised.'

"According to Megan, her parents constantly provoked her, saying they would not give her the money to go to the exclusive Quincy Academy, because 'you're too stupid to profit from it.' Further, they taunted her, saying, 'When we're dead and the money is yours, you can do anything you like.'

"'That started the idea,'" Megan told police. 'I figured, if they were dead, I'd get all their money and use it for boarding school. I'd be free at last. It was sort of a fantasy at first. Jenny and I would talk about it for hours. We'd plan all sorts of ways—funny ways to get rid of them, like pushing them off a cliff or getting them onto a ladder and sawing off the legs, electrocuting them in the tub by tossing in a radio—you know, all those things you see in the movies.'

"The girl said they first started talking about a fire when they heard on the news about a large apartment fire in Chicago, where sixteen people were killed and twenty-three injured. 'It seemed like the easiest, best way to go,' said Megan. 'Jenny got the gasoline.'"

Another article focused on the girls' intelligence, the paradox of brilliance and evil contained within the same brain.

KILLER GIRLS CALLED SUPERIOR STUDENTS

"According to school officials, both girls were outstanding students, and extremely bright. Said school principal, Herman Rosenbloom, 'Jennifer, especially, is extremely creative and precocious. So much so that the other students find her a bit intimidating. She and Megan were inseparable.'"

Kim did not move, nor did I, except to turn the crank.

DRUGS INVOLVED IN ARSON-MURDER OF PARENTS

"Both Jennifer Rouseau and Megan Wynant admitted, under intense questioning by police, that they were 'a little giddy' from marijuana the night they set the Wynant house on fire, killing both parents of Megan Wynant. 'We were feeling good,' said Megan. 'We were laughing and running across the lawn. We got the kerosene from Jenny's garage.'"

Oh, yes. Jenny—Jasmine—Mother was always so logical, so very particular. She'd never take a chance on just gas alone, even with a lit candle. No, add a little gasoline just to make sure that the fire spreads fast, that the whole house ignites and blows up so that nothing remains, no flesh on the bones, no hair, nothing even to be identified, except for teeth, which don't burn.

I began to shake and heave. Suddenly I felt as if I were coming apart. I ran, blindly searching for the rest room. The librarian, seeing my frenzy, pointed, squeaking out, "The little girls' room is over there!" I made it into the stall, felt my insides exploding.

The violence of the killing was what shattered me. And the certain knowledge that my mother had stood there watching it all. Yes, I knew, as if I had been there in the flesh, exactly how it happened. Mother would have watched, because she'd have left nothing to chance. Meticulous, plotting, controlling—she would have watched and masterminded every detail.

They had planned it for weeks, oh, so carefully. How delicious, those long nights of lying awake, talking, plotting, imagining. They were no longer bored—oh, no. When you're planning a murder, it sort of takes over everything, life becomes pretty challenging. Exciting. Having a secret makes everything special. People treat you as if you were just an ordinary person, but no, you're God. You're playing God.

Days ahead, they'd set the stage: Megan would sleep over at Jenny's. "She slept over here last week," Megan would say, to clinch it. "We always take turns."

"All right, fine, if it's all right with Mrs. Rouseau." The Wynants would be glad to get rid of their pestering girl for a night, not to have to hear her whining and complaining and fussing. Ah, peace for the night. They'd put out the dog, as usual, in the doghouse out back.

But it was unusually cold that night, a frigid snap coming in from the north, with strong winds.

The papers had reported it. The girls used it. Everything was going their way. The wind would fan the flames, speed up the inevitable. Except that they hadn't counted on the dog being indoors.

One of the articles had said it, in brittle irony:

KILLER GIRL MOURNS DOG, NOT PARENTS

" 'I never meant to hurt Sasha. She was supposed to be out in her doghouse. We never meant for her to die.' "

On that night, with the wind slamming into their faces, the two girls had crouched down low behind shrubs, behind the cinder-block wall, watching the sudden burst of fire, thrilled by its brilliance, the flames' magnificent progress. Gold, red, orange, crackling, roaring, smoking—ah, it was like a thousand Fourth of Julys, and they had executed it, moving for weeks toward this conclusion. But then—what was that? Could it be...? Then came the sudden shattering of glass, together with the wailing cry of the dog as it burst out into the night. It was a living torch, blazing, flaring as it hit the wind. The dog streaked across the lawn, its howls mingling with the roar of the fire.

Oh, the girls would have moaned and screamed, muted behind their hands, "No! No!" and they stared at each other in silent horror, knowing they would never, never forget the sound of those animal howls, the agony of a dog on fire. Every time they saw a dog—or any creature with fur and feelings, dependent on the goodness of humans, they would remember.

I heard footsteps, a door opening, banging shut. "Laura! Laura, are you in there?"

"I'm here, Kim," I said, muffled, my mind and heart still in that other time with that other girl, my own mother. She and Megan had run back to Jenny's house, jumped into bed after swiftly getting out of their smoky clothes. They had lain under the covers, silent and stiff, appearing to be asleep when the parents came, amazed that the girls had slept through the chaos, dreading to awaken them to the terrible news.

Later the investigators found gasoline stains on Jenny's shoes and on her jeans. Megan, of course, had the key to the back door, had let herself in, turned on the gas in the oven, lit the candle...it was so easy to piece it all together, almost like child's play.

"Are you okay?" Kim asked.

"Oh, sure." I almost laughed, I was so far from being okay.

I came out, washed my hands and face and borrowed Kim's comb for my hair. My face in the mirror looked a little wild, hair all over the place, eyebrows knotted, intense.

"I feel," I said at last, "as if there are a thousand things I need to do. But none of them will make any difference."

"What do you mean?" Kim looked frightened.

"Nothing I do will ever make a difference. Because of what she did."

"That's silly," said Kim. "You're separate from her. Different people. You can't be responsible for what your mother was—or did."

I held out my arm, my hand. My fingers looked foreign to me, my feet, body, face, all seemed inhabited by some other spirit, no longer mine. "I'm part of her. She's part of me. Her blood, her genes, even her thoughts are inside me."

"This was such a shock," Kim said. "The point is, Laura, we have to stay on target. We were doing this to find out about your grandparents. The point is, they might still be alive."

I shook myself, as if I were just awakening from a drug or a dream. "Yes, they might be," I finally said. And now I realized that more than ever I needed to find them. "And if they are alive, they can tell me what really happened. All the details."

"Why do you have to know?"

"It's how I am," I said simply. "It's just the way I am."

Kim put her arm around me, the way she used to do when we were little, even when we were walking on the street. Back then, it was so natural for us to show affection.

Now, I held myself away, for I felt dirty, as if I were diseased and contagious. "Let's go back," I said, mustering my strength. "Let's finish this."

We walked back to the microfiche room, and a surge of anger gripped me as I saw the man from the picnic sitting on my stool in front of the machine, staring at the screen with rapt attention.

"Excuse me!" I called out loudly. "I wasn't finished with that!"

The man stood up and backed away, his hands clenched nervously.

"Who are you?" I asked. "What are you doing?"

He nodded toward the machine, the pages from the past. "It was a terrible tragedy," he said, his voice trembling with emotion. "I remember it. Oh, God."

"Then you *did* know my mother," I said, my heart racing. "You knew all about her and…"

He looked straight at me, and to my astonishment I saw tears in his eyes. "Yes. Of course I knew her. I know everything. And the minute I saw you at the picnic I knew you were her daughter. You look like her. The hair and eyes."

"But, why didn't you say something?" I cried. "Why did you let us go like that?"

"You have to understand," he said, hands outspread, a gesture of helplessness. "This is a small town. People talk. I heard you kids were snooping around at the high school. I knew you went to the historical society. I figured you'd be back."

"You mean—people have been spying on us?" Kim exclaimed.

"This is a small town," the man repeated. "Everybody talks. I've sort of been watching for you. You see, I—oh, I'd give anything to know what happened to Jenny. Beautiful Jenny." He took a handkerchief from his pocket and wiped his face.

"You were her friend," I murmured, seeing the pain in his eyes, his sorrowful face.

He nodded, his eyes downcast. "I worshiped her. I had the biggest crush on Jenny Rouseau! And then she vanished. I wanted to talk to you at the picnic. But the others—I couldn't. Everyone wanted to forget what happened here."

"So they all lied to us!" I exclaimed. "They just go around pretending my mother didn't exist."

He rubbed his neck, his chin. "You have to understand," he said. "It was the crime of the decade. Some called it the crime of the century. It was in all the papers, not just here, but all over, even on TV. A horrible thing. It put Birch Bend on the map. Nobody wanted that kind of publicity."

He put out his hand. "I'm Lester Shane. You can't imagine how I felt when I saw you at the picnic, looking so much like Jenny. All these years I've wondered what became of her. I hoped she'd be okay, that somehow she'd gotten over what happened. I didn't know she was married. It's terrible that she died so young. But at least she had you. She had a life, a family. I'm glad she got away. There's so much hatred here."

I looked at Lester Shane, the light hair, the very bright blue eyes, still filled with tears.

"If this town is so hateful," I said, "how come you stayed?"

Lester smiled slightly. "Sharp. Just like your mom. Always the question, right on point, right for the jugular. I stayed because my family has a business here. We sell and service business machines now, along with selling office furniture and supplies. I come here to the library once in a while to check on their machines. My family has been in this town for four generations. I wasn't about to break the chain, even if I had the guts, which I don't."

Lester Shane motioned Kim and me over to a long work table. "Have a seat. You've come a long way." He peered at me closely. "You want to know, don't you?"

"I have to know," I cried out passionately. "I have to know the truth. Imagining is so much worse!"

"Yes. You would want to know. She was like that—so curious, even if it hurt. Always making plans. She was so smart. Too smart for her own good, and too committed."

"Committed? To what?"

"You'll see." He sighed to himself, glanced at Kim. "This your girlfriend?"

"Yes."

He nodded. "Jenny and Megan were best friends. Inseparable. Do you know Megan?"

"I just met her."

"Nastiest little bitch in the world," he said. "Always scheming."

"She told me her parents died in a car crash."

"That girl wouldn't know the truth if it came and slapped her in the face. She was a pathological liar. Lied for the fun of it. Messed up Jenny's life—your life, too, I guess. I mean, what happened to Jenny was..." He stopped, wiped his face again. "Jenny got a raw deal."

"Why? What happened?"

His brows lifted in astonishment? "Didn't you know your mother was in prison?"

"She was fifteen, just a child."

"No." Lester Shane gritted his teeth together, a grimace of pain. "That year the legislature of Virginia, in its infinite wisdom, passed a new law. Juveniles over the age of fifteen could be tried and punished as adults. Jenny had just turned fifteen. She was tried as an adult and sentenced to twelve years in prison. Accessory to murder. It came out at the trial that it was Megan who actually turned on the gas, struck the match that blew up the house. Your mother was the youngest female ever to be put into that place."

I stared at him, unable to look away, unable to imagine what prison was like—yet imagining it all the same.

"Megan got juvenile detention until she turned twenty-one. Only seven years. Easy time, I'd say, compared to what your mom must have gone through."

I felt Kim's hand on my arm, the arm on which I wore the bracelet, FRIENDS FOREVER.

"You sure you want to hear all this?" Lester Shane asked.

"I want to hear everything," I said, pulling away from Kim, drawing my arms tight across my chest, like making a cocoon, although I knew that nothing could help me or comfort me now. I had opened the door, like Pandora's box. All the evils, now, would come flying out.

chapter / 17

Lester Shane sat with his back to the window. The light projected a glow behind his head and shoulders, like a halo, making him look fragile and otherworldly.

As I sat across the table from him on the hard wooden chair, waiting, I tried to imagine this man as a boy in high school, in love with my mother. I glanced at his full face and corn-silk hair. There was a soft, gentle look about him. Had she loved him, too?

Lester wiped a handkerchief across his forehead, folded it carefully, and placed it in his pocket, then sighed. "I followed this case in the newspapers every day for weeks. I think I memorized every detail. You can imagine, people around here hardly talked about anything else."

My heart was thumping so wildly that I almost thought Lester Shane and Kim could hear it, too. What might it have been like here, with that terrible news flying from person to person, the gossip, telephones ringing. *Did you hear what those terrible girls did? Is it possible?*

Lester Shane was nodding, wiping his face. "At first, I

didn't believe Jenny had anything to do with it."

"You supported her," I breathed. "You were her friend."

"Of course. But then the evidence came in—it was a nightmare," he said heavily. "I still can't quite believe it, even now. I still choke up, after all these years. The thing is, all kids *talk* about doing things—bad things, you know. Usually nothing happens. It's all just talk. And these were basically good kids from good homes, you know, nobody really abused them or neglected them. They were just normal kids."

"Until they burned down the house and killed two people," I said, my voice steely, for I was still numb. Every word of Lester's was a blow; I had to brace myself against them.

"Well—yes." Lester Shane looked down at the table, at his hands, the fingers laced tightly together. "I kept trying to figure it out, thinking that somehow it was a mistake, that maybe Megan did it alone and pinned it on Jenny. But the evidence kept rolling in, and Jenny wouldn't deny it. Jenny's parents hired that lawyer from Alexandria. She wasn't supposed to say anything until the trial. Then she said—they had her give a statement, and of course, it was in all the papers. All over the country. She said she did it out of love."

"Love!" Kim and I cried, both together. "*Love?*"

"Love for her friend," Shane said, breathing heavily, "and pity. Oh, they had her interviewed all over the place, and then there was the trial. The place was packed. Reporters—everyone. I got in, stood there for hours. I wanted her to see me, so I could give her—well, I'm not sure she even knew I was there. She was so cool! Gave her story, blow by blow. It sounded almost—almost logical. Megan was determined to kill her parents. Megan had convinced Jenny of their cruelty, implying much more, I guess, than the fact that the father took a strap to her. If you ask me, he should have taken that strap to her more often! She was a hellion, that girl. Anyway, Jenny figured that Megan would botch the thing, would somehow get herself killed in the bargain."

"So she decided to help," I said.

"I'm not sure it was a cold-blooded decision like that." Lester Shane frowned, still looking at his clenched hands. "You know how kids get to talking, they make believe, especially girls like that, so smart and creative. After a while the thing takes on a life of its own. Maybe reality and fantasy get kind of fuzzy. And if you're smoking pot and drinking your father's whiskey…"

"They were doing that?"

"Oh, yes, they admitted it. According to Jenny's parents, it wasn't the first time, either. The girls had been warned and they'd promised not to do anything—uh—bad. Well, I don't know of any kid who hasn't swiped a cigarette and taken a nip when he wasn't supposed to. Seems like it's just part of growing up. But these girls—you have to have known them. The way they were, everything they did always took them a little further than anyone else. If they were supposed to write a report, it turned into a whole damned book, you know? They made a mural once, a backdrop for a play in junior high, and it was a regular masterpiece. They worked on it for sixty hours, I think. Extremists. Gifted, brilliant extremists."

"So she admitted it," I said, bringing him back to his tale.

"Yes. They set the fire. They had it all planned, for that Friday night when Jenny's parents would be out at the square dance festival across town. Megan's parents always went to bed early, right after the ten o'clock news. The girls waited until about eleven-thirty. Then they got dressed in dark clothes and went out…"

Kim spoke out. "Did they mean to kill them? Maybe they

just set the fire thinking to scare them, to make them give Megan the money—or if the house really burned down, there might be insurance money, and then Megan's parents would let her go…"

Lester Shane nodded wearily. "Yes, all those things were thought of. They were brought up. Nobody really knows what the girls were thinking. But the fact is…the fact…. In law they have a term, *res ipsa loquitur*. The thing speaks for itself."

"You studied law?" I whispered.

"I started to. I wanted to." He sighed. "Anyhow, when Jenny's parents came home, there was this terrible commotion, engines and crowds of people and the streets hosed down. The fire was out by this time, but there was still smoke, and the smell of it, and everyone talking about the tragedy, because they had pulled Mr. Wynant's body out, and a few hours later they found a pile of bones…" Lester glanced at Kim, then at me. "I'm sorry. This is upsetting you girls."

I could only stare at him, nodding slowly, but he was already continuing with his tale, breathing heavily, squeezing his hands together.

"Of course, Jenny's folks knew right away whose house it was that had burned down, and everyone said thank God that at least Megan was spared, because she'd been sleeping over at the Rouseaus'. So the parents rushed home, and they saw the girls fast asleep, or so they thought. A few minutes later the fire marshal came over and said he had to wake them up and tell them. That maybe they had some information. Megan went hysterical when they told her." Shane puffed out cheeks in a look of disgust. "She was some actress, that girl. By the next day, when they started really questioning the girls—separately, of course—the whole thing came apart. They couldn't hold up under that kind of pressure. Who could?"

"They admitted it?" Kim whispered.

"Of course they did," said Lester Shane. "Finally, Jenny's lawyer couldn't do anything but plead for mercy. He pointed out that neither girl had ever been in any trouble with the law before. He begged the court to consider Jenny's age, to at least send her to a juvenile facility. But the judge was adamant. Young people all over the country were running wild, he said, burning their draft cards, doing drugs, no respect for parents or for any authority—now this. The ultimate crime, killing one's parents."

I recalled Megan's recital, how she had told me of my mother's hatred for her parents. Megan had transposed her own feelings onto Jenny. A liar. Pathological liar. Hellion. Nastiest bitch in the world, Lester Shane had called her. Why hadn't I seen it?

Lester Shane exhaled deeply from between pursed lips. "Well, Megan said it was all Jenny's idea. She said they were just talking, playing. It was Jenny who put the plan into action, suggested the candle, got the gasoline and spread it all around the house. It was Jenny who was so desperate to leave town and take Megan with her, that she'd do anything to get Megan free, even to killing her parents. She said Jenny had done other things—stealing, setting a car on fire once. That was never proved, but it all added up to make Jenny look like a monster. Oh, Megan was crafty. I don't think Jenny ever really knew how Megan did her in. In court, at her hearing, Megan wore a pink checked dress and a hair bow, looking like a sweet, innocent young girl. It all had its effect. Finally, Megan was sent to Youth Authority, and your mother was sent to women's prison. Your mom got out for good behavior after nine years. There was a small item in the paper about it. She never caused any trouble, they said, she was a model prisoner."

I felt a terrible pressure in my throat.

Lester reached for his handkerchief. I saw that his shirt was stained under the arms with sweat. My body was still cold, the chill holding me together, I thought, as if I were made of ice and snow.

"But when we saw you at the picnic," I said, "why didn't anybody—I mean, everyone said they never knew her."

"Well, nobody actually knew who you were. Not for sure. Some of us guessed—Monte and Geraldine, the redhead. We talked about it later. Nobody really wanted to get into this again. What would we have said? Told you this whole story?"

"I suppose not. It would have been…"

"Who wants to tell someone a thing like that about their own mother?" Lester Shane exclaimed, his hands pressed into fists now. "Look, I'm sorry. I would never have…" He bit his lip, looked straight at me, as if for forgiveness. "You have to realize what it's like in a small town like Birch Bend. There are business interests in this town. People couldn't afford that kind of publicity, especially Monte Ward. You saw him at the reunion—that big-shouldered guy."

I nodded. "I remember him. He was trying to get us out of there."

"Monte's family had this training camp at the edge of town, for pro baseball players. Monte's dad was about to open up a spa for the general public. This was when personal training was still new, people were just getting into the physical fitness thing. All the emphasis was on wholesome, clean living. A lot of people had invested with Monte, and a lot of others were planning to ride on Monte's coattails, like opening a new restaurant to handle the crowds, gift shops, even a small theater. People in a town like Birch Bend are always looking for opportunities like that. What we didn't need was this kind of publicity, strangers coming to stare and cluck their tongues, like they come to other shrines of crimes."

"Shrines of crimes?" Kim echoed. "What's that?"

"Like the town of Fall River in Massachusetts where Lizzie Borden axed her folks—that's what I mean. Like that place in L.A., where Charles Manson and his gang did those killings. People come there to gawk and talk. We decided we didn't want that here. Bad image. Bad for business, for raising kids—just bad. So we all agreed to keep it quiet, let the whole thing die. If anybody ever came poking around for information—and a few reporters did come, years later, looking for a follow-up story—we all agreed we'd give them the silent treatment. Act as if it never happened. That's how things are laid to rest."

"Unless it was your mother," I whispered. "Then, it's hard just to lay it to rest."

"But you have to!" Lester Shane cried out. He rose from his seat, began pacing along the table to its end, then turning back again. "You have to let it go, Jenny. I-I mean Laura. Let it go. Learn to forgive."

I got up, went to the microfiche machine. I didn't want to hear another word from Lester Shane, and I guess he knew it. I heard his footsteps receding, and I knew I'd never see him again.

The microfiche machine still gave off its greenish glow. I stared at the screen and read:

COLD-BLOODED KILLER BURIED TREASURES

"A thorough search of the premises of both girls accused in the arson killing of Mr. and Mrs. Hugo Wynant revealed that Megan Wynant, daughter of the murdered couple, had secreted certain treasures in a small suitcase in a ravine behind her home.

"Apparently fearful that her keepsakes would be destroyed in the fire she was setting, fourteen-year-old Megan, along with her friend, Jenny Rouseau, gathered together certain items and hid them beyond the fire's range. When detectives opened the suitcase they found several items of jewelry, three sweaters, a small book of photographs, a school essay on "What My Country Means to Me," which apparently won a creative-writing prize, and a pair of nearly new black suede boots.

"Megan Wynant is quoted as saying, 'I didn't want to lose everything.'

"Court-appointed psychologists have examined both girls and concluded that both were in full possession of their faculties when they committed the crime, that the small amount of marijuana and alcohol they consumed could not have affected their capacity to understand the consequences of their acts."

I felt Kim beside me, heard her breathing, and I found myself saying in that cold, dead tone, "They saved Megan's stuff."

Kim said nothing. I felt the warmth of her body close beside mine. I knew she was crying.

"Let's go," Kim whispered. The touch of her hand on my arm seemed to burn through the flesh, and I winced.

"What?" she cried.

"I don't know what to do. I have to learn everything all over again, even how to breathe." And it was true. My breathing was erratic and sharp. My arms and legs felt heavy, my mind dull and blank. Yes, I had to learn all over again who I was, and the task was too great, too hard.

Almost listlessly I continued to turn the crank on the machine, and the articles flowed past my line of vision—the verdict of guilt; the sentence; explanations of prison life; how it would be for my mother, the youngest inmate in a maximum-security facility. There were analyses by social workers and criminologists, statements by neighbors, teachers, friends, then the dredging up of other, similar cases, comparing this "heinous crime" to others the world over. My mother had made news. Big time. I shuddered and at last turned away.

Somehow Kim and I made our way through the building, past the cheerful librarian, outside to the bus station. All the way back in the bus we sat silently, letting the turns and bumps jostle us, feeling them with a kind of gratitude, as if the act of sitting in a bus and being moved about was enough to make talk unnecessary.

But of course, it wasn't. When we got back to the hotel we rushed to our room as if demons were chasing us. We put out the DO NOT DISTURB sign, and we flung ourselves on the beds, and we both knew, I think, that we would not sleep at all that night, but that it would be a night of vigil and of torment.

chapter / 18

"We have to talk," Kim said.

"I know," I said.

Only talk could help me. But the moment we began, there was a rap at the door.

"Don't answer it," Kim whispered, settling deeper against her pillows.

"Laura! Kim! Open the door. It's Roz."

I ran to open it, and Roz moved into the room. "What's wrong? Why didn't you answer right away?"

"I was in the bathroom," I lied. "Kim was asleep. We had a long day."

"Did you? I was worried," said Roz, looking anxious. "Did you find what you were looking for?"

"Oh, yes," I said, my voice high-pitched, almost giddy, as if I'd been laughing all day. "Yes, I saw some wonderful photographs of my mom when she was young..."

"And we went all over town," Kim chimed in, "with Mrs. Armenta—what a nice lady. She was Laura's mom's best friend."

"It must have been warm and wonderful," said Roz. "So now you can bury those ghosts," she said.

"Yes. Yes." I nodded and smiled brightly, thinking of stage lights, music, applause. There were two of me, one standing here nodding, the other dying inside, inch by inch.

I felt Kim watching me, trying to take her cues from me.

"Better hurry and get dressed for the banquet," Roz said, going to the door.

"The banquet!" cried Kim and I together.

"You haven't *forgotten!* It's at seven sharp, in the private dining room. And don't forget your commentary."

After Roz had left, Kim and I stared at each other, stupefied. "We have to go," Kim said.

I said, "I forgot all about it."

The banquet had been planned for months, for the next-to-the-last night of our trip, because tomorrow, the last night, we'd be packing. Tonight at the banquet, each person would tell about the most memorable experience on this trip. We'd planned the food, even entertainment. One of the boys would do a magic act. Two of our classmates would play guitars, Tricia Geyer would sing, Cissy Cane would do her usual impersonations of Barbra Streisand and Lily Tomlin and Dolly Parton, complete with a pillow stuffed down her front. That always cracked everyone up.

"There's no way we can get out of it," Kim said.

I shrugged. "It doesn't matter," I said. "I just—won't—think about—it." I lay down on the bed, limp, exhausted.

Kim stood there looking down at me. I felt sorry for her. I moved my hand, heard the jingle of the little hearts that said FRIENDS FOREVER. Soon Kim wouldn't be around anymore. Oh, she'd break it off gradually, make her getaway. Who wants a crazy person, the daughter of a criminal for a friend?

"Laura," Kim said, as if she'd been reading my mind, "Don't worry. It's okay. We're best friends. Nothing can change that."

"Best friends?" I cried. "What does that mean? What are best friends supposed to do for each other? Commit murder?"

"Laura, please don't…"

I sat up with sudden energy. "Oh, I'll tell my most memorable experience here!" I cried. Something seized me, a kind of vengeance. "Oh, yes, I'll tell them, then they'll have a good reason to talk behind my back—can't you imagine Cissy and Marlene and all those guys—oh, yeah, they'll really have something to talk about."

"Don't—Laura, don't," Kim whispered. She looked scared.

"Why not? This is big news. This is different, exciting, isn't it? Nobody else's mother killed two people. And she was only fifteen when she did it, ladies and gentlemen!" I stood up, gesturing like a TV-show host. "Imagine what she might have done just a few years later, older and smarter, imagine! She might have blown up the whole damned Empire State Building! Hey, let's hear it for Jenny Rouseau, alias Jasmine Rogers, and for her daughter. What can her daughter do to top this?"

"Stop it, Laura," shouted Kim. She strode toward me angrily. "Stop it!"

"I'm—sorry." All the breath and bravado had gone out of me. I sank back down on the bed and, more than tears, a terrible weakness flooded over me. I lay down on my side, curled like a baby in the womb. Kim came to lie beside me, without touching, but I knew she was near.

Finally we heard the people talking in the hall, and we got up slowly, as if it were the middle of the night and we'd been asleep for hours.

We washed our hair and got dressed. I'd brought a black

skirt to wear tonight, with a black top and a print vest, and boots.

"You look great," Kim said.

Someone knocked at the door. I jumped, then went to answer. "A message for you," said the clerk from downstairs. "Came while you were away."

I tore open the small notice. "It's from Thomas!" I breathed, remembering his voice and his touch. Then I realized, with a jolt, that today's revelations meant that everything between Thomas and me was over. We could never be together as we were, never innocent, never just Thomas and Laura. No, the ghosts of Megan and Jenny would always hover between us, accusing, blaming, hating.

"What's he say?" Kim asked eagerly.

I read the message. "He left his phone number, at least," I said. "It just says he called this afternoon. Wants to talk to me to make plans."

"What are you going to do?"

"I can't see him now," I said. "He doesn't know anything about the—the crime. He thinks his mother is—he doesn't know."

"What are you going to tell him?"

"I guess I'll tell him that..." I sat down on the small sofa. Yesterday seemed years away, yesterday when Thomas and I had walked together in the park, looked into shop windows, kissed.

"I'll tell him that I've gotten together again with a former boyfriend."

"Spider?"

"It doesn't matter. Thomas wouldn't know. I can't see him again, Kim."

"But you have to call him back."

"I can't stand to hear his voice!" I cried.

"You—you've *really* got a crush on that guy," Kim said in amazement. "He really got to you."

"Yes. Loveless Laura. She fell in love."

I stared at the telephone, a plain beige instrument on a small nightstand. It seemed alive. I picked up the receiver.

"Want me to leave?" Kim asked.

I smiled slightly. "Of course not. I'd tell you everything anyhow."

Kim nodded and went to stand before the mirror, pretending to be fixing her hair, and then she gave up the pretense and sat down on her bed, waiting.

I placed the number through the hotel operator, using the credit card my father had given me. It occurred to me that I'd have a hundred things to explain to him. Somehow, I wasn't worried. It felt as if nothing could ever bother me or worry me again, not after today. I had hit the bottom.

Except that when I heard Thomas's voice, my body sprang back to life. I felt a flush on my face, a surge of joy. "Thomas!" I said, breathless. "Oh, I…"

"It's so great to hear your voice, Laura," he said ardently. "I called three times. Did you get my messages?"

He sounded so eager, it almost made me laugh. I'd have given anything just to touch his hand.

"No, I just got one of them. The clerks here aren't very efficient. It's just a small hotel."

"It doesn't matter. I've reached you now. I thought about you all night. All day."

"I thought about you, too."

Kim stood beside me, frantically gesturing, mouthing the words, "I thought you were breaking up!"

Thomas said, "When are you going back to California?"

I felt an ache spreading through me. "Thomas…we're going back on Saturday. Thomas…" I just wanted to hold on to this moment a little longer, to hear his voice, to imagine his smile, and those eyes. I remembered how his lips had felt against mine, how when his arms were wrapped around me, I felt beautiful. Never again would I feel that way.

"Did you go back to Birch Bend? I was hoping you would get some information for us."

"Yes. I went." Why had I said that? My head felt light. Why hadn't I just lied and said I didn't go?

"Laura, I asked my mother about this car accident she had told me about. About her parents?"

"Yes, yes…did she tell you anything?"

"She got so furious with me! She's in her room now with a migraine. I guess the whole subject—I asked her whether there was a fire. She said she never knew anything about a fire. We had this terrible scene…"

We heard a strange noise, a click.

"Mom?" Thomas said sharply. "I've got it." He paused, said sharply, "Is someone on the line?"

I froze. Megan. Words came back into my mind, whirling like a cyclone—*pathological liar, nastiest bitch in the world.*

"Laura!" Thomas called my name, as if I had evaporated and he was calling me back. "Laura! Are you still there?"

"I'm here," I said, my voice soft. "Thomas, I have to tell you something. I—" I glanced over at Kim. She gazed at me, her sweet face so sad, feeling my pain. "I've gotten together with—um—a guy I was going with. Last month. That is, we broke up last month, but we decided—well…"

There was dead silence on the other end of the line. Then Thomas's voice, completely altered. "Laura, did you go back to Birch Bend? Did you learn something?"

"No!" I cried. "I didn't…"

"You just said you did!"

"I mean, I didn't discover anything. How could I? Thomas, all this was years ago. It doesn't matter. Look, we're having a banquet. I've got to go now."

"Wait!" I could imagine him reaching toward me. His tone was urgent, desperate. "Laura, listen, there are things I've never talked about—but you seem to know. There are things…I can't explain how I feel, but the minute I saw you, there was this connection. I've got to see you again, Laura. I could come to Washington. I could be there in the morning."

I glanced at Kim. She was staring at me, listening.

"I told you, Thomas," I said, "this won't work out. I just called back to tell you…"

I heard another strange noise on the line, or maybe I imagined it.

"I can't see you, Thomas," I said.

Again there was silence. Then Thomas's voice, filled with perplexity, coaxing me. "What's wrong, Laura? What's really wrong? You can tell me. Did you…"

"Can't you understand I don't want to see you!" I cried, shrill now, anguished by my own lie. "Look, we had a good time yesterday, but that's it. I'm going home, and I'm going to be involved with my friends. It would be—awkward if you came. I don't want you to come to California. I'm sorry."

"You're sorry!" he shouted. "Okay. No problem. I'm sorry, too."

I put down the receiver before I could say or hear any more. I picked it up again, half expecting to find Thomas and me still connected, but I heard only the buzzing dial tone. He was gone.

"We can't be—friends," I whispered. "Not after what

happened. It would be too awful. I mean, how could I tell him? It's better if he never knows. There's no advantage to him knowing. Is there?"

Kim shook her head. "No. It would just hurt him. We have to go. To the banquet."

I turned to glance at myself in the mirror, amazed that my exterior could so well camouflage my inner self. I looked okay, even more than okay, while my heart was breaking.

Afterward, when we were back in our room, I realized that during the entire banquet I had actually removed my thoughts from Jenny Rouseau, my mother, from Birch Bend, even from Thomas.

Going through the motions of eating, smiling, listening, I had been able, somehow, to divorce myself from that other reality. Maybe that's how people manage, I thought, they just stop thinking and feeling. Maybe that's what I'll do, put my feelings away somewhere, like Mother did.

I was stunned. Yes. That's what she did. Of course, once in a while they gushed out, and then she ran and hid in her room, stopped up her ears with the screaming, wailing chorus of the Beatles, filled the ache in her body with cakes and sweet breads and cookies, made sure she never looked attractive enough to encourage friendships—oh, friendship was the last thing in the world that Jenny Rouseau wanted, either for herself or for her daughter.

Spider had sat beside me at the banquet. He praised the food, the trip, the day—oh, he loved everything. Several times he reached for my hand. Then he said, "What's wrong, Laura? Did I do something?"

"No. Nothing."

"What's going on with you?"

"Nothing."

He said, "I thought you and I were getting along. You know, the other day…" He sighed, flexed his fingers.

I gave him a look. Icy. Too much was coming at me—Mother, Megan, Thomas. I wanted to tell Spider things. I just couldn't.

After a while he started talking to Cissy and some other kids. They laughed and joked. I saw them as in a circle, spinning round and round. I had bounced off, was stationed somewhere in outer space, like those astronauts standing there on the edge of their capsule, connected to it by a cable that could, at any moment, snap.

Spider talked about the day at the FBI and visiting Arlington Cemetery as the most memorable, for him. "All those graves," he said. "It makes you think. I mean, most of us would never even kill anything. Those guys weren't much older than we are. They'd just gotten out of high school. I can't imagine coming face to face with someone—even an enemy—and killing him. It's awesome. My dad was in the war. My grandfather too. I feel—like I want to talk to them about it now."

When it was our turn to comment on our most "memorable experience" on this trip, Kim and I got up together, and we gave the clichés about the attractions, the history. Darryl Lapkin looked at me with a strange smile—did he know this was just a bluff? Afterward he actually came up to me and spoke. "Hey, Laura, that was good, what you said. About the space center."

I stared at him. I couldn't remember what I'd said. "Why, thanks."

Now Kim and I lay in bed in the near-darkness of the small hotel room, with the vague clatter of the city beneath us, and from down the hall, the soft halting moans from the elevator, the occasional crackle of someone using the ice machine. All around us, life was proceeding; no barrier had been set down from on high, the world still turned as before.

But we were stuck in the process, needing to puzzle it out. We talked, offered up our thoughts like scattering seeds, waiting for something to take hold and germinate.

"Well, maybe they thought…"

"Or they didn't mean to…"

"Or someone else put them up to it. But who? Who?"

"Or they got carried away, you see, just to the brink, and were going to stop, but then something happened, the gasoline spilled, it ignited somehow without…"

"But no, no, they admitted it."

Always we were stopped by that fact. Both girls had confessed. One of the articles had said they confessed "with smugness, owning the crime, the enormity of it."

Yes, they owned it. Forever. They owned it and passed it on down to their children.

At the banquet, Diane Letton got up and gushed about her experiences. She had loved, adored, the White House. She'd had her picture taken with the congressman. "It's something I'll always remember," said Diane, breathless, smiling. "I've got tons of pictures. I'm going to put them in an album for my grandchildren."

I said to Kim in the darkness, "There will always be this stain. For generations. That's what this means."

"No. It's not your fault what your mother did. Every person starts fresh."

"No, they don't. We're all infected by other people's genes. Didn't you learn that in biology? Don't you remember about the inherited characteristics? It doesn't matter whether it's the environment or the genes. We still resemble our parents."

"Not in all ways."

"You never know. We pass things on to our children."

"You don't have to tell them."

"Then I'll be lying. I'll be pretending their grandmother was normal and virtuous. She had all these rules! She was certainly no angel herself."

That made us laugh—I had not thought we could laugh.

Kim said, "Why do we expect our moms to be angels?"

"We don't expect them to...to kill, to be capable of it."

"Oh, anyone is capable. You heard what Spider said, about people fighting in a war."

"This wasn't a war."

"Yes it was, in a way."

"Why do you defend her?"

"I'm trying to help you, damn it!"

"Don't yell. Don't cuss. Please. I've got this horrible, horrible headache."

"Want an aspirin? I brought some."

"Sure. I'll take twenty."

"Come on, Laura. Quit it."

"I know now why she couldn't love me."

"She loved you."

"Maybe. But she couldn't show it. She was afraid."

"Of what?"

"That if I got too close to her, I'd turn out like her."

"Go to sleep. Please, it's so late. I'm so tired."

"It's true."

"Go to sleep, Laura."

But I couldn't sleep, felt I'd never sleep again. Scenes kept sprouting before my eyes, from the distant past, from yesterday, today, from a year ago. Kim knew, but she hadn't focused on it. She'd remember it some day soon, we'd talk about it. She'd see I was right. The blood, the genes, the DNA, whatever you call it, those rivers of stuff inside us, they are never pure; they carry other people's junk, their sins, their weaknesses.

I was capable of it. That was the darkness that I knew, and of which Kim wouldn't dare speak. The scene stood before me, exact in every detail—the little theater at the school with the shiny floor, those purple curtains, the white-and-gray backdrop, with its odd design of Grecian pillars; the scant stage furniture used for that scene—a battered bookcase with several dozen ragged volumes inside, that pea green old sofa with the bulging middle cushion, a straight chair, a weird little iron table...we had rehearsed it for weeks. How Darryl was supposed to back away from me, trip over the little table, and I, Moira McQueen, dressed all in black with that long, black wig, cold, sultry, murderous...

"Work into the piece, into your character," said Miss Stafford, our teacher and director. She talked us into our role, pushed, cajoled, shouted, provoked. "He stole something precious from you. He lied, deceived you—he is vicious and evil. You have to kill him. Do you understand? Think of something that is precious to you, something vulnerable, then think of the worst, the most disgusting crime..."

"But that's not in the play at all, Miss Stafford," Darryl protested.

"Silly boy!" the teacher tore into him. "What does that matter? We look for the ultimate! We play for the highest stakes! If you're supposed to be sad over some loss, think of the greatest loss of your life, and in that way dredge out the emotion, the deepest emotional content you can muster. Do you understand?"

"Yes, yes," said Darryl. He was perfect for the part of this man, an obvious victim, pale and timid. Darryl didn't need to psyche himself up, he just acted what he was.

For me, it was different. I moved into my role, immersed myself for hours, thought, breathed, felt the thing, until I had achieved the mind, the heat, the hatred I needed in order to be Moira McQueen, the vengeance-seeking queen of night, who stalks and kills her imagined enemy.

So I put on her clothes and her wig, and I poured in her emotions—fear, hatred, and fury. I said the lines, moving slowly as Miss Stafford had taught me, hands clutched at my chest, face half turned toward the audience so that they could see the intensity of my rage. I confronted Darryl who, in his terror, trips backward against the little table. I reach out, then I grab his hair, yank up his head (gently, don't really hurt him! the teacher had warned) but I was in the role, truly, fully, and I pulled him up, took one last step, grasped him by the throat and squeezed and squeezed all the while screaming, "You devil! You'll pay! You devil!"

The lights beamed red into my eyes; my pulse beat fearfully in my ears, and my lungs seemed about to explode with my cries, "You devil! Devil! Devil!"

I still don't know the full sequence of what happened. Kim was at that rehearsal. She was, in fact, wardrobe mistress for the play. I never asked her about it afterward, and she never said. I only know that I lay on the stage, gasping, with the coach, Mr. Barnard holding me down. Time stretched, strained, and then someone said, "Are you okay?" And someone laughed and said, "My God, I thought she was really going to kill him!" And I saw Darryl, his pale face, the terror in his eyes.

They canceled the play. The principal said it had been a

poor choice from the start, not an appropriate drama for young adolescents—we should do a musical, he said, something light and pleasant.

Kim walked me home that day, all the way up the hill. When we parted she gave me a slight smile. "You're a great actress," she said. "You really are, Laura."

I stared at her. I remember seeing spots of bright sunlight filtering through the oak leaves. I said, "I wasn't acting, Kim."

She stood a moment longer, watching me. Then she turned and began to jog down the hill.

I thought she'd never come back to my house, never walk with me again. I wanted to die that night, not only because I thought I'd lost my only friend, but because I'd found someone else living inside me, someone so ugly I couldn't bear the thought, yet neither could I expel that other person.

I had lain in bed that night holding my breath, wondering how long it would take for me to suffocate. But of course, the mechanism that longs for life took over. I breathed. I lived.

I realized now that I was holding my breath again, and that beside me, Kim was sound asleep. Tomorrow, I thought, wishing I could formulate some plan. But tomorrow seemed like a vast dark canyon, and I was falling.

chapter / 19

From some poem I had learned long ago, the words came back: "A single night, a thousand years..."

I lay there in the semidarkness of our hotel room, Kim's and mine. I heard Kim's soft breathing; I stared out into the shadows, asking myself question after question.

Why was I so obsessed with my mother? Why couldn't I just move on and be myself? Maybe, I thought, because she had been so distant from me. If we had known each other better, if we'd had real time together, I wouldn't be so needy.

Cycles of emotions came over me. I was angry. She had lied to me continually, while from me she had always demanded the truth. I was angry at her teachings, her reprimands—how dare she tell me what to do and how to behave!

I wanted to scream at her. "Why didn't you tell me? Why didn't you trust me?" If I'd known, we could have talked about it and grown close. I might have been sympathetic. I might have understood. Yet even now i rebelled at the thought. What is there to understand? She killed, premeditated, in cold blood, as they say.

After anger, came a flash of relief. She was gone now. There was nothing more I had to do or feel or think—I could disengage myself from her.

Still, I didn't sleep. I was half awake, half dreaming, moving into my mother's mind and her memories. How did I know her memories? I knew, because I was part of her. I knew, because I'd read about these things. I knew, because somehow her life and mine were entwined.

They did unspeakable things to her body. Once, they strapped her legs to an iron chair. After seven hours, she fainted. Later, she learned to conform.

Those in charge know what matters most, what humiliates most. All private things are made public and carefully regulated. They decide when and how. Your body no longer belongs to you. It has been given to the state, to punish.

At first she was rebellious, trying to manipulate her keepers. Soon that ended, and she curled herself up, like sow bugs you see on the sidewalk, protecting their soft interior. They lie motionless and dormant, waiting for an end.

Nine years is a long time, eternal time. Nights must seem like forever, never quite dark, never really light. A dim bulb burns continually, obliterating any thoughts of privacy.

Privacy was a big thing with her, always. Private in the bathroom, in the bedroom, in her thoughts, in her being. Privacy and clean underwear, soft panties and bras, pink, pale blue, pure white. What had she worn in there with those women? Hard cases, felons. What had they done? Everything. And they'd done it to husbands, lovers, and friends, even to their little children.

She belonged there, with the other killers. The judge said so. It was her punishment. Her cure. Yes, it changed her. She never killed again. Neither did she laugh much, or make any plans.

Nine years is a long time, a long time to be without flowers.

"I had the gardener plant half a dozen jasmine…" Father had planted them outside her window. Knowing about her past, he gave her this fragrance. She knew the names of every plant and flower. She inhaled their perfume, making up for that other air, foul beneath the smell of disinfectant, contaminated air that no amount of chlorine or Lysol could freshen.

At night the wardens walked along the hallways. They shone flashlights into faces of the guilty sleepers. Awake or asleep, nobody cares. All night echoes of crimes are repeated in the tortured minds of their perpetrators; there is no forgetting.

After that, of course, she would not want to sleep with anyone, but claim her privacy, her own space. She and her Ivan developed a different intimacy. They sat together quietly reading, doing puzzles. Maybe that was enough. Maybe that was, to her, heaven.

Sometimes in the night she screamed out. He ran from his bedroom to hers; he held her like a father, cradling her gently. He knew the terrors that pulled her awake.

They had not expected a child. Probably it shocked them that their union, centered on their own needs, brought them a child. He, at forty-four, was so lonely, too intellectual to attract women. Then she came along. Spoke Latin. Talked about such things! Where had she learned all this?

She must have told him, "There was a library at the prison—I read every minute I could."

Nine years is a long time. You learn things; how not to let any feelings show. You learn vocabularies, both streetwise and highbrow; you learn trivia because there is so little to read, you devour the oddest information. You learn how to amuse yourself playing solitary games. You learn to smoke. Cigarettes are the only luxury here, acquired for favors, for the pocket money earned by sewing pillowcases made of fabric so tough you could pack potatoes in it. (You must hand the shears back to the matron, making certain she has them in her custody. Missing shears mean one month in solitary. Needles are doled out, counted. Thread is rationed; someone could make a rope.) A small article had explained it all. A candidate for congress had accused the Virginia legislature of creating a "country club" atmosphere in the women's penal institution. The article made it quite clear: Prisoners are treated exactly like wild animals, never allowed to roam, always caged. Like wild animals, they become tense and wary. They learn to take nothing for granted. They are always afraid.

Are you afraid, Laura? Afraid of the dark? Of dogs? Afraid to be alone? No? Brave girl!

Jenny wasn't afraid, either. But that was before. Afterward, at twenty-four she came newly into the world, confused and scared. She had been locked away. Now, emerging, she was alone. Mother and father—how could they bear to look at their killer daughter? Bad seed, monster—or maybe it was she who couldn't face them.

She went to London; cold, damp city with its incessant traffic and soot and crowds. Where did she meet her Ivan? Where did he find his Jasmine—Jenny—what name did she use?

Perhaps it was at a gallery. He stood beside her, watching her face as she was transported into the colors and revolving forms of the joyous van Gogh.

"I love van Gogh more than anything…" she had said. "He was crazy, you know. Ended up killing himself—once, cut off his ear. A genius, you know."

She should have been a critic, a poet, a professor, an

inventor. But she hid in the house. She ate. She smoked cigarettes and solved crossword puzzles. She knew many esoteric
words and the meanings of things. Only, she didn't know her
own daughter.

"Play with me, Mom! Let's play dolls, we'll dress the dol-
lies—we'll make up stories. Pretend they are going skating—
pretend they're sisters or cousins—come on!"

"I don't like pretending," she said.

She was frozen in time, her life divided into two definite
portions. Everything that had happened "Before" was on one
side; everything "After" was on the other. She loved only the
music of "Before." All music that came "After," she found
horrid, the yammering of cats, the crashing of trains. "Turn it
off, Laura, for God's sake!" she would scream.

The old tunes comforted her. If only she could hold on to
them, they might keep her safe. Why hadn't she immersed
herself, drowned herself in the music? Instead of pulling on
that dark sweater, instead of running across the wet grass in
her sneakers—shrieking with excitement as her hand grasped
the gasoline can, inhaling the fumes that escaped from the
spill on her shoes and her jeans, the spill that later con-
demned her—why hadn't she stayed indoors, turned on the
stereo, let it surround her with its loud, melodic, enfolding
presence? She had screamed at them later, locked into her little cell, "Where were you, Beatles? Why didn't you save me?
Why didn't you help me? God! Where were you?"

Did she think about God? Speak to Him?

She went to church. Not often. "Churches are rather
creepy, don't you think?"

In the corners, amid some overlooked cobwebs, sins are
tucked away; here, in the church, they peer out, like spiders,
demanding to be noticed.

"Why do you go to church, if you don't believe in it?" Questions resonated, and her cool answer. "Oh, I don't know. Just to keep in touch, I guess. My parents used to go."

On that night with the howling wind and the blazing torch of a dog, she had crossed a bridge, a chasm, had assigned herself a new role, that of a stranger on the planet. She no longer belonged with the "real people." So she did odd things.

"Come help me in the shop, Jasmine, I need help over the Christmas rush."

"Sure, Harley. I'll help you."

"Don't the clocks drive you crazy?"

"No. I rather like them—what do you suppose they are saying?"

Don't. Don't. Don't.

They cry out warnings, but we don't hear them.

Time stopped for her on that night. Life stopped, because she had stolen a life. Two lives. She would spend forever trying not to remember, but remembering with every tick, every tock.

It was her penance, just as it was her penance not to feel, not to kiss, not to compliment, except with oozing sarcasm, "Ah, my perfect Laura—you are the only perfect person in the world."

Except that there is a terrible flaw, Mother. You put it there. We are killers, you and I. We are missing something very basic.

How could you have done it, Mother? How could you?

Oh, it was easy. The hard part is not doing it. Staying sober, keeping control. Don't you understand? It's easy to get carried away.

Suddenly I sat upright, saw the green hands of the clock: three A.M., that deathly time when the night still stretches too long, and there is no possibility of sleeping. My nightgown was drenched, my hands and legs tingled.

I lay there, flat on my back, the blankets kicked off onto the floor, and I thought. No more visions came, only the cool questions: Had she planned, ever, to tell me?

I didn't know. Couldn't tell.

What sort of a person was she?

I didn't know. Couldn't tell.

Was she evil?

She wasn't all-good. I knew that.

Did I love her?

I felt myself dissolving. The question was too great to bear. Did I love my mother before? Could I love her now, knowing what she had done?

I turned and, from the pale streetlamp glow I saw Kim lying on her side, sleeping peacefully. Lucky Kim, I thought.

chapter / 20

I had thought I'd stay in that last day and pack and sit around—I didn't feel like seeing anyone. Kim was planning to spend the entire day at the Smithsonian. At six in the morning, there was that banging at our door. Spider. I opened the door just enough to tell him, "Shh! I'm sleeping."

"No, I see you," he replied with a wide smile.

"Go away. I mean it. I'm not running today."

"You should. It's good for…"

I shut the door in his face, locked it, heard his footsteps receding along the hall. I stood there against the door, wishing it were a wall tall enough and large enough to separate me from everyone and everything. I understood now why people who are not even religious will join monasteries or convents. There are times when the clatter of the world, combined with the clatter inside one's head, is simply too much. I wished now for a place, any place, where I could be utterly alone, never needing to explain anything.

Oh, yes, now I understood my mother's sudden retreats into her dark bedroom, and the hours when she lay listening to her music, drowning out those other words that must have hammered in her head as now they hammered in mine.

In desperation I rummaged through my bag, gasping with relief when I found it—my Walkman. I slipped in a cassette, Alanis, and I pulled the earphones over my head and sat on the small sofa, my legs bunched up under my body, and I listened, transporting myself into the sound, waiting for breakfast at seven. And as I waited, I focused my mind on words, synonyms, beginning with "breakfast," and I listed them in my mind: food, repast, meal, brunch, snack, feast, banquet.... I went on with another word—kill: slay, vanquish, murder, execute, destroy.

My mind floated to the chant from childhood:
> *"Sticks and stones may break my bones*
> *But words will never hurt me..."*

Yes, I could live by words and by music, only that. I could live in peace, then, never having to explain anything, never having to feel or react.

I glanced at my watch, saw that it was just after seven. The breakfast bar downstairs would be open now.

Softly I opened the door, went down to the lobby. Several early bird tourists were there, nobody from my group. This made me suddenly very happy, to be anonymous, to smile blandly at the tourists, to think my own thoughts without interruption while I took a plate and helped myself to two slices of banana bread, a croissant, a blueberry muffin, a cranberry tart, and a large, glazed "snail."

I brought the food up to the room, thankful that Kim was still sleeping and, almost joyfully, I curled up on the small sofa with my breakfast, put on my earphones again, and retreated into my new, safe world.

I must have fallen asleep, because next thing I knew, Kim

was standing over me, hand on her hip, asking, "What's all this food for? You never eat anything but cornflakes in the morning."

I glanced up at her, watching her mouth move, intent on the song that was in my ears. I could hear her beneath the music, of course, but it was easy to pretend otherwise, simply to shut her out.

I closed my eyes and lay back. "Go on without me," I said. "I'm just going to mellow out today."

She stood looking down at me, and I saw her mouth move again, but I turned up the volume on my Walkman, and I waved her away, closed my eyes and thought how wonderfully simple it was just to be alone.

Later, when I woke up, I turned on the TV and watched some dumb morning shows, slowly eating all the muffins and cakes I'd brought up from the breakfast bar.

Oddly enough, it didn't fill me.

I went to the window and looked out. From here, everything was different, all colors blending into a pale blue-gray, the sky and the sidewalks and boulevards, the people rushing along. Now and again I saw a splash of red—someone's jacket or scarf, or a bright blossom. The buildings and monuments were large chunks of granite, hard and imposing, yet they would someday tumble down. Someday the streets would be torn up. Every automobile, truck, bus, and bicycle, would eventually end up in the junk pile. Every piece of clothing that all the people wore would someday be discarded and broken down again into fibers, then dust. What's left? I asked myself.

Only this: Love remains, and hate.

I thought of my love for Thomas, irrational and maybe even absurd. No matter how many people I met, I'd always love him. A deep part of me would always feel what I'd felt when we walked together and when we kissed. We were like twins, like clones, meant to meet, because we alone could understand each other.

I felt suddenly charged with energy, glancing at the empty plate—all that sugary cake! I pulled on my black tights, long shirt, running socks and shoes, and I tied my hair back with a wide band.

Outside, the air was warm and caressing. It was already noon, the sun high in the sky, and as I ran and ran and ran, I felt the color coming into my cheeks, the blood and breath pushing through my body. I felt a strange, free joy, and I thought of myself as a horse, a jaguar, a lion, running along the African plains, alone but yet not alone. There was a strange sense of connection now, to everyone who has ever suffered or been deceived. I thought of every parent of every person buried in Arlington, of every descendant of every victim pictured in the Holocaust Museum, in the African Museum, on the Vietnam Memorial. All of them, I thought, are like me. They live with pain. They know what it's like to be sick with disappointment. Still, they carry on, and they can even laugh.

I remembered how sometimes I'd come home in the afternoon, and Mom and Mrs. Sheffield would be in the kitchen together, laughing and laughing, and I'd see Mother's red cheeks, her eyes wet from laughter. It made me jealous. They could never quite repeat the joke. Now, I hugged that memory tight.

Deliberately then, I turned along G Street, where several days earlier I'd seen a large public library. "Everything you'd ever want to know is in the library." My mother used to take me to the little library in Mill Valley, and occasionally to the large main library in San Francisco, where I sat for hours in the children's room, looking at books. The library was her haven, like her music.

I searched through the biographies and histories—from our trip to the Holocaust Museum I knew exactly what I was looking for, and swiftly I found several books, rifled through the pages, hardly breathing as my eyes scanned the words and my mind grasped them perfectly:

"...when I discovered later what my father had done during those years, I couldn't believe it. To me he had always been gentle and kind. He taught me how to fish, being so very careful extracting the hook, so that the fish would feel little pain. And now they wanted me to believe that my father had given the orders to murder...even babies...in cold blood..."

"...it was a different time. He was a different person then, under the control and influence of people who had no conscience. What could he do? He followed orders..."

"...my parents were involved in it—my mother, too. They considered themselves patriots, acting out of love for their beliefs and for their Nazi leaders..."

"...it made me sick to my soul when I found out what my father had done. How could I possibly atone for it? Was this to be the entire meaning of my life, to make up for his sins?"

I read on and on, reaching across years and miles. It was amazing to me how close I felt to those writers. I knew them better than my schoolmates, I thought; we had shared the same experience, the sudden sickness of soul, the quick shift from feeling like a normal, ordinary person, to being a monster, the child of a monster.

It grew shadowy in the little alcove where I sat reading. Reluctantly I began to put the books aside, then my eye caught another entry, written in italics, as if the words were meant for my special attention:

"Whatever happened in the past, and whatever echoes from it remain, I must remember that I am the same person now that I always was. I am separate and alone. I am the one who will determine what this life shall be."

By the time I got back to the hotel, snacks had been set up in the lobby, sodas and tea and coffee, and a platter of sandwiches and cakes. A small crowd was gathered, including a few of my classmates. I walked around the edges of the room, thinking to make myself invisible, but I heard someone calling.

"Laura! Wait."

Darryl came toward me, holding a plate filled with tiny sandwiches and cookies. "Roz was looking for you," he said. "We were all over at the Hirschorn and the Women Artists Museum. I thought you were interested in all that stuff."

"I just went for a run," I said. "And to the library."

I glanced at Darryl. He looked sturdier, more robust than in my memory of him, pale and cowering before my onslaught.

"I never got to talk to you," he said now, awkwardly looking down at his plate, then back at me. "After your mom died, I wanted to tell you—I felt very sorry about it."

"Thanks. Don't worry about it. I know it's hard, sometimes, to talk about things like that."

"I know. My mom died when I was ten."

"Oh!"

"It's okay. She'd been sick ever since I was born, so I guess I expected it. She had M.S., really bad. The last three years she didn't even live at home."

I stood there unable to think of anything to say. Then we both spoke at once, laughing slightly in embarrassment.

"Did you ever..."

"I wanted you to know…"

"Darryl," I said, "I'm really sorry that I…hurt you that night. In the play. I wanted to tell you, but I felt like such a jerk, and…"

"You didn't *hurt* me, I guess," he said. "I don't really remember. I was just—shocked. I mean, that anyone could act like that. You should get the Academy Award."

I laughed. "I got carried away," I said.

"Well, I guess it's like when I'm playing the cello. I forget everything. It's like—it gets into me, you know? Like, I'm part of the instrument."

I nodded. I knew what he meant.

"Hey." Darryl stared at me, and I saw his color deepen. "Are you going with Spider Margolis?"

I found myself grinning. "Nope. We're just friends."

"Oh. I didn't know. I thought maybe we could—do something together sometime." His tone rose on the last word, a question, a hope.

"Sure. I guess so," I said, marveling at the moment, the incident, this sudden reconciliation. All this time I'd thought Darryl hated me.

A group of girls came in—Diane, Kim, Cissy, and Marlene, and several others. They were laughing and talking. Then they saw me, and their sudden silence sliced through the air. I went up to them. "Hi, guys," I said. "Did you have a nice day?"

They all started to talk at once about the sights, the music, the people, the excitement. "I wish we could stay another month!" Diane exclaimed dramatically.

"I'm ready to go home," said Cissy. "I'm really tired."

I saw the tiredness in Cissy's face, pale shadows beneath her eyes. I felt a surge of sympathy. She always seemed to be working so hard at being peppy.

"Oh, come on, Cissy, you're always wound up like a rocket!" said Marlene.

"Yeah, yeah," Cissy said. "You're right. Hey, why don't we go to a movie tonight? They've got some great things playing."

"We've got to get up early," Kim said.

"Oh, forget it, we can sleep on the plane tomorrow," said Cissy.

"If you can get a group," said Roz, breaking into our circle. "Be back by eleven, though."

"Want to go, Laura?" Kim asked.

"Sure," I said. "Why not?"

"We'll get some of the guys," said Marlene. "We'll ask Spider and Jordan and…"

"Darryl," I offered.

Marlene shrugged. "Whatever."

Kim took my arm as we went through the lobby. "I'm glad you're feeling better," she said.

"I guess I am," I said. In truth, I was exhausted and numb, empty of words and thoughts and ideas. I was, like a jellyfish, just floating along.

We stopped for the key, and the clerk said, "Wait a minute. There's a phone message."

Kim reached for the message. "Probably from my mom," she said, "confirming our arrival time." She scanned the message, looked up, and silently handed me the note.

"What is it?"

She only stared at me.

I read, "I'm coming to D.C. to see you. I have important info. Meet me at the Lincoln Memorial, 9 P.M. I love you. Thomas."

"Girls, girls!" Roz's voice came crowding into my space. "I want you to be sure and sign out tonight. Laura, I looked for you today at the museums."

"I was at the mall and the library," I said. "You told us we were okay alone within three blocks."

"Just be sure you follow the rules," Roz said.

Roz, Kim, and I rode up the elevator together. Thomas's note felt like a hot cinder in the palm of my hand. Kim's eyes were locked onto mine. We spoke volumes without opening our mouths.

In our room, Kim spoke first. "What are you going to do?" She was breathless.

"Nothing," I said.

"What do you mean? He's coming *here*. How can you just ignore him?"

"We talked about this," I said. "I can't see him. Especially, I wouldn't go out to that place alone at night. Roz and Langfeld would kill me. And if I went, what would it prove?"

"He loves you," Kim whispered. "He loves you."

"Sometimes," I said, "love isn't enough."

"Oh, Laura. How can you be so—so cold?"

Cold? My heart was beating to make my cheeks burn, my body was on fire. In truth, I was incapable of thinking beyond this moment and Thomas's words, "I love you." Nobody had ever said that to me before.

Darryl was right: I should have won the Academy Award. I was the life of the party. We all went to dinner at a Chinese restaurant, and I sat at the head of the table, telling anecdotes, making up stories, ordering side dishes and green tea, and cookies. I played my part of the bright, happy, well-adjusted, high school girl. I laughed and called across to people, asked their opinions, used their nicknames, made fun of our chaperons, imitated Roz and the Langfelds and our principal back home. We sang the Mill Valley song, and I clowned and sang in a high voice, as if I was a little kid in kindergarten:

> *"I'm gonna talk about a place*
> *That's got a hold on me,*
> *Mill Valley*
> *A little place where life*
> *Feels very fine and free,*
> *Mill Valley..."*

After dinner we all walked over to the theater, and as we stood in line, Spider came close beside me, and he put his arm around my shoulders. Darryl watched us from across the way, his eyes intent upon my face, and I gave him a smile. Spider doesn't own me, I thought. Nobody owns me. I'm free. I'm fine and free.

We bought popcorn and Cokes and we watched the show, Spider still holding on to my arm, my hand, my shoulders.

I glanced at my watch. Quarter to nine.

"Excuse me, Spider," I whispered.

As I passed Kim I whispered, "Ladies' room," for a moment thinking she'd want to join me, but she only drew her feet in and snuggled closer to Jordan.

I worked my way to the aisle, careful not to step on any toes, and I walked out to the lobby, through the exit door to the street. For a moment I felt turned around and confused. Then I focused on the light patterns along the boulevards, and I knew exactly where I was and where I was going.

I began to jog a slow, steady pace, my backpack rocking lightly against me. I turned down Virginia Avenue. From there I could clearly see the Lincoln Memorial, stately and strong.

I could imagine Thomas standing there on one of the steps, waiting for me.

chapter / 21

The streets were moist with a light sheen of rain that must have begun sometime while we were in the theater. It was cold and quiet. The Saturday night crowd hung out at clubs and theaters and restaurants, leaving Lincoln, George Washington, and Thomas Jefferson pretty much to themselves. Only an occasional car came by, a few lone pedestrians hurried along, their shoulders hunched against the weather, heads down.

I checked my watch. It was after nine. I had underestimated the distance from the movie theater. The wind blew specks of debris into my eyes. I blinked, hard, and looked toward the Lincoln Memorial, a warm nest of light set among the black outlines of trees and shrubs. Lincoln looked stern, worried, like my father on the worst days. Thoughts of Father brought a surge of regret and pain. Why didn't he speak to me? Why hadn't he ever held me?

And suddenly the answer came: He knew everything about my mother's past, and if he and I drew close, mightn't he forget himself, let something slip? Mightn't he even be tempted to explain things, to draw me into their net?

So they kept me out, innocent, alone.

My hands felt icy. I stuffed them into my pockets. I thought now of Thomas, only of Thomas. Soon I would see his face and feel his arms around me.

Thomas, son of Megan. For an instant I shuddered. Might he, somehow, have inherited her evil? No, no, I quickly answered myself. I trusted my intuition about Thomas, his goodness.

I walked faster, with the feeling that I was breaking a barrier, crossing a boundary. Thomas—Thomas—his name filled my senses. With Thomas, everything was new and honest, no history of deceit or neglect, no bitterness. Whatever Thomas asked of me, I thought recklessly, I'd do it. Like a moth to flame, like metal to magnet, I was moving toward Thomas. I wanted to call his name. Thomas! But the wind and the darkness and the cold dampness kept me quiet. I would find him—another minute or two. Then I'd be warm in his arms. He'd run toward me, calling my name.

Briefly I wondered whether Kim would be worried, looking for me in the ladies' room. Of course, she would—but she'd realize that I was doing what I had to do. She'd know I'd be all right the moment I found Thomas. Maybe, I thought, he'll come back to the hotel with me and meet my friends. Maybe…

I found myself standing straight in front of the Lincoln Memorial, Mr. Lincoln's immense form illuminated from the back, so that he seemed even more stern and imposing, a godlike figure, all knowing, all seeing, infinitely wise. I could smell greenery, moisture on stone, and from somewhere nearby, damp soil.

Thomas? I looked about, saw a solitary figure, a tall figure, someone dressed in dark clothes, ski pants and a knitted cap.

The figure moved with a heavy gait, like an old woman, and I wondered why someone like that would be out here in the night.

I walked around to the back of the monument, hearing the wind lash the branches of trees that lined the walk. There, it was very dark, like the forest in fairy tales, where the unexpected happens, usually evil. I caught the swift whisper of a remembered phrase, "Aren't you afraid of the dark, Laura? My brave girl!"

From here the monument looked like a tomb. I must have heard something, a scratching sound, for the hair rose up on the back of my neck, and I froze.

In that moment before the final moment—that infinitesimal space of time between calm and terror, there was that awful premonition of danger. There was that sudden spring of tension, every muscle tight and hard, breath held back, ears and eyes pitched to the slightest stirring, as if by awareness I could possibly hold off the inevitable. Thoughts flashed like bits of bright metal into my brain: Run! Fight! Scream!

But it was already upon me, like some jungle creature, springing from behind. Within an instant I was wrapped in pain, my head pulled back by my hair, so tight I felt my scalp tearing away. A knee slammed into my back, a blow so strong I would have doubled over, except that the iron-fierce grip held me bent backwards, and another sharp blow to my calf made me sag down to my knees. Words rushed from my throat, screams.

"Shut up. I've got a knife." He dragged me to the trees.

Blood-red terror gripped me, flowed before my eyes. I felt the point of a knife against the left side of my throat, knew it could be over in an instant, my life draining out here on the ground—for what?

"Take my bag," I gasped. "Take it. Everything. Please."

Around my throat the grip tightened, cutting off air, so heavy on my chest that I imagined weights of iron pressing me flat.

Wetness poured down my face, blood, rain, or tears, I don't know which. I was only dimly aware of the form that had fused itself with mine—the dark clothes, knitted cap, the sharp breath against the side of my face—I felt something bite into my ear, harder, harder. "Please. Take it. Leave me..."

The voice was strangely contorted, as if its owner were missing some apparatus of speech. "I don't want your money. I want you."

Mugger. Rapist. The words slid across my mind, warnings, instructions—I had heard enough of them to know that only one thing counted. Stay alive. Stay alive.

Within my chest a pounding began, all my energy and terror were locked into that small cavity. I remembered, from some distant time, that there are ways to seize the advantage, but my mind could not focus on them. Languor and limpness pulled me down, drained every trace of strength from my limbs. So this is the way it ends, I thought in wonderment and sorrow and surprise. This is the way I die.

I realized, suddenly, that the arm around my throat had loosened slightly. The attacker had stepped back a little, regaining balance. My limp body had become dead weight; maybe it seemed I had fainted or totally acquiesced—the balance, the balance, I thought numbly.

Every ounce of resolve rose up in me. The body knows, somehow, the thrust, the turn, the force that makes the difference between being killed or staying alive. Alive! Alive! Every fiber of my being screamed the word into every nerve and cell in my brain, giving me strength.

Like pistons my feet shot out. My head, fists, elbows, knees all became weapons. I kicked, jabbed, fought, bit, felt the slash at my back, spun around, screaming.

Screams spilled out into the air, exploded like shrapnel from a bomb. "I'll kill you! Kill you. Couldn't. Let it. Be. Couldn't leave—it alone." The words meant nothing, only the intent: Kill you! Kill you! There were screams. Whose? Mine or his? Who was he? Nobody. No person. A creature. A thing, detestable, evil.

We struggled. How long? Time wavered. A moment. An hour. Forever. Time ceased to be, it hung over us as we were locked in battle, our bodies clashing, our fury merging with our blows. I tore at his face, I bit, I gouged his nose and throat with my fingernails. My own face felt numb, my back was on fire.

I had never fought before. This was new—no, this was old. The oldest thing in the world, the struggle to the death—I knew it, tasted it, wanted it, needed it. To kill. He was down. I leapt on top of him, seized a handful of hair, slammed his head down on the concrete. Suddenly the knife lay there on the ground, within reach, and the killer in me grasped it, felt the rage, the urge, the joy of it. Now I was the attacker. The dark shape lay beneath me, eyes wide, the whites of them gleaming, the face motionless, as if death had already come, setting the features like stone.

I held the knife up, ready to let it plunge. I screamed out sounds without words. My strength, now, was supreme. My hand held the power of death. We were alone in this greatest intimacy. I understood all at once what it means to take life, the terrible thirst for it, the lust. It is why the soldier runs to take the enemy hill; it is why the night stalker waits in the dark corner. It makes the only real difference. Everything else is only a game. What counts is life—or death, only those two, nothing in between.

But I saw those eyes, human eyes, staring at me. The head turned slightly, as if to avert my hand. Dark hair lay against the pale concrete, curling, damp. I saw the lips part, the moist softness within. I saw lines about the mouth, the glint of gold on a tooth, the pinkness of the inner lip, and my heart pounded unbearably. No. I can't. My eyes burned. There was a beating in my ears. No. I can't kill.

"Laura!"

My name came to me as in a trance.

"Laura."

As if a mask had been torn aside, I now saw the face.

How could it be? Thoughts ricocheted through my mind, confusion held me immobile, still poised, the knife raised. I knew the face and the voice. I knew her name. The name pulsed through me, "Megan. *Megan.*" In that moment I knew everything about us both, and that I had the power to take her life, as she had tried to take mine. "*Megan.*"

Lights beamed into my face, a voice called out, "Halt!" Two men ran toward us. "Halt! Halt!"

She was up, her dark form scrabbling, running, wavering from side to side, trapped, then she ran to the officer, clutched at his arms, "This—girl—attacked me! She held a knife on me. Oh, my God—oh, thank God you came!"

Faintness washed over me. The lights seemed to waver before my eyes. From a distance I heard a man say, "This girl's bleeding, bad. Quick, call paramedics."

Someone laid me down. Hands pressed against my face and arms, as if I were a toy about to fall apart, being held together by someone's hands.

Shrill, her fingers stabbing at the air, Megan accused, "I

don't know where she came from—I was just walking—it's a horrible thing when a person can't even walk in the early evening…young people are vicious. She had a knife. Almost killed me. I screamed—why did it take you so long?"

"We'll get your statement at the station, lady."

People came running, shouting. "Laura! Laura! Laura! Oh, my God, what happened to her?"

Screams, pushing, faces staring down at me—Kim and Spider and Jordan all staring. "Laura!"

"You know this girl?"

"She's our friend. Oh, God! Is she…?"

I was in the middle of a swiftly revolving universe. Sounds came to me like echoes in a cave. I heard all their voices jumbled together, wavering and spliced like dissonant chords.

"Laura! My God, what happened to her?"

"She's so pale!"

"Stand clear—who are you?"

"She's our friend. From our class. We're here on a trip."

"What's her name? Where are her folks?"

"She's Laura Inman."

"What was she doing out here alone?"

"She was meeting someone."

"She sure met someone. Nearly got killed."

"Will she be all right? Is she going to…"

"Don't know. Lost a lot of blood…"

I heard the siren, saw booted feet, a stretcher. Someone lifted my unyielding body; I felt as if all my muscles had collapsed. Tears formed, oozing from my eyes, a huge, deep sorrow, and I murmured, "I'm dying. I'm going to die." And it was a wonder to me, how easily life can slip away, how swiftly everything ends, how fragile all of it is….

"Take her to E.R."

"Good thing you patrol guys came by."

"Hey, here's Secret Service! Must have heard the yelling all the way up at the White House."

Inside the ambulance, everything was white, stretched tight, glaring into my eyes. Something clamped over my nose and mouth. Someone pushed up my sleeve, stabbed the muscle in my arm. A bottle wobbled above me.

"Easy. Just take deep breaths. You're going to be okay."

"Okay. Let's go. Stand clear, please."

"Let me go with her. Please! She's my friend. My best friend."

"Where's your chaperons? We'll need consent…"

"I will take protective custody. Probably needs surgery. I'll take the responsibility."

"Let's go. We'll get statements at the hospital. Take the girlfriend. We may need her to tell us…"

Someone took my hand. Slim fingers, soft, and I heard someone crying. Kim.

Blackness fell over everything.

chapter / **22**

In the well of darkness where I found myself, I lived it all again, only this time with a bright clarity. I knew everything, as if all the information had been stored forever inside me. All I had to do was provide the words, like filling in the blanks of a large crossword puzzle.

Meet me at the Lincoln Memorial, at 9 P.M. I love you. Thomas. She had known it would bring me out.

It was Megan who had summoned me, to kill me.

Why?

Because I was my mother's child. Because I knew everything. I knew the worst of her, and I could tell it to the world. Her husband and her son were completely ignorant of her past. I alone knew her life, could piece it all together.

Megan, at twenty-one, had re-created herself. Released from juvenile prison, she went to Canada to start fresh. She still had that pixie smile and bright eyes. Above her small, pert nose, two odd little vertical lines had formed, giving her a look of some distress, which drew people to her in sympathy, especially when she told them, "My parents both died in a dreadful car crash when I was very young."

So Megan created herself, middle class and proper, matronly in her dress, a little extravagant, as befits a woman of some means and status. Everyone knew Megan Meistrander; her name was on the letterheads of half a dozen charities. Except, nobody knew her well enough to imagine her terror at receiving a letter out of the blue, a letter from California.

How she had trembled at the postmark! California. Jenny had always said she would someday live in California. The dreaded moment had come. All her life Megan had found herself, even in the happiest moments, looking over her shoulder.

When the letter came, she stood there at the mailbox, holding it in her hand, weighing it. It was not Jenny's hand-writing, but a well-slanted, firm penmanship. The return address in the corner said Laura Inman.

She brought the letter into the house. She set the kettle to boiling, held the envelope over the steam. At last she was able, gently with her fingernail, to peel the flap away. She slipped out the letter, stood there reading it while the kettle hissed and screamed. "...sad news that my mother died on February 8 of this year..."

There was another letter, this one familiar in its handwriting, the large, graceful loops, the periods like tiny circles.

"Dear Megan, I'm sure you'll be surprised to hear from me..."

Megan trembled. She watched the little clipping flutter to the floor. She bent to pick it up—that damned photograph! It was the one, the *only* time she had ever stood with her husband at a lectern, target of photographers with their insidious flashbulbs. Now there it was, in that news magazine—where in the world would Jenny have found it? Well, she always was a reader, read anything that came her way. How like her to have written! Especially that sentimental line, "When all is said and done, there are only a few things worth mentioning, a marriage, the birth of a child,…and, finally, forgiveness."

How like Jenny to slosh around like that in sentimentality. Forgiveness! She would never forgive Jenny for botching it, for spilling the gasoline on her clothes. Weakling, coward, Jenny had cracked under questioning. Jenny had doubled over when they showed her a photograph of charred bones and that skull with teeth still stuck in the jaw. She had lost her nerve completely, screaming, crying to heaven for forgiveness—they said at the trial that she had fallen down on her knees, entreating Jesus.

What tripe! Megan had planned it so carefully, to pin it on the handyman, that fool who came around twice a year to clean out the gutters and fix broken hinges and things. Muldoon was his name, a half-wit; he used to bring Megan peppermint candies when she was small. She had counted on Jenny to finger Muldoon, to say she'd seem him around the house that night, with a can of gasoline. But no, Jenny had fallen apart. Megan saw her afterward, pale as a ghost, her eyes glazed over.

She read the note again focusing on the line, "—what if Megan and I were to meet again?" and the word, "forgiveness."

Megan stood in her kitchen, and she began to laugh, softly at first, then with abandon. Dead. Jenny's gone and died! Oh, lordy, good riddance.

Deftly she had resealed the envelope, then printed the words, "RETURN TO SENDER. NOT AT THIS ADDRESS."

How shocked she was to see a strange girl in her house that morning! To hear the name, Laura Inman, to read that letter once again, having to pretend it was the first time.

Yes, there was that catch in her breath, the swift fluttering of her eyelids. Swiftly she recovered her poise, controlled her panic.

She had always been imaginative and bright. Her story unfolded as she spoke, the various elements fitting together as if she were writing a play, creating outrageous characters—a young girl who hates her parents, runs away, threatens her friend. How cleverly Megan devised her tale, making Jenny the rebel, the one who could be so cruel. And how sincere she had sounded. And when Thomas wanted to take the day off from school, how furious she became, playing the concerned mother, worried about her son's future, his grades. Of course, she didn't want her son near that girl, child of her co-conspirator. What if she knew something? Thomas didn't even know the name of her hometown, Birch Bend. All these years she had kept him at bay, deflecting his questions. By now, he was no longer curious. Until this girl came along.

She didn't trust the girl, nor did she trust her son. She spied on him. It was in her nature. She had not changed since childhood; manipulative, a "pathological liar," as Lester Shane said. Unknowingly, Thomas himself had set the snare. He asked her about her parents. He questioned her about the fire. They had a terrible fight. What right had he to inquire? Who made him wonder? Of course she knew who—Laura Inman. That girl.

She counterattacked. When did you speak with Laura? Did you disobey me? Did you cut school? She called the school, using a ruse to discover that Thomas had, indeed, been absent. Now she was filled with rage and fear. How much did Laura know? What had she told Thomas? Suddenly Thomas had come around with questions—the fire. How come you never told me about that fire? Why did you say your parents were killed in a car crash?

She went to bed, pleading a migraine. She lay there, trying to invent something plausible, but somehow she was drained of ideas, exhausted from all the years of subterfuge. She had spent a lifetime trying to erase her past. Now, in a moment, everything would be laid bare. What would become of her? Her husband, a purist, might not abandon her, not outwardly, but she knew his hardness, his stern morality. He would put her away, if not out of their home, then out of his life. Of course, his career would be destroyed. Her own reputation, all those years of making herself creditable and giving—everything would come apart. Where were all the friends when things go bad? Friends run away, she knew that. Nobody wants to stick around when there's trouble. She lay there with a cold cloth on her forehead, inventing a migraine, her mind racing over possibilities, all terrifying. And Megan focused, finally, on a single solution. Eliminate Laura.

First, she had to get her out into the open. How?

Oh, that was so easy! In Thomas's room was the brochure with the number of the hotel in D.C. Then, a mere phone call, insisting, "No, I don't need to speak with her. I just want to leave a message."

She left the message: "Meet me at the Lincoln Memorial...I love you. Thomas."

Night, out in that city, was filled with dangers. Muggers and shooters and criminals of all sorts hung out, preying on tourists.

She thought briefly of using a gun, rejected the notion. Too difficult to obtain, application and waiting period—too complicated. No, the easiest thing was a knife, the handle smooth and strong, the blade sharp and long, six inches at least, to go deep enough, through clothing and muscle to its mark. Aim for the lung or the heart. Gain ascendancy by attacking from behind. Surprise is the biggest factor, and speed.

So she bought a plane ticket, dressed in dark pants and sweater and cap, looking almost like a man, surely like a man in the shadowy light.

What about the knife? How'd she get the knife?

Oh, easy to buy a knife at any sporting shop in Washington, D.C. A gift for my husband, she'd say. He likes to go fishing.

Her husband, Jacob, was usually out at night, what with all his ministerial duties. It suited her that his life was so full. As for Thomas, he'd never even know she'd been gone. All those nights out, attending committee meetings and events—he was used to her absence. It was only a matter of a few hours, all told. How perfectly she would coordinate every aspect! She'd be back home before midnight. Time to change into her suit. Time to compose herself.

Now, to the crime: How delicious, the plotting of it, just like old times. Only this time, she would do it solo. Even if the girl screams, who would hear? Traffic noise, wind, rain—everything combines to mute the sounds of struggle, and besides, it is over so fast. It doesn't take long to thrust a knife into the throat, into the back. Drag the body into the shrubbery.

The body would be found at dawn, probably by some jogger, or a dog sniffing about. It wouldn't be big news. Certainly, it wouldn't make the news in Canada—why should it? People in the States are always getting mugged or killed. One more schoolgirl, one more mugging—nothing to talk about.

The cops would investigate, looking for a motive. Well, that was obvious. Robbery. Missing would be the girl's money, watch, and bracelet. (Friends could testify to the loss of the bracelet, that sentimental silver thing.) Missing, too, would be the cash from her backpack, fifty-four dollars and some coins. A typical mugging. Megan would keep no mementos of the crime, though it occurred to her to keep the bracelet. No, she would resist the temptation, toss the thing into the waste-can at the airport. She would even take the precaution of wiping it clean of prints first. Nothing could ever connect her with this unfortunate incident. Nothing.

Thomas might never even know of the girl's death. He'd been wanting to go away to school. Well, then, she would let him, send him to Oxford or, if it was the States he wanted, insist on some eastern school, Yale or Princeton. She would tell Jacob that if their son were going anywhere, it had to be Ivy League. They'd agree, so relieved that she finally approved of his leaving.

Then, he'd forget all about Laura Inman. If ever he did call Laura's home, he'd hear there'd been this terrible accident. He might even mention it to his mum. She would be sympathetic; forehead creased in sorrow, she would pat his back and say, "What a terrible thing! What a vicious, awful thing!"

So Megan went down to the airport. Never mind phoning a travel agent, leaving a trail. She dressed herself in casual clothes, dark slacks, and sweater; the knitted cap was in her bag. She studied her image in the restroom mirror at the air-port. She looked different in these clothes—tough and strong. And she was strong, thanks to the twice-weekly ses-sions at the gym, where the trainers expressed appreciation of a woman past middle age caring enough to keep her body in shape.

Smiling casually, she bought a ticket to Washington, D.C., with a return at eleven in the evening. Plenty of time to get it done. She was meticulous in her planning; took a cab to the center of town, searched in a telephone book for the store, bought the knife, then waited until dark, sauntering about town like any tourist, speaking to nobody, taking no souvenirs.

As it grew dark, she felt that familiar exhilaration mixed with dread and fear. Once you have stood on the edge, there is no forgetting that thrill.

I awoke to a stiffness in my arm and shoulder, a sour, dry taste in my mouth.

"Don't try to sit up yet," someone advised, a dry, calm voice. "You'll get a terrific headache if you do."

I turned my head slightly, saw a nurse, and beside her, Kim.

I called her name. "Kim. Oh, Kim, I'm so sorry."

She came toward me, half smiling, but frowning, too. "Oh, Laura. I was so scared when I saw you there—all that blood. What happened? Where's Thomas? Oh, Laura, I would have come with you!"

"Some—water," I whispered.

"Can she have water?" Kim asked.

"Here's a cup of shaved ice. Give her that."

Kim put the cup to my lips. I took a piece of ice into my mouth, let it melt slowly. "I was going to meet Thomas," I said. My voice sounded strange, weak. "He wasn't there. It was all a trick. I feel so stupid! Megan lured me out to kill me."

"Megan! That was Megan? Why would she want to kill you?" Kim's eyes were wide, startled.

"She thought I'd tell Thomas. About the fire. The—murder. It would all be over. Her terrible secret. She's—" I sighed. —"really a killer. Always was. Could be she s…"

"Insane," Kim said. "Or maybe just bad. A bad seed. She has no conscience. There are people like that."

"Sociopaths," I said.

"If you say so." Kim smiled slightly.

"Kim, I'm sorry I made you cover for me. It wasn't fair."

"It's okay, Laura," she said.

"No, no it isn't. It isn't right for one person to manipulate another, to make them do things, to make them feel they have to prove their friendship."

Kim nodded and silently moved a chair nearer to my bed.

"Where are the boys?" I asked. "Do they know…?"

"They went back to the hotel. I never told them anything, Laura. When Spider saw you down on the ground, I thought he'd pass out."

From the hall I heard the nurse saying, "Yes, she's awake now. You can talk to her."

Kim said, "Roz and Mr. Langfeld are here. They're pretty upset. They had to sign all sorts of papers and explain why you were out alone."

"I'm sorry. I guess I really messed things up. Probably they'll never take another school trip again."

Kim sighed. "You didn't mean any harm. You couldn't have known this would happen."

"But I broke all the rules. I got Roz in trouble."

"Look, you were on a—a mission. You made some mistakes. Don't beat yourself up about it now. You're beat up enough already." Kim smiled slightly, and I wondered how I looked, but before I could ask, Roz came rushing in. She looked exhausted.

"Laura! Oh, honey, you're going to be okay. The doctor said it was just a flesh wound. They took some stitches and gave you antibiotics, to prevent infection. Just take it easy."

Mr. Langfeld knelt down beside my bed, looking very concerned. "We were able to reach your housekeeper, Mrs.

Sheffield. She wanted to fly straight here to be with you, but we told her it wasn't necessary. The doctor said you could travel home with the group tomorrow if you want to. Of course, if you feel too weak, we'll make other arrangements. It's up to you."

"I'll be okay," I said. "I'd rather go with the group."

"We'll see how you are tomorrow," said Mr. Langfeld, patting my hand. "There are two officers outside who want to talk to you. Do you feel up to it?"

"Sure," I said, though I found I couldn't nod or move my head without pain.

Mr. Langfeld stood back. He gave me a long look, as if he were about to say more. Then he sighed, put his hands into his pockets and said, "You've certainly had a rough time, my dear. I hope things work out better for you now." He turned to Roz. "We'll just wait here while the police talk to her." They stood aside, watching me anxiously.

The two officers came in and stood at the side of the bed. They wore tan uniforms and their expressions were sober. The one nearest me smiled and he spoke gently. "How're you feeling?"

"Okay," I said. I tried to smile, but the movement hurt the side of my neck. "I guess I must look pretty beat up."

"Well, you've got a shiner," the officer said matter-of-factly. "It could have a been a heck of a lot worse. Fortunately, you're a real fighter." He pulled up a chair. "I'm Dave Luna. This is my partner, Oren Sommes. We need to ask you a few questions. Okay?"

"Sure."

Dave Luna continued. "What made you go out to the Lincoln Memorial? We heard you were with friends at the movies."

I told them about the message, the proposed meeting with Thomas, being attacked there at the Memorial.

"Kind of risky," Dave Luna said, "going out alone at night in a city like Washington, D.C. You're from a small town. I guess things are different there."

"Mill Valley," I said, with a swift vision of the green hills, the small, friendly shopping plaza, our school on the hillside. "Yeah. It's pretty nice, very safe."

"So, why do you think Mrs. Meistrander attacked you?"

"I knew something about her that she was afraid I'd tell." And as briefly as I could, I told them the story of the crime from over twenty-five years ago, the double murder.

"Who was the other perpetrator?" Officer Luna asked, frowning, leaning toward me.

"My mother," I said. It was hard, saying the words in front of Roz and Mr. Langfeld. I felt ashamed, as if I were standing naked in a crowd. Then, with a jolt, I realized something, and I burst out with it. "Megan had no remorse at all. But my mother paid for that crime all the rest of her life!"

"I'm sure she did," the officer said softly. "This Megan Meistrander is quite some piece of work. We've had her in the station only two hours. In that time she's accused you of every crime in the book, besides trying to bribe the watch commander, and when that didn't work, she threatened an international incident, complete with atom bombs! Only kidding—but she has gotten everyone in an uproar, made three calls to Canada, tried to tell us that you were part of a gang..."

"At any rate," said the other officer, "we knew from the start that she was lying about you."

"How did you?" I asked.

"The moment she saw us, she tried to run. Victims don't

act like that. She saw she couldn't get away and quickly changed course, accusing you of attacking her. Well, it was a good try. But we've got enough to hold her for attempted murder."

"She's left-handed," said Officer Sommes. "Your stab wounds could only have been made by a left-handed person."

Officer Luna nodded. "As it turns out, the receipt for the knife was in her wallet. Came from a sporting goods store right here in D.C."

"What will happen to her?" I was thinking of Thomas, how this would hit him.

"She'll go to trial, of course," Luna replied. "We might need you to come and testify, or we might just send someone to California to take your statement. It depends on how the D.A. decides to handle the case."

"Let's let this young lady get some sleep now," said Luna. He rose, smiled down at me. "Take it easy."

Mr. Langfeld and Roz came near once again. Roz laid her hand on my forehead. "Good night, Laura, dear. We'll see you in the morning."

Mr. Langfeld cleared his throat, thrust his hands into his pockets. "So, we'll go back to the hotel and tell your classmates that you're all right. Everyone will be glad to know that. Especially that fellow, Spider. I called over there, and Mrs. Langfeld tells me he's still hanging around the lobby waiting for news."

"Tell him—what will you tell him?" I closed my eyes against the thought that everyone in school would know the whole ugly story.

"I'll tell him you're doing fine. Anything that was said in this room," Mr. Langfeld added with a glance at Roz and Kim, "is certainly going to remain private between us."

The word "private" made me think again of my mother, how she valued privacy. She had hidden everything of hers, kept it sealed in a box, even that picture of Megan and her. If I hadn't been snooping, I thought, I wouldn't be here in the hospital now. But then, I realized, I'd never have known myself either.

"Mr. Langfeld," I said, holding back tears, "I'm sorry I was so—rebellious. I didn't follow the…"

"We forgive you," said Mr. Langfeld with a smile. "Though I'll admit, you gave us some bad moments."

After they all left I lay in the hospital bed, listening to the night sounds from the corridor—faint, muted tones, things being wheeled along the hallway, someone calling out, footsteps, a distant chime. I felt under my eye. The flesh was tender and bruised. The side of my neck stung, and I could not lie on my left shoulder, where the doctor had stitched the gash left by Megan's knife. I felt, however, more whole and healthy than I had in weeks. As if from some hazy photograph, there came the vision of me and Megan, my body poised above hers, the knife in my hand. I could easily have killed her. But I didn't.

Once I heard a nurse enter the room, and I felt something being wrapped around my arm as she took my blood pressure. I opened my eyes.

"You'll be fine," the nurse said.

"I know," I replied.

chapter / 23

What amazed me was how all the kids gathered around me with little gifts and expressions of sympathy. Cissy and Marlene and Diane had bought me half a dozen magazines. Some of the other girls gave me flowers. Jordan gave me a packet of postcards of Washington, D.C. Everyone in the group signed the postcards, wishing me "get well."

Spider had insisted on coming along to the hospital to pick me up. The doctors ordered me to use a wheelchair until I got home, just for precaution, and Spider insisted on being the one to push it. Kim came to the hospital, too, of course. She brought my makeup and a change of clothes, but when I looked in the mirror I realized that no amount of makeup could camouflage the fact that I'd been in a terrible fight.

When Spider came in he did a double take, then he kissed me lightly on the cheek. "You look great," he murmured.

I laughed. "Thanks." I had seen the purple bruise under my eye and the way my mouth went lopsided when I tried to smile.

When we got to the van, where all the other kids were

waiting, Darryl Lapkin came up to me, offering a Power Bar. I took it and thanked him. "Guess I need to build up my strength again."

Darryl nodded knowingly. "I could have told that guy not to mess with you," he said. "I hear you really decked him. Held him down until the cops arrived."

"People tend to exaggerate," I said modestly.

"Oh, no," Darryl said with a grin. "Not about you."

I got to fly first class, so I could stretch out and sleep. It was great, but as we began our descent into San Francisco, I began to feel very queasy, from my wounds as well as from apprehension.

I had trespassed. I had opened a door long closed to me. Now I would have to face my father with this new knowledge. I had no idea when he was coming home; I rather hoped for a reprieve.

But, to my astonishment, there he was, standing at the gate with Mrs. Sheffield, rushing up as an attendant wheeled me from the plane.

"Laura! Laura! Thank God, you're safe."

I had never seen my father cry before. It shook me terribly, so I, too, had to brush the tears from my face. Mrs. Sheffield bent down to kiss me. "Oh, child, child," she said over and over again. "We'll take you home now, safe and sound."

My father had flown in from Tokyo only two hours earlier. I could see his tiredness, his pallor and the slight trembling of his hands.

At home, I lay on the sofa in the living room, while he sat in his large leather chair, both of us sipping mugs of hot broth that Mrs. Sheffield had prepared before she left.

"We need to talk," my father said. His long arms hung down over the sides of his chair. He looked pale and tense.

"I know," I murmured. "I found out things about Mother." I did not look at him, but tried to steel myself against some consequences I couldn't even imagine.

"I know you went to Birch Bend," my father said. "When Mr. Langfeld spoke to Mrs. Sheffield, he told her you had gone there and discovered...our past."

I started at the word "our," then realized that, of course, he had always known, from the beginning, from the time he met her. Now the words in that love letter became clear: *We need to learn to forget the past...how can anything about you ever repel me?"* I was astounded at this new vision of my father. He could simply have walked away, but he had willingly shared all those guilt-ridden, difficult years.

I felt flushed as I asked him, "When they told Mrs. Sheffield, what did she say?"

"Laura, Mrs. Sheffield has known about it all along."

"She *knew?*" Again, I felt cheated, a stranger in my own home, kept ignorant all this time. "Why did you tell her?"

"I didn't. It was your mother," my father said, eyes half closed, as if to look back over the years. "It was just a few months after you were born, when Mrs. Sheffield came to us. We needed someone reliable and calm, and Mrs. Sheffield seemed perfect from the start. I'm not sure what triggered it, but one day your mother went into one of her depressions. She retreated to her room, into her music. After a time Mrs. Sheffield went in to her with a cup of tea, and your mother told her everything."

"Why did she tell her?" I breathed. "She never told anyone else, did she?"

"No. Mrs. Sheffield was the only one. I suppose she needed to tell someone. Also, they needed to trust each other. Maybe your mother just wanted for another human being to understand, even to forgive her. At any rate, Mrs. Sheffield simply gathered your mother into her arms and held her, and as far as I know, they never spoke of it again."

"Mrs. Sheffield didn't—" I sighed as I thought the word. "She didn't judge Mom. She just loved her."

"Yes." My father looked up at me. "Mrs. Sheffield is quite a remarkable woman. She was heaven-sent to balance your mother's moods. A past like this," he said, "leaves scars."

"I'm aware of that," I said dryly.

"And I'm aware," he said with equal lack of passion, "that you also suffered. Your childhood was not carefree, although we tried, Laura, truly we did."

"I wasn't as good as Mrs. Sheffield," I said, feeling tightness in my throat, guilt and grief together. "I—I couldn't understand how Mom could have done it, and I…"

"Blamed her?" His voice was suddenly loud, his body darting forward in the chair. "Of course you did! Murder is blameworthy, Laura, and don't ever forget it. We have to look evil in the eye, call it for what it is. Otherwise, how can we steer clear of it? What your mother and Megan did was horrible, horrible. Nobody can ever deny that. And neither of us could ever forget it."

"So you traveled," I said dully. "You got away."

"Yes. Sometimes I simply had to get away. It was fortunate that my job took me. I had an excuse. I'm not proud of it, Laura, but I needed the respite. Yes, I needed it, so I could go on with the—the masquerade."

"You never have to pretend again," I said softly, seeing how vulnerable he suddenly looked, how aged.

"Was Mother ever going to tell me?" I asked.

"I don't know, Laura. It was up to her to decide. I'm sure she agonized over it, not wanting to hurt you. Of course, a thing like this does hurt everyone. How it happens—who can say? Who can ever know?"

"They just went over the edge."

"Yes. That's it."

We sat silently for a time. "I want to show you something," I said, and after a moment I ran to my room to get the letter, returning to show it to my father. "This is the letter that started it all, the letter Mom wrote to Megan."

I stood back while he read the letter, then he handed it quietly back to me.

"She forgives Megan," I said softly, trying to find comfort in that fact.

"The difference between the two of them," said my father, "is that Jasmine did have a conscience. She was weak, and she let herself be used—but after the thing was done, she took full responsibility for her crime. Megan never did. We know that by what she tried to do to you. Megan never had any sense of shame. She is one of those people who thinks she can play God."

I picked up our cups to take them out into the kitchen. My father stopped me, saying, "Your mother loved you very much."

I turned. "But she never—never said…"

"She was afraid of so many things. She never thought we'd have a child. Didn't feel—worthy, was the word she used. Worthy."

"Why didn't she ever see her parents?"

"Same reason. Shame. She didn't want to cause them any more pain. She felt she had to disappear. Maybe she was wrong."

"Oh, Dad," I said, moving to go to him. "I loved her, too."

"She knew that," he said. "She was so proud of you, Laura,

of all your abilities, the drama, your success in school, your many friends. You gave her all the things she couldn't have anymore. Do you understand that?"

"I think so," I whispered.

My father's eyes were closed, his breathing deep. I thought he'd dropped off to sleep. A faint fog swirled around the window, painting a silvery layer on the branches and leaves of the maple trees and pines. Our little valley, Mill Valley, is often steeped in fog; it makes it seem like a secret place, closed off from the rest of the world.

Suddenly my father opened his eyes and smiled at me. "You and I," he said softly, "need to spend more time together. Would you like to, Laura? Maybe we could go somewhere for a vacation, unless you'd rather..."

"There's nothing I'd rather do," I said, filled with emotion. "Maybe this summer?"

"Yes. We'll do something special. Maybe rent a houseboat. Or go on a bike trip."

I was amazed. This was exactly what I had always dreamed of, never daring really to hope. Now I said, "I wonder what to do, Father." I couldn't remember when I'd last asked my father for advice. "I haven't told any of my friends about the—about Mom. Except for Kim. Is it wrong to hide my past?"

"No," said Father. "In a way it is your past, too, but that doesn't mean it has to affect your future. Your mother paid for what she did. You don't owe the world anything on her behalf—except, maybe, to take care never to hurt anyone. But that's true for all of us."

Now I told my father, "I want to find my grandparents."

"I think you should," he agreed. "We could try to locate them on the Web."

We went immediately to his computer and typed in their names but we came up blank. "Maybe they aren't in the phone book," Father said as we walked back into the living room. "I'm so sorry, honey. I wish…"

"It's okay," I said "I have an idea." I glanced at the stack of magazines that my friends had given me, and which Mrs. Sheffield had thoughtfully arranged on the coffee table. "I'm going to try to make them contact me."

Nearly two months later, I received the following letter, postmarked South Carolina. It said:

> *Dear Laura Inman:*
>
> *Concerning your ads in Earth Craft Magazine and in Modern Pottery, it is possible that we are the persons you seek. Our daughter, Jenny, disappeared from our home in Birch Bend, Virginia, when she was in her early twenties.*
>
> *We did not know whether she had ever married, or indeed, whether she was dead or alive. We would like to speak to you by telephone to check on certain details of our daughter's experiences, to ascertain whether we are, in fact, the family you are seeking.*
>
> *Please call us collect as soon as you receive this note.*
>
> > *Yours hopefully,*
> > *Jeanette and George Rouseau*

My father stood beside me as I dialed. My hands were trembling so that I thought I'd drop the receiver.

The woman answered. My heart leapt. "Hello? Hello?"

"Hello. This is Laura."

"Laura. I—it's very—shocking to—imagine that…"

"I didn't know how to find you."

"It was so clever of you to…"

"How can we know whether we are really…my grand-mother made pottery."

"Yes, yes, I am a potter, too."

"Mrs. Armenta in Birch Bend showed me some of her pottery…"

"Tell me about your mother, Jenny. What she was like. Oh, this is so hard!"

"She loved—the Beatles. All their music. She had all the songs."

"Yes? What else can you tell me?"

"There was a picture, a photograph of her and her friend. She was wearing jeans and her hair in a ponytail. Her friend, Megan…"

"Megan, you say? You have a photograph of the two of them?"

"Yes, it was among her things, and a bracelet, a silver bracelet…"

"Wait! Little hearts, engraved with alternating words—let me think. Yes, Megan gave that bracelet to Jenny for her fifteenth birthday! It said—it said FRIENDS FOREVER."

"I am wearing that bracelet now," I said.

Silence made its own sound, heavy and full of meanings and possibilities. A whole lifetime of possibilities.

"We can catch a plane and be there tomorrow," she said. "I'll make the reservations and phone you back straight away. I—we can't wait to see you. Oh, my dear. My dear! We can't wait."

I said, "I can't wait, either, Grandmother."

* * *

There was one more letter I needed to write. Kim sat beside me as I wrote it, helping me form the right words. It said:

> *Dear Thomas,*
>
> *I'm writing to let you know that I am thinking of you, knowing how difficult this time must be for you and your dad. When I gave my deposition here in California, I was thinking of how all this will affect you. The attorney who came said that it's possible your mom would go into treatment at a hospital instead of prison. I hope that will be the case. He also told me you would be going to Harvard in the fall. Congratulations, and good luck. I know you'll make a great Harvard man.*
>
> *Maybe we'll meet again some day. If not, I wish you all the very best. Not many people in the world know exactly how it feels to share a certain past. Even if we never meet again, we will always have a special bond. And that day we spent together was one of the best ever.*

I sat there with the end of the pen in my mouth.

"How should I sign it?" I asked Kim.

"How about your name?"

"You know what I mean. 'Sincerely' sounds too cold. 'Yours truly' is much too formal."

"What about love?" Kim suggested.

I looked at her, grinning. "Somehow, I knew you'd say that."

"There's nothing wrong with love," said Kim.

"You're right," I said. I wrote the last two words, and I sealed the letter. "There's nothing wrong with love."

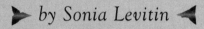
I guess you want to know why they sent me here for this—what do you call it? Encounter group?"

Luke grinned. "We call it a workshop. 'Encounter' is a seventies' term—not a bad one, but what we are doing now is working together to find whatever each one of us is seeking."

Michelle glanced about, moistened her lips. She did not like being looked at, and she was aware that Luke faced her fully, his entire body posture open for listening. She felt a sticky sweat under her arms. She had to speak, to give him something, so he would stop staring at her.

"I was going with this guy. He turned out to be a—he took drugs. Not a whole bunch, but he—he sold some, too. I guess everyone knew except for me. New girl."

Luke nodded. "So, what happened?"

"He got a little too persistent. Thought he owned me.

I told him to get lost. He threatened me." Michelle glanced at Luke.

Luke leaned toward her. He looked genuinely interested.

Michelle went on. "I told him I wasn't scared of him."

"Was that true?"

"I don't know. Anyhow, he's got another girlfriend now, so it doesn't matter."

"Did you sleep with him?"

"No!" Furious, Michelle rose from her chair.

Luke nodded mildly. "Sorry. I needed to know…"

"I'll tell you what you need to know," she snapped.

"Thank you," he retorted, his tone sarcastic.

They faced each other for a long, frozen moment. Then Luke asked softly, "What else?" His gentleness made Michelle almost ashamed.

She said, "I fell asleep in class. Big deal. My teacher made a big deal out of it."

"Why can't you sleep at night?"

"Who told you that?"

Luke smiled slightly. "I have spies."

Michelle sighed. "I don't know. Strange room. Strange bed."

"Do you like your new house?"

"Oh, it's beautiful. My room is downstairs next to the living room. It has its own little deck, overlooking the canyon. My mom's bedroom is upstairs, and she has her office up there, so we each have privacy. My room is really large. I got all new furniture, wicker, which I love, and this great bedspread, mostly red, a print with leaves and birds and…"

"My, my, I ask a simple question, and I get a whole visual tour of your house. Might that be seen as avoidance?"

Michelle said nothing, but inside she fumed.

"You don't miss the East?" Luke asked. "You don't miss your father?"

"No. Not at all." She looked away, bit her lip, overwhelmed by the sudden pressure in her throat.

———————